29 Years

Robin Stow

Copyright © 2015 Robin Stow

All rights reserved.

ISBN-10: 1515253619

ISBN-13: 978-1515253617

DEDICATION

To my wonderful children whom I adore.

ACKNOWLEDGMENTS

My thanks to the following:

Squadron Leader Jeffry Brain RAF a WWII Spitfire pilot, friend and raconteur.

Group Captain Hugh Verity DSO, DFC for the wealth of information about 161 Squadron in his book 'We Landed by Moonlight'

Sarah Helm for the insight provided into the world of Vera Atkins and the SOE agents in her book 'A Life in Secrets'

Chapter 1

Early 1944 – Above The English Channel

The side canopy of the Lysander shattered as cannon shells tore through the fuselage. The pilot, Flt Lt Graham Knowles, knew immediately that they'd been jumped by a German. Hurricane trained, he slice-turned, slammed the stick right, booted the rudder left and shoved the throttle wide open diving for the clouds below. His head urgently swivelling from side to side looking for his attacker in the moonlight. Having swooped on its target from behind, the hunter was climbing high on the right side, exhausts burning bright blue-red in the night sky.

The Messerschmitt Bf110 is a heavy twin engine fighter. The Germans called it Zerstörer, or destroyer. Top speed over 340 mph, maintaining engagement with the much slower Lysander would be difficult; Knowles was counting on it. As he dived, the Bristol Mercury engine sounded strong and the dials indicated all was normal, the airspeed rose steadily to 200 mph. No smell of petrol; he guessed that the main fuel tank, directly behind him, was undamaged. He kept the nose down, engine roaring, the needle went past 210 mph, the German was banking down off the top of his climb to re-engage. Both planes were racing for the clouds, into the red at 3,000 rpm, 220 mph, 240 mph, needle past the end of the scale, now off the clock. The German was quickly closing on the little Lizzie.

The clouds were wisping up towards them as the 110 opened fire, Knowles waited one heartbeat then banked hard right, the tracer hammered past, ahead and left of him. It was immediately dark in the cloud.

The moonlight gave a weak glimmer overhead then was gone. Knowles eased out of the dive and flying on instruments turned east roughly at right angles to his previous track when the German had spotted him. It was raining heavily in the cloud, huge pebbles of rain blattered against the canopy and the air was turbulent with gusts and sudden drops.

The altimeter showed 2,000 feet, the met forecast had promised cloud to zero feet over Brittany. Knowles knew that the night fighter would have climbed back out of the cloud and would be waiting for him to resurface, somewhere between his disappearance and the coast of northern France. Watching the compass, he eased onto heading 090, flying east hoping to put as many miles as possible between himself and his pursuer. The weather was deteriorating in the cloud. He heard the intercom click on;

'Are we safe now?' It was a woman's voice with a strong French accent.

'Yeah, safe enough, are you alright?' He replied.

'Yes I am alright but your aeroplane has some bad damage, there are holes in the sides and the wind and rain is coming in.'

'She'll be alright, these are very strong little planes, a few holes don't matter too much. I'll stay in the cloud a bit longer and hope the German has gone to look for us somewhere else then we can head for home.'

'Where is your home?'

'Our airfield is on the south coast near Chichester; about 100 kilometres from London, d'you know it?

'No I don't, I don't know England very well.'

'I hope you enjoy your visit; it's a beautiful country. Are you going to London?'

'Yes, I hope so, I am meeting my colleagues tomorrow.'

'Well, I'm just the taxi driver, my job is to get you out of

France and over to England in one piece if the Boche will leave us alone tonight.'

'Will we go all the way in clouds? The weather is getting worse.'

The little plane was bucking in the downdraughts; the rain was so thick they might have been under water. Up front a rubber seal had come loose and a steady stream of water leaked into the cockpit where the large side window joined the windscreen frame. The water was working its way behind the instrument panel and there were occasional flashes and sparks as it found exposed electric contacts.

'No, I need to get back above it. The forecast said the weather in the clouds was going to be bad with very strong air currents. I'll turn South; away from the direction that they expect us to be going. Then slowly climb until we are just in the top layer of the cloud. This plane is painted grey on the top so we should be hard to see from above.'

Knowles opened the throttle and started to climb, banking around to the south. He completed the turn and looked for the shimmer of moonlight that would indicate the cloud thinning. At 11,000 feet the cloud started to break up, tendrils of smoke blowing across the windscreen, the wingtips appearing and disappearing through the mist.

'Keep a sharp look out, I need your help, I can't see behind me.'

'OK, it's all clear behind' called out the French voice.

The big black cross of a 110 slid silently into view almost directly above and in front of Knowles. By adjusting his speed and direction he was able to keep station directly below and astern.

'It's not so clear up here; there's a night fighter directly above us! I'll have to sink back down into the clouds and lose him.

There's enough fuel for ninety minutes and it's one hour back to base so we can't wait around for too long.'

'Where did the plane come from? Is it looking for us?'

'I don't think it's the same aircraft that shot at us. I guess the first 110 has radioed his controller and they've vectored in more aircraft to find us. Each plane will have a sector to patrol, that's why this one is going slowly. Loitering to save fuel and stay airborne for as long as possible, they can't see us below because they only have aircrew in the cockpit on the top of the plane. Make sure you pull your seatbelt straps tight, it's going to be a wet and bumpy ride.'

Knowles stared red-eyed at the instruments as he flew blind into the cloud again. Once more the plane bucked and corkscrewed through the turbulence. He eased the stick to the right, feet dancing gently on the rudder bar. Eyes glued to the artificial horizon and compass. Banking round through 180 degrees to head north to the English coast. He set the throttle to maintain 150 mph and rotated his shoulders to ease the tension.

'I am going to try and stay hidden just in the top of the clouds, once we're over the Channel I'll try the radio to let them know we're on our way back and our estimated time of arrival.'

'Okay, I'm looking forward to seeing your England.'

Knowles was sweating after ten minutes wrestling with the controls. He knew that the Gestapo and the Abwehr hated the fact that the RAF flew secret missions into France. They would scramble all available aircraft to shoot down a Lysander.

Unexpectedly the cloud started thinning and suddenly they were in clear air. He could see the Channel twenty miles ahead. The Cherbourg peninsular was on his left; there was no cloud over the Channel. He pressed the radio switch to transmit:

29 Years

'Hello base this is G GEORGE do you read me over?'
'Hello G GEORGE I read you loud and clear over.'
'G GEORGE I'm on my way home. There's bandits looking for me, do we have any air cover available?'
'Base, there's a standing patrol out at the moment I'll let them know. What's your location?
'G GEORGE twenty miles east of Cherbourg.'
'Base roger out.'
Knowles opened the throttle and dived for the deck, as the plane picked up speed the passenger shouted 'plane above us, plane above us now!'
Where is it? What's it doing?
'It is above and behind, flying level and heading to the left, to the east.'
'OK, maybe he hasn't seen us, watch him but keep looking out for other planes.'
Knowles levelled out at 1,500 feet.
'Plane above left! Plane above left! I think he's seen us, he's turning to follow us!'
'Hello G GEORGE this is base.' The unhurried voice of the operations officer at RAF Tangmere announced himself.
'G GEORGE I've got two bandits on me, they're about to engage.
'Base, roger, air cover with you in thirty seconds.'
Knowles anxiously scanned the night sky through all sections of his cockpit, looking for the enemy, praying for Spitfires.
''e's behind us, behind us!'
'How far?'
'Three kilometres.'
'Tell me when he is at five hundred metres.'
'Ok now two kilometres.'
'Now one kilometre.'

'This is Blue Leader; two bandits at three o'clock, two thousand feet, follow me!'

The three Spitfires in a tight arrow, three gloved hands shoved their throttles forward in unison to full boost. The fighters leapt forwards, supercharged Merlin engines screaming at the night as they speared in to attack.

'Five hundred met..' she was flung against the side of the cockpit.

Knowles wrenched the plane left in a raw skidding turn. The Bf 110's high rate of fire blazed a storm of tracer past the Lysander. Most of the 20mm canon shells hosed off into the darkness but there were some heavy strikes to the rear of the airframe. Knowles felt the rudder and elevator controls become slushy and heavy to operate.

'Where's he now!' he demanded.

He heard her laboured breathing and a thick swallowing then softly 'I don't know, I can't see. I'm hurt can you help me?' She groaned deep and low.

'Sorry, I can't get to you; the petrol tank is between us. How badly hurt are you? Where are you hit?'

She moaned other disjointed words, sighs, stifled chokes and sobs and then the intercom went silent.

The Lysander had been on a mission to drop explosives and money to resistance agents near Angers and to bring one agent back to England. Knowles knew it was important, he had to get her back alive and there may not be much time. He guessed she'd been hit by the heavy canon shells that can tear a body apart.

'You must try and stop the bleeding. There's some bandages in the locker on the floor. Talk to me, tell me when you've found 'em'

He tried to keep her awake while he focused on the job of staying alive.

He could see that the Bf110 had overshot; the big plane was going round for another try.

29 Years

Above and beyond, moonlight flashed off the canopy of a banking, diving fighter, then another, then another. The three Spitfires separated, two going for the 110 that was turning to attack. They came streaking round underneath and from astern. Tight, one behind the other.

Deadly close range, the words of their gunnery instructor sounding in their ears;

'Wait 'til the target fills the gun sight; wait 'til you feel you can touch the plane; then thumb down on the joystick fire button'.

Cannon shells tearing through the underside of the 110 and ripping up through the cockpit. The first fighter flicked right and his wingman engaged, Under the hail of 20mm solid steel shells the 110 broke apart; separated from its tail plane, spiralling into oblivion.

The single Spitfire went for the 110's unsuspecting wingman. Direct, killing bursts of tracer; there was an explosion and brilliant fireball as the fuel tank was hit. The 110 fragmented, filling the night with flaming debris.

Blue Leader came alongside to inspect the damage. Knowles waggled his wings to show he was OK then switched to the short range R/T on the radio and heard the Spitfire pilot.

'Are you OK? You've got some tail damage is she still flyable?'

'The controls are heavy but I should be OK if the Huns leave me alone.'

'Roger, we'll give you cover back to the coast, out.' The fighter surged away, climbing in a wide arc to re-join his wing.

Knowles switched back to the command net and called Tangmere.

'Hello Base this is G GEORGE, the standing patrol will shepherd me to the coast. I've got some tail damage but my passenger is seriously wounded.

Can you arrange to have a medical team stood by?'
'Base, roger, I'll see what's available, out'
Knowles gently eased the stick back, opened the throttle and started a slow climb. He needed to gain height in case of further problems over the Channel. The more height he had, the further he could glide if necessary. It was getting cold in the cockpit, after the fear and excitement of the previous thirty minutes he could feel the sweat cooling on his skin below the silk undergarments. The Spitfires ranged themselves in patrol formation out in the sky above the Lysander, ready for any further enemy action. Knowles switched to intercom;
'Hello, are you there? We're safe now.'
She coughed and groaned then whispered;
'It is bad, there is much blood from my legs, I cannot move.'
'Did you find the bandages? Did you try to stop the bleeding?'
'I try but I cannot reach, I am so tired. I'm so sleepy.'
'No, no, don't go to sleep, keep a lookout, stay awake watch the Spitfires. Can you see them?
'I, I can see one.'
'Look out for the other two, I need to know where they are.' Knowles invented the task to keep her awake.
'We'll soon be over the English coast, I can see the white cliffs not far away now.'
'Hello G GEORGE this is base over.'
'Go ahead base.'
'We don't have a medical team available for your passenger. We'll reroute you to Little Rissington. They've got a secure unit with doctors standing by. Turn onto heading three four zero, distance ninety miles, you should be there in about thirty minutes. Switch to channel E on your RT and let them know your ETA, over.'
'G GEORGE, thank you for your assistance, wilco out.'

29 Years

No problem, Knowles knew 'Rissy' well enough, he'd flown in and out a few times, it could be quite windy up there though. He checked the instruments, fuel, enough for 45 minutes, oil pressure steady, airspeed 180 mph, height 7,500 feet. Compass heading, due North.

The reassuring steady throb of the radial engine had a calming effect. The night sky was quiet and clear, the south coast stretched out across his front as he banked smoothly left onto the new heading.

His main worry was getting the passenger back alive.

'My name is Graham Knowles, what's your name?'

There was no answer.

He clicked the intercom on and off to try and rouse her then repeated himself.

'My name is Graham Knowles, what's your name?'

'Oh, arhh je m'appelle Jeanne. I'm sorry, I am called Jeanne.'

'Is that like Jeanne D'Arc?'

'Yes, just the same.'

He continued to keep up a simple conversation with her, often having to repeat his questions as she slid in and out of consciousness.

With thirty miles to run he switched to channel E.

'Hello Little Rissington this is G GEORGE, do you read me? Over.'

'Hello G GEORGE this is Little Rissington, I read you loud and clear. We're expecting you, what's your ETA? over.'

'G GEORGE my ETA zero two twenty over'

Roger, you're cleared to land on grass runway zero six, the flare path is for you, Barometer one zero one zero. Remain where you are when you roll to a standstill, the ambulance and medics will come to you. Note that we're seven hundred and thirty feet above sea level over.'

'G GEORGE roger, thank you, out.'

He adjusted the altimeter to the correct atmospheric pressure.
'We're nearly there, landing in about five minutes.'
Silence.
'Nearly there, can you hear me?'
There was no reply.
'Oh shit.' he muttered.
As it came into view on top of the hill, Knowles throttled back onto the glide path into Rissy. When he could see the flares through the right hand window he turned onto heading 06, keeping a bit lower than a normal approach, ready for the updraughts that come from the wind around the hill. Wary of the slushy controls, he was concerned that the landing might be a heavy one.
As he closed the throttle and the airspeed dropped, the Lysander sagged and wallowed, the damaged controls slow to respond. The plane sank, the flares rushed up either side to meet them, when it looked as if they were at shoulder height he pulled the stick back and the aircraft dropped onto the grass. As the damaged tailplane touched, it dug into the grass slowing the plane very quickly. Knowles realized that the tail wheel was either damaged or shot away. He kept it straight with the footbrakes and came to a standstill. The flare path went out, extinguished by the ground staff.
Knowles swiftly went through the engine shut down procedure. As the last coughs clattered away into the night the dimmed lights of an ambulance came alongside.
He pushed the side window down and climbed out, parachute dangling from behind.
'Morning sir, understand you've a casualty on board.'
'Yes but I haven't heard from her for a while, I think she's unconscious, she maybe dead.'
The medic climbed up the aluminium fuselage ladder, shoved the smashed canopy back and looked inside.

By the light of his torch he could see a young woman slumped in the rear cockpit. The harness and the parachute that she was sitting on were covered in blood. There was wet blood all over the floor and on the lockers. A half-opened field dressing lay in the blood on the floor; he spoke softly;
'Alright love, we'll have you out of there in a jiffy.'
Her head was laying on her right shoulder, her throat white and exposed. He found the pulse in her neck; weak and fast. Her breath was coming in irregular heavy gulps and pants. The medic undid her harness then reached down and got his arms around her for the lift onto the coaming.
'Jump up and give us a hand will you?'
The other medic climbed the short ladder and between them they carefully lifted, then lowered the wounded woman. Once on the narrow canvas stretcher she was loaded into the ambulance. Doors shut, it ground slowly away in low gear across the grass towards the hospital.
'Can you give me a lift to the Ops Room?'
'Yessir, hop in.' The night patrol Jeep creaked over the grass and onto the tarmac perimeter track. In the Ops Room he asked the Duty Officer if he could call Tangmere.
'Yes indeed, the secure line is on the desk over there under the window.' Once he'd reported in to his Ops officer and advised that he'd send in a damage report in the morning, Knowles got a lift over to the Officers' mess. The steward showed him to a bedroom and pointed out the bathroom down the hall.
'What time shall I wake you sir?'
What time does breakfast finish?'
'Eight thirty sir.'
'Eight fifteen then please.'
'Right oh sir, sleep well.'

Knowles dumped his 'chute on the floorboards, took off his sheepskin Irvin jacket and flying boots and sat on the bed. His mind was full of the flight and Jeanne's chances of survival. After a minute he shook his head and stood up to finish undressing. He got into bed and pulled up the covers, switched out the bedside light and turned on his side. A last look at his watch, 3.03 am; exhausted, he went straight to sleep.

Chapter 2

Early 2014 – The Cotswolds

John had known Dave Chatham since they were at Bourton on the Water primary school. He'd gone on to the secondary school next door in the same large village but John's schoolteacher parents had wanted better for their son. They'd tested, taught and nagged him to do better with the result that he passed the 11 plus and won a place at Pate's Grammar School in Cheltenham.

John had to suffer the usual jeers of derision at the bus queue for his new school. Those primary school friends now shunned the grammar school pupils. Because of the different uniform, they were no longer part of the same tribe. Their rituals and goals were different and he was no longer part of their society. Their paths continued to diverge through their teens, John struggled at such a high achieving school where his exam marks made him a regular visitor to the lowest quartile in each GCSE and then each A level subject. Nonetheless, to his and his parents' surprise he was offered a place at Oxford Brookes to read Geography.

Dave meanwhile had his future sorted for him by his dad. He was a quick-witted boy but had little interest in schoolwork. Dave was well liked, a bit of a lad but kind and with a smile that endeared him to his mates and teachers, he had charm too which had helped get him out of trouble on several occasions. Young Dave followed his father into the legal world to discover the disappointments of life as a junior barrister's clerk.

Dave reflected on yesterday's meeting. He'd known John for a long time, since they were six.

He'd thought of him as being a bit of a clever dick, grammar school, university and everything. He felt a bit insecure in his own lack of education but knew that he'd got more of a talent for understanding real life and business than John. Yesterday, out of the blue, John had come round to his office on the High Street at Moreton-in-Marsh. John said he had some ideas that might be of interest; Dave made mugs of instant coffee, they sat and chatted, catching up on the missing years: 'so how was it working in the Law? You were a barrister's clerk weren't you.'

'Yeah, my dad got me into his chambers; they had a set in Oxford and one in London where Dad worked. I started in Oxford that was alright, but the hours took a bit of getting used to. He gave me a lift to work in the morning then he got the train to London. In the evenings I took the bus home. It meant I was always in early but I didn't mind, I used to read up on the cases and sometimes chat to one of the barristers. I found I had a bit of a knack for the game and got on well with the senior clerk who was a mate of my dad's. When I was about twenty there was a vacancy at the chambers in London. My boss put me up for it so I went for an interview and got the job. It was very different, very old fashioned, at the Inns of Court.

The hours and the commute was a killer, I used to kip on the train but I got paid a lot more so I just got on with it. I learnt a lot about the Law, even more about people and the way they behave under pressure. Once I found my feet I enjoyed the buzz and banter in Chambers. You have to be quick or you get eaten alive, there's some sharp boys working up there I can tell you.'

Dave leaned back in the executive leather chair behind his desk. It was a small room but with two large sash windows looking out over the wide High street. Gallen sat the other side of the desk holding his coffee mug.

'I bet you met some real characters, what sort of business did they handle in your Chambers?'

'They did all sorts, I was on the criminal side, a lot of it was to do with financial fraud. Tax, currency and VAT scams, our barristers were normally defending and had quite a good reputation for what they called "innovative defence" he laughed, 'I think some of those barristers were just as dodgy as the crim's. If they hadn't gone into the Law they could just as easily have ended up on the other side!'

He smiled at the memories his words triggered.

'I met a lot of the clients; some of them were very successful businessmen who'd just got greedy. Some were hopeless at business and could only make money by fiddling the books and not paying their taxes. Others found a loophole and created webs of front companies to create what was called the European VAT carousel. Hundreds of millions of VAT went missing which should have gone to European tax authorities.

The Silks were experts on the VAT front and I got quite involved with some of the cases. When I was about twenty-five I was given more responsibility and spent quite a lot of time helping the clients. Normally it was because they were in custody and just couldn't get on with running their businesses and organizing their family and personal lives. So I started with the occasional errand and then as they got to know me the jobs became more important. Not really anything to do with the case, just stuff that needed doing. Organise a car to take the wife or girlfriend shopping in the West End. Arrange a nanny to look after the children for a day. Just run of the mill stuff but it meant that I sometimes got to meet family members. Some of these guys were really grateful, it took a few worries away during a very stressful time for them and they remembered me.

I often got invited to family events, birthday parties and suchlike. Some of them stayed good friends.' At that point he felt he had shared enough of his history and said; 'so tell me then, what's these ideas that you want to talk about?'

'It's a property deal so probably easiest if we go up to the site tomorrow.'

'Sounds good, I've got meetings 'til eleven let's meet here at half past, we'll go in my car.'

After John had left Dave continued to reminisce, there was a lot he'd not shared with John. There was a lot he'd not shared with anybody, not even his wife Liz.

About eight years ago he'd got a call on his mobile, it was one of the chambers' past clients; a very clever Maltese guy named Matthias Nasim. Matt wanted to see him, to talk about the future. They met in the American bar at the Savoy Hotel on the Strand.

Matt greeted him enthusiastically, hugging him like a long-lost brother. After reliving some old tales Matt explained what he was up to. He'd made a lot of money from property in southern Spain and wanted to start an operation in England. Due to an earlier failed enterprise and a run-in with HMRC he had been declared unfit to act as a UK company director for fifteen years. Now he was looking for someone he could trust to run a company for him in England, to act as a front for Matt as a foreign investor. Matt had access to a lot of cash and he needed a way to put it to work. Property is a lightly regulated industry that needs a lot of capital. Matt thought that Dave could be the right man for the job. He wanted Dave to leave chambers and set up a small property development company with ambitious growth plans. They could work out the details later but Matt would double his salary and give him a share of the profits. Was Dave interested?

29 Years

You bet Dave was interested, he'd had enough of commuting, waiting another twenty years to become a senior clerk and not being able to afford a decent family house.

They were standing in the centre of RAF Little Rissington airfield. It had been a major RAF station during and after the 2nd World War. The fenced perimeter enclosed an area of about two square miles, it had been much larger in the war years but successive governments and defence cuts had trimmed the site. Property developers had been the main beneficiaries, though homeowners were the obvious ones. You couldn't miss the bright yellow, freshly cut cotswold stone of the new houses. Hundreds had been built on the north side of the airfield creating a new dormitory village named 'Victory Fields.'

The chain-link airfield gate was open, John pointed the way and with a determined lift of his jaw, Dave eased his Jaguar XF off the B493 onto the single-track tarmac entrance road. This led to a perimeter track where a knee-height signboard said left to 637 Volunteer Glider Squadron and right to the kart racing circuit. Dave slowly negotiated the potholes all the time aiming for the control tower.

He parked and they got out of the car, even though it was April and the sun was shining it had little heat and the temperature drop was noticeable. John put his hands in the pockets of his Puffa jacket.

They admired the view, behind them stood the unoccupied control tower, its angled green glass and metal window frames looking very much of the 1970's. There was one huge black tarmac runway about 100 metres in front of them joined to two smaller runways running at 60 degrees to one another forming an A shape with the control tower at the centre.

The main runway was very long, in fact from ground level they couldn't see either end of it because the airfield was built on the top of a shallow rising hill 730 feet above sea level.

They slipped back into the midnight blue Jaguar, Dave turned on the ignition and as the engine woofed into life he tapped the control for heated seats to warm the cream leather. Dave undid the buttons on his coat and leant back in the driver's seat. The engine idled almost silently whilst the sun lustered off the dark metallic paint of the powerful bonnet.

'So, tell me again how d'you see this, err opportunity?'

'Yeah, well, I heard you're interested in property development around here and in particular on ex-RAF airfields. They're always moaning about the lack of housing in the local papers. I've picked up a lot of landscaping work on the new estates that have been built in the last few years. Through the tendering process and design and build stages I've got to know a few of the directors of the house-building companies. As you can see there's been a large development on the north side of the airfield. The developers bought and built on the area of the old RAF barrack buildings, you know, the offices, married quarters and some of the old maintenance hangars. So far they've built about four hundred homes, say the average price is three hundred thousand – well you do the math's that's a hundred and twenty million quid. Now what's interesting is that the government plans for this airfield have changed quite a lot over the years. I don't know if you know much about the airfield's history but I used it as an example in the dissertation that I wrote for my Geography degree.'

Dave just looked at him, eyebrows slightly raised; he didn't have to say anything. John could guess exactly what Dave thought about further education.

29 Years

He could just hear the words heavy with sarcasm 'Dissertation, Geography degree... huh, and look where that got you.'

Ignoring his expression, John carried on telling the background story. John knew it so well that he gazed out of the windscreen and imagined the airfield going through its various evolutions as he spoke of them. From its opening in 1938, the aircraft developing from canvas covered bodies, engines spluttering as they wobbled towards landing. Through the bombers and Spitfires to the jet-powered aerobatics of the Red Arrows. In the 1980's and 90's the huge transport planes. The RAF C-130 Hercules and the USAF C-5 Galaxy. With the arrival of the United States Air Force in Europe, Little Rissington became the largest military contingency hospital in Europe, prepared and ready for the thousands of casualties that might result from operation "Desert Storm" the war on Iraq.

Noticing from the corner of his eye Dave's start of alarm, he reassured him, 'of course, as you remember there weren't actually many casualties and none came here.'

'So what happened to the hospital then?'

'All the equipment was dismantled and removed by the Yanks when they left, then the hangars that housed the hospital were condemned and pulled down. Even though it looks deserted, the RAF still use the airfield a bit, there's some powered gliders used by 637 Volunteer Gliding Squadron, we saw the sign on the way in. I think it's also used as a satellite for Brize Norton and sometimes I saw helicopter pilots training when I was at my lock-up storage in the hangars down there.' He indicated with his thumb over his shoulder down the hill behind them. The car had warmed up and he unzipped his jacket. John knew the history very well and a fair bit about the landscape.

'When I was seventeen or eighteen, on fine days I used to cycle over here and lie on the grass watching the aircraft. I was supposed be revising for exams but often I just wasted time daydreaming. The airfield was mowed once a week; I remember the smell of fresh cut grass. There's hares here you know, great to watch, you see them sometimes when it's quiet, just sitting in the sunshine.

If you look towards the eastern boundary over there, you can see a long, low hump. That's an ancient burial ground called a Long Barrow, they say it dates from three to four thousand BC. It was dug into during the war and they made it into an air raid shelter. I also heard that part of it was used as an underground hospital for wounded pilots and aircrew.'

'So what's the property angle here then?'

'Well, the area on the eastern side of this site might become available so there could be a chance to build another housing estate like Victory fields.'

'Why won't those developers get first crack at it?'

'The Council wants to see the work get spread around a bit. It could help if your local firm was involved rather than the big boys.'

'What size is the area the MoD are thinking of selling?'

'It's about twenty, maybe up to forty acres it includes those old hangars where I have my lock-up.'

'So how d'you fit in?'

'Through my landscaping business I know the property side at MoD, I could introduce you.'

'Alright but if it's a government sale won't it go to public auction?'

'Yeah but it's not clear if planning permission will be granted. The MoD won't sell to a bidder who puts conditions on the purchase. With your contacts on the Council you'd be better placed to know what type of development they'd give consent for.'

'OK, understood, have you got a plan of the proposed development site?'
'Yeah, I can email it to you.'
'No, best not, when can you drop it round to me?'
'Tomorrow afternoon if you like.'

Chapter 3

Early 2014 – The Cotswolds

'Laydeez and gennlemen!' The PA system scythed with piercing treble through the chatter and clattering of diners at the County Council annual dinner. The Master of Ceremonies, a well-fed citizen wearing a boxy suit gestured anxiously at the sound system manager. In the semi-darkness of an alcove, face visible only as a green mask, the master of the PA toned down the distressing pitch. The MC greeted them once again, this time with a little more warmth. 'Ladies and Gentlemen of the Gloucestershire County Council, I am delighted to welcome you to the Holiday Inn where I'm proud to be the manager. I hope you enjoyed the dinner and I'll now introduce your speaker for the evening, Leader of the Council, Geoffrey Dent!'

There was a light pattering of applause, Dave gazed around the function room. There was some hurried activity amongst the diners, swift refilling of wine glasses, some beckoning and miming to waiters that more booze was needed. The urgency clearly demonstrated by those who waved their bottles upside down, one thirsty humourist waggling the inverted empty over his head.

Geoffrey got to his feet and looked at his notes, his voice was as dry as his subject and style of delivery. Dave tuned out and looked around at his table companions. They were a table of eight, their host was Joanna Davies; Jo was a friend of his wife Liz from way back. Jo was doing well in her career and was now a Councillor responsible for planning.

On Dave's left was Allie Shiffton, Dave immediately warmed to her and during dinner they'd got on well.

29 Years

Allie was in her early fifties with two children at university, there was a third child, a boy of six. The youngest had been unwell for the last two years and had recently been diagnosed with Crohn's disease. Dave had never heard of Crohn's. Allie explained in too much detail that it had been very distressing to see their beautiful boy James, who admittedly had been a bit of a surprise when she found she was pregnant at forty six, become so ill from the age of four. She said the symptoms come and go but James had suffered from stomach cramps, fever, fatigue, loss of appetite and difficulty in putting on weight. As Allie relived the stress and worry, so she drank more of the Chilean Sauvignon Blanc but ate little. She continued to describe the situation that had been made worse because there was no useful treatment available in England. There were experts and medication that helped in USA. They'd been to Duke University in Durham, North Carolina six weeks ago but it was so expensive. Fights, hotels, consultants fees and medication that she didn't see how they could afford a programme of treatment.

Dave had become uncomfortable and actually been glad when Brian interrupted and moved the conversation on to holiday plans for Easter. He said that he and Jo were going down to Somerset for three days walking and relaxing away from work. As their conversation took off, Dave turned to Jo on his right. She shifted slightly on her chair and smiled at him, she had a very engaging smile 'I'm so glad that you and Liz could make it this evening.' She lifted her chin and rounded her shoulders. It was a girlish pose that had the probably unintended effect of enhancing her cleavage in an eye-catching manner. 'Sorry about the last minute call but my other guests dropped out on me yesterday morning, the wife wasn't well.'

'No problem, I'm glad you thought of us.

You know we're always up for a late invite; who was it that let you down?'

'He's a director of Liberty homes; they're looking to break into the region. I thought of you because you're in property development and you might make some useful contacts here.'

She leaned forward confidentially; 'of course you know the Council are behind on the new homes requirement, we're interested in good proposals.' She looked directly into his eyes 'you should let me know if you've got anything big coming up.'

Dave couldn't help himself, his eyes flashed down across her pale cleavage; he glimpsed her pointy breasts hanging freely under the loose-fitting silk shirt. Jo sat back and looked carefully at him;

'If you've anything big coming up.' she repeated softly.

'Well, as it happens, I'm looking into a project in the Cotswolds, it's an old airfield site'

'Excellent, I like brownfield developments. So much less complicated than farmland and helps to avoid the Area of Outstanding Natural Beauty arguments. When would you like to get together so that we can talk about it in more detail?'

'Let me call you next week, I need to do some more work on the proposal before I show you anything.'

'That's great, I'll look forward to hearing from you.' Jo nodded to confirm her interest, then sat back and picked up her wineglass. She drank neatly and put the glass on the tablecloth, rotating the stem in small movements between her thumb and forefingers. 'Now, tell me about your lovely boys, what have they been up to?'

The conversation moved into the well-charted shallow waters of schools and children.

Dave became aware that Allie was silent beside him, as he turned his head she said:

29 Years

'I'm so sorry for going on about James and our problems.'

'Oh no, don't give it a thought, I'm sure it's on your mind all the time, I wish I could do something to help.'

'Well, if you could, we'd be so grateful. It just seems like everything's against us at the moment.'

Dave remembered that one of the barristers in his old chambers had a kid that had similar problems. He'd call him on Monday; see if he had any information that might be useful.

~

While Dave and his friends were at the council dinner, John was at home in Fifield with his girlfriend Rachel. They carried their plates of food through from the kitchen to the sitting room in the one bedroom cottage. Rachel was a cheerful, outdoorsy girl who worked in a garden centre near Burford.

They'd met through John's frequent visits to the centre buying landscaping materials. Now they saw each other on an irregular basis since getting rather passionate at a New Year's Eve party. On New Year's Day they had woken up together to a wintery morning under the duvet in John's bedroom.

The evening was surprisingly warm, normally the temperature dropped as the sun went down but tonight the heat had stayed in the air as the earth released the sun's energy. The sky had started to cloud over, trapping the warmth. They sat either side of a small oak table, placed in such a way that they could both see the view eastwards over the valley. The weak evening sun layered through the thickening clouds, lighting up random fields and hedgerows in the distance.

Robin Stow

As Rachel started to talk about her day's events at the garden centre, John suddenly interrupted;
'Oh dammit, I left my tools at the lock-up on the airfield, I need them first thing over at Northleach. I'll have to go and get them after we've eaten, sorry Rache, go on, what were you saying?'
'No, no, it doesn't matter, look I'll come with you later if you like.'
'That'd be great, it shouldn't take long; we could stop at the Lamb for drink after if you like.'
'Yeah sure, that'd good.'
That chatted about their days and after a quick tidy and washing-up went outside to leave. John had an old Porsche 912 parked under the lean-to at the end of the terrace.
'You never finished telling me the story of how you come to have this old car.' They got in and as they looked at the darkening view, before starting the engine he recounted the tale.
'I won it. I was playing poker with some other guys in my third year at Uni. It was about three am; we were all a bit pissed and were playing the last hand. There was a lot of money on the table. I had a full house, queens on kings and was feeling very confident. All the others had folded except a PhD student named Chip from Texas. He'd run out of cash but said
'I'll see you.' John laughed at the memory.
I told him: 'you've got to pay to see, but you, my friend, you ain't got no more money.'
'Wait, wait I'll put up my car.'
'What car?'
'My little old coupe back in Dallas.'
'You can't be serious.'
'I sure am, I've got the vehicle title document right here in my pocket-book.'

29 Years

Everyone was laughing. Chip was well known for his extravagant statements.

'This is crazy, how much is it worth?'

'More'n a thousand bucks I'm sure'

'What type of car? Does it work? What sort of nick is it in? – Everyone had a question, caught up in the excitement revved up with Export lager, Red Bull and Jagerbombs.

'How do we know if it's any good?'

'You can call my uncle, it's stored in his garage right there in Highland Park. Hey, here's the number, use my cellphone.'

'You can't call now, it's three am.'

'Yeah, sure but they are six hours behind so its only nine in Dallas.'

'OK, OK, so who here knows about cars and what to ask?'

'Steve, Steve knows'

'Right then Steve you better make the call and explain what's going on here.'

'Hey, look guys. Steve, if my aunt Mavis answers the phone just say you want to talk with George Martins'

'No problem, I'm on it' said Steve.

So Steve made the call, which went surprisingly well in the circumstances. He spoke to uncle George who confirmed what Chip had said. He added that the little coupe was just fine and he'd driven it a few days before. So Chip put the title on the pile of cash and said; 'see you.'

I sighed sadly and put down a pair of kings and a pair of queens, Chip shouted 'yes' and put down a pair of kings a pair of aces and a four of clubs.

He was so chuffed but when put I down the third queen his face fell.

'Oh crap, you done me! Well played my man.'

Robin Stow

So I'd won a car and probably enough cash to pay for shipping it over to England.

'That's a great story, and I love the car, so get it started and take me for that drink you promised.'

'Sure we'll just drop by the hangar and get my tools.'

The headlights cast weak, pale yellow beams and she was left hand drive but it was always a pleasure to drive the old Porsche across the hills; the rasping exhaust barking in the dusk. He opened the front boot and clunked the tools in; they pulled away from the hangar and wheeled away down the hill to The Lamb. The sun had almost set and the sky was wide and flat over the distant hills.

'Hello John, what can I get for you two?'

John looked questioningly at Rachel who nodded.

'Pint and a half of Best please.'

The full, wet glasses were slid across the varnished bar top, John was telling Rachel some more about the history of the airfield. He pointed at the broken propeller blade on the wall saying that it came from a Wellington bomber that overshot the runway and crashed into the pub garden in 1943. 'Only the tail gunner survived, the plane finished up standing on its nose leaning against the back wall over there. The airman had climbed onto the pub roof and got down by sliding down a drainpipe.'

'That's right' said the barman 'if you're interested in the old stories you should talk to Ed Collins, he was there in the war. That's his nephew Tom in the blue jacket over at the other bar.'

Tom heard his name, looked over and grinned 'are you taking my name in vain again?'

'No, not me mate, just saying your uncle was at Rissy wasn't he?'

'Yeah, that's right – why d'you ask?'

'These two are interested in stories about the airfield during the war.'

29 Years

Tom walked around the corner of the bar holding his pint.
'Hello, how d'you do? I'm Tom Collins'
They introduced themselves and Tom leaned against the bar beside Rachel.
'So are you local then?'
'Yeah, from Fifield' said John 'so it was your uncle who was at the airfield in the war?'
'He was, he used to come in here a lot but he's rather old now and can't see that well either so he doesn't get out much.' Tom took a swallow of his pint and wiped his grey moustache outwards with thumb and forefinger.
'What's your interest in the war?'
'Well I wrote about the airfield in my Geography degree. I know a lot about the land but I don't know much about what went on there in the war.'
The three of them talked for a while then Tom said 'I need to head off home now but there are so many stories. If you'd like to meet Uncle Ed, why don't you come over for tea next Sunday afternoon? He loves a chat about the old days and you'd be a very welcome change for him.'
'That's really kind, we'd love to.' John glanced at Rachel. She shook her head 'Oh, I can't, I'm working on Sunday at the garden centre, but never mind, it sounds like more of a boys' thing anyway. You go ahead John, I'm sure you'll have a great time.'
'Great, we'll look forward to seeing you, come to Brook Cottage in Sherborne at four o'clock next Sunday. D'you know the village?' John nodded
'Right then, if you're coming from Windrush, turn off the main road opposite the gates to Sherborne House, follow the lane towards the river and you'll find us at the end on the left.'
The Lamb was almost empty when said their goodbyes and walked away across the heavy, ancient flagstones to the black oak door.

Chapter 4

Early 1944 – The Cotswolds

Occasionally, before breakfast, Collins cycled around the perimeter track, the early morning breeze on the hilltop was cold but the exercise kept him warm. He was wearing a thick blue serge battledress uniform with black shoes; their heavy leather soles skiddy on the wet metal pedals. He looked across the huge airfield, his eyes slid over the half-round Nissen huts and stopped on a small plane marooned in the middle of the grass runway. As he completed his circuit, he turned towards the little plane, curiosity aroused. Aircraft weren't his responsibility but this one was definitely not in the right place, he knew it should be parked in dispersal or in a hangar.

He decided to take a closer look and pressed on over the grass, his shoes getting wetter with the heavy dew. He came alongside, stopped and laid the bike down. It was a high wing monoplane, painted matt black underneath but with grey topsides. The left wing and rear of the fuselage were punctured with many tears, the canopy starred and smashed with bullet holes. There was a long skid mark from the rear of the aircraft. He looked at the tail plane, the wheel was missing; just the strut remained, bent sideways and dug into the ground.

He walked around to the front of the plane and saw a fitters' truck approaching. Ed waited until they stopped and climbed out.

'Mornin' sir.'

'Morning Corporal, what's happened here?'

'I dunno sir, we was just told to carry out a damage inspection.'

29 Years

He strode swiftly around the aircraft eyes flicking everywhere.

'Right then you two, nip off and get the tow truck; the tail wheel's fucked, we'll put a sling under the tail and tow 'er backwards to 'angar nineteen.'

The Corporal continued his inspection, lips pursed as he noted the bullet holes.

'She come in early this morning.'

He climbed up the short ladder attached to the fuselage and slid back the rear canopy.

'Cor there's a mess in 'ere, some poor blighter's copped a packet I shouldn't wonder.'

He stepped back down again saying 'well we can put 'er back together again easy enough, 'ooever was in the back is going to take a bit of mendin' though.'

They turned as the tow truck growled towards them. They could just make out two heads through the fogged-up split windscreen.

'What type of plane is it?'

'She's a Lysander, but I never seen one painted black before. And she's got no armament; there should be twin Lewis guns just 'ere.' He pointed at the rear cockpit.

'Don't know what she's been up to but whatever it was, it didn't go too well.'

'Yes, it looks as though they got an unfriendly reception from Jerry doesn't it? Good luck with your repairs.'

'All in a day's work sir, nuffink we can't fix.' The Corporal grinned and saluted as Collins picked up his bike.

'Right you dozy twats get out of that nice warm cab and get this fucking crate shifted!' The stream of abuse continued as Collins pedalled away towards the Officers' Mess; looking forward to hot tea and a cooked breakfast.

Once he'd finished eating and thanked the steward, he went into the anteroom for a cup of coffee and a cigarette.

He picked up the Daily Telegraph and sat down to enjoy a quiet ten minutes.

Relaxation over, he put on his hat and cycled to the office, he left his bike in the outside shelter and entered the Nissen hut.

'Morning sir!' chorused the clerks as he went by and entered his office. He sat down and eyed the paperwork that was sitting in his in-tray, the first task was Duty Rosters; he sighed and pulled the file towards him.

The Station Commander's phone rang.

'Group Captain Pearce' he announced.

'Guardroom here sir, I've got a Flying Officer Atkins here to see you sir.'

'Who? I don't know any Flying Officer Atkins, what's he want'

'He's a she sir and won't say what it's about but she's from London and says it's important.'

'Oh very well, send her over then.'

He replaced the receiver and looked at the wall clock, 10.45; something was up, visitors from London were rare at Rissy. It was mainly a maintenance station; there was very little operational flying.

Five minutes later there was a knock at his door.

'Come in, come in, good morning, good morning.' She saluted. 'Good morning sir, I'm Vera Atkins, would you mind if I close your door?'

'No, no by all means, may I get you a cup of coffee first?'

'No thank you, I'd just like to talk to you.'

Vera closed the door and sat down. She was an elegant figure in her well-cut, blue WAAF Flying Officer's uniform, blonde hair worn in a stylish roll at the nape of her neck. 'What I am about to tell you is secret and is not to be shared or discussed with anyone other than with my prior agreement.'

Pearce bridled slightly at the junior officer's words. He laid his forearms on the desk and leaned forward.

'And you are who, exactly?'

'I'm second-in-command of the French Section of the Special Operations Executive, the SOE. My Commanding Officer is Colonel Maurice Buckmaster, you may telephone him if you wish.'

'And what does the SOE do?'

'I'm afraid I can't tell you that.'

'And what is it that you want from me?'

'I expect you know that a damaged Lysander landed here last night with a wounded passenger on board?'

'Yes I know about that, an unconscious young woman was taken to the field hospital, she's still there.'

'I'd like to see her and the doctor who's treating her.'

'And why is that may I ask?'

'Because she's one of my operatives, I need to assess her condition and decide what to do with her.'

'I see, well, before we go any further I'd better have a word with your C.O.'

She gave him the number and he spoke to Buckmaster.

'Hmmph, well that all seems to be in order, I'll come with you and we'll see what's what.'

They got into her waiting car and he directed the driver to the field hospital. It had originally been created as an air raid shelter by digging into the side of an Anglo-Saxon burial mound. The shelter had been enlarged inside the mound to provide space for a small ten-bed hospital. They entered and found a medical orderly sitting at his desk in the underground cavern.

'There was a female casualty brought in early this morning. I'd like to speak to the doctor who treated her' said Pearce.

'Yessir, if you go down the hall you'll find Major Rogers along there on the right.'

As he finished speaking a man appeared in a white coat, blue uniform trousers below.

'Hello, are you after me? I'm Kit Rogers.'

'Hello Kit, yes we are, we'd like to talk to you about one of your patients. A young woman who was brought in early this morning.'

'Ah yes, the French girl, I wondered who might come to claim her; she won't say anything to me. How can I help?'

'Is there somewhere we can talk?' asked Vera.

'Not really, no, it's just as you can see.' He gestured at the open ward.

'Hmm, perhaps you would follow me then.'

As they walked away she said 'we can talk privately in my car.'

They reached her Riley and she suggested to the driver that he might like to go for a walk and have a cigarette. Once they had closed the doors she explained the reason for her visit. The doctor answered:

'I can tell you that she's semi-conscious, very weak and in shock from blood loss. We gave her a transfusion, four pints. She's on a drip to make up the rest. There are some severe flesh wounds to her legs caused by metal splinters. I think that one of the cannon shells hit a metal spar in the fuselage and sent splinters through the rear cockpit. She must have bled for quite a while before she got to us.'

'Will she make a full recovery and can you say how long it will take?' Asked Vera.

'There's no reason why not and I expect at least three to four months maybe more before she is a hundred percent. You might bear in mind that she'd have died if she'd been left any longer.'

'Thank you, may I see her now?'

'Yes you may but please be brief and don't distress her. She may not be very lucid.'

29 Years

Vera walked toward the slight figure in the bed; black hair spread out on the pillow. White face, white sheet. Her eyes were closed, her dark lips slightly parted. A transparent tube from a drip snaked across the blanket to her thin pale arm.

'Hello Jeanne, it's Vera.'

The young woman on the bed slowly rolled her head from side to side and became still.

'Jeanne, c'est moi; Vera.'

The woman opened her eyes briefly, as they closed again she murmured.

'Ah, enfin. Vera.'

Vera pulled a chair to the bedside and gently took Jeanne's hand.

'Can you hear me? Can you understand me?

The head nodded once. Vera spoke clearly, slowly and kindly to the wounded woman:

'you're safe here in an RAF hospital. You've had a bad time and lost a great deal of blood but now you're out of danger. The doctors will make you better but you need lots of rest. I'll arrange everything for you so you musn't worry. I'll leave my telephone number with the Station Commander so you can easily talk to me if you need to.'

The head nodded again and the dark lips might have smiled very faintly.

'Merci Vera.'

'Do you have any packages, a bag for me?'

She nodded again, Vera looked at the doctor questioningly

'Her belongings are in my cubicle.'

'Excellent, I'll have a look presently. Good bye my dear you can be sure I'll be keeping my eye on you.'

Vera stood up and replaced the visitor's chair, as the group moved away from the bed she said:

'Thank you sir, I can see she's in very capable hands.

How long will you need to keep her in hospital and what convalescent facilities do you have?'

'I expect she'll be with us for a week or two, at least until she can get up unaided. Then she'll need somewhere quiet and peaceful to mend and get her strength back; I am afraid we don't have any convalescent facilities though.'

'That's fine, I understand.' They went into his cubicle; Vera swiftly went through the contents of the suitcase and packages. Having found what she wanted and transferred it to her satchel she turned to Group Captain Pearce.

'May we go back to your office now?'

'Yes of course. Thanks Kit, do let me know if you need any help with the, err patient. He nodded in the direction of Jeanne's bed.

Back in Pearce's office they resumed their seats: 'thank you sir that was very helpful. Now I need somewhere private for Jeanne to convalesce, d'you have any thoughts as to where may be suitable?

'What? Me? Around here? Don't you people have access to all sorts of, err all sorts of places?'

'Sadly not, I'd prefer her to convalesce near here where Major Rogers can monitor her progress. The fewer people who know about her the better. Is there a discreet family that she could lodge with that you know and can trust?'

Pearce opened his leather tobacco pouch and ruminatively started filling his pipe.

'Well I do know a few people nearby; I've been stationed here for nearly three years now. I suppose you want somewhere quiet, out of the way, no children that might gossip in school, that sort of thing?'

'Yes, that sort of thing, does any one spring to mind?'

He struck a match and sucked strongly on the pipe, satisfying jets of smoke squirting pungently from the corner of his mouth.

'Possibly, mmm the best one I can think of is a chum of mine who's a solicitor, he is or was a partner in a firm in Cheltenham, he's semi-retired, in his sixties I'd say. Both children are away serving; their son's in the RAF and their daughter's in the Wrens. They live down at the end of a lane in Sherborne, that's a little village about five miles from here.'

'Sounds like a good possibility, how do you know him?'

'I like to go to Evensong at Sherborne, it's a splendid church, built for the Earl of Sherborne you know and they've a good choir. Tim Smith is a Church Warden, that's how we met. He introduced himself and made me very welcome when I first went there. We often chatted after the service then one evening he invited me to his house for supper afterwards. Excellent food, his wife's French actually, Monique, she's a super cook, oh, and she speaks very good English but with quite an accent.'

'That's very interesting and may be helpful, thank you very much sir.'

'Now talking of food, I expect you had an early start coming down from London, would you like to join me for lunch in the Mess?'

'That's very kind, I'd like that very much, err, d'you think we could go and visit the Smiths afterwards?'

'I should think so, I'll give Tim a tinkle, make sure they're both about.'

He phoned and found both the Smith's at home; they were invited over for three o'clock.

Pearce directed the driver: past the turning to Great Rissington, down the hill to Great Barrington, turn right at The Fox 'nice pub that one' on through the narrow winding street that was the main road through Windrush then when they were almost opposite the gates to Sherbone House. 'Turn right here and follow the lane to the end, careful, mind it's a bit tight in places.'

Tim Smith had heard the car and was standing in the open front doorway.

'Hello James, lovely to see you, do come in and tell me what brings you and your young friend out on a chilly day like this.'

The log fire was bright and it was warm in the sitting room. Tim and Monique welcomed Vera and offered them tea. Once they were settled Vera admired the magnificent view over the deer park on the far bank and away northward to the hills.

'Yes we really are very lucky; that's the Sherborne brook, more like a little river really. Good fishing; trout, grayling and so forth. Not a house in sight is there? The deer park belongs the Sherborne Estate, we hardly ever see a soul down here do we darling?'

Having established the suitability of the location, Vera explained that there was a young wounded Frenchwoman who needed somewhere to recuperate for two or three months and asked if the Smiths would be prepared to look after her.

'My dear girl we'd consider it an honour, we've often talked about how we could be a bit more use and do our bit. You tell us exactly what you'd like us to do and it shall be done.'

As they drove away Vera said: 'I think they're ideal, Jeanne will be very happy with the Smiths. I really like the idea that she can move into the flat over the garage when she's stronger, she'll feel a bit more private there. Tell me, what's the house called?'

'It's called Bennett's Farm.'

'Well, I like Bennett's Farm very much and I like your friends too. One other thing, I'm sure that you and Major Rogers don't have time to keep an eye on her day to day; so would it be possible for you to appoint a liaison officer for Jeanne?

29 Years

Someone she can talk to, someone who can help her with her recovery. And, when she's able to, to go for long walks, get her fit again. Do you have someone you can spare?'

Pearce immediately thought of his admin officer, a young bomber navigator who'd been blinded in a flak storm over Berlin. He'd regained most of his sight but was no longer medically fit to fly. He was still serving but in an office job; he was a bright young man and Pearce knew he was bored senseless with the paper pushing.

'Yes I do have someone we could use, I think he'll be just the ticket.'

'Excellent, can I drop you back at your office? I need to push on back to London.'

They parted, Pearce promising to stay in touch with progress reports.

The following morning Collins found himself in the Station Commander's office.

'Come in and sit down; now, how are you enjoying your admin duties?'

'All pretty routine thank you sir' was the non-committal reply.

'Then I think I may have something that's a little less routine for you.' Things were looking up, Collins didn't know Pearce very well but he had turned out for the Station Commander's cricket side at the end of last summer. He wasn't much use against fast bowling due to his eyesight but he was still a handy leg-spinner and had taken a few wickets.

'No, I don't want you to start organising the cricket nets quite yet.' He leaned forward across his desk. 'As a matter of fact I need you to act as a liaison officer on a very discreet, actually a very secret matter. We're reporting directly to London on this one, it's all very hush, hush so keep it under your hat.'

Pearce went on to share what little he knew about Jeanne and to explain what was going to be required of him over the next few months, then:
'So firstly, what I want you to do is go over and meet the Smiths, I've told them about you and they're expecting your visit. I expect you'll be seeing a lot of them, they're good friends of mine so don't go letting the side down will you? Then go and introduce yourself to the MO, Major Rogers, I've briefed him about your role and when he thinks she's ready for it, he'll introduce you to Jeanne and you can get started. Does that all seem clear to you?'
'Yes it does thank you sir, does she speak English? I'm afraid my French is of the Standard English schoolboy variety. Bomber Command didn't provide much by way of language training.'
'I'm told her English is pretty good so you should be able to get along alright, might even be an opportunity for you work on your fron-say' he laughed. 'So I suggest you pop along to the Smiths and get the ball rolling.'
Collins walked back to his office buzzing with excitement. After months of twiddling his thumbs here at last was something interesting. Wow, a French agent and a girl to boot. He wondered what she would be like; fairly hard-bitten, probably seen some pretty rough stuff. Poor thing, sounded like she was badly hurt. He'd cycle over to meet the Smiths after lunch then check with the Medical Officer afterwards.
That afternoon saw Collins pedaling through the quiet, wintery countryside. After they'd shown him around, the Smiths sat him down to a proper farmhouse tea; they treated him as if he were their own son who they said was away flying in the Middle East. 'It'll be so nice to have some young people in the house again' said Monique. 'I do hope we'll become great friends and we'll help you to get our wounded girl fit again.'

29 Years

Collins had stayed much longer than he expected, they really hadn't wanted to let him go. It was after six when he got back to the station, too late to see the MO that day so he went over in the morning.

It was the first time that he had been to the hospital. It was a strange set-up, underground and rather dark and gloomy. The floor was smooth polished concrete, the roof was curved corrugated iron supported by unpainted steel girders and stanchions.

'Is Major Rogers about?'

'Yessir, if you go down the hall you will find him along there on the right.'

He stood in the gap in the curtains and saluted. 'Good morning sir, I'm Ed Collins, the Station Commander told me to come and see you.'

'Hello, yes indeed, I'm expecting you, our patient is still very weak but making progress, leave it another two or three days and give me a ring. I'll let you know when she's strong enough to meet you.'

As Collins went back to his office he saw the Fitter Corporal who had towed the Lysander away.

'Hello Corporal, how did you get on with your repairs?'

'Hello sir, yeah we 'ad some 'elp as it 'appens. They needed the plane back toot sweet so they flew their own fitters over with a complete new tail wheel assembly. While they fitted it we patched up the fuselage and control wires.'

'That took some work off your plate then. D'you know where they came from and why was there such a rush to get the plane back?'

The Corporal wasn't happy being questioned, he sucked in his breath over clenched teeth and leaned forwards confidentially 'they come from RAF Tangmere, some sort of special operations outfit.

They needed it back quick, something to do with flying during the moon period.' He straightened up. 'That's it sir, nothing I need to know about I'm sure.' He saluted and headed on over towards the NAAFI.

Collins reached his office and sat there musing on his new task. Was there anything he could do to prepare for it, practice his French? He couldn't ask anyone or even tell anyone what he was going to be doing. Actually he could, he needed to tell the clerks something to explain his future absences. He'd tell them that he was doing a French course at Brize Norton that should cover it and he could do some French revision in the office without it causing any comment.

He went into the Chief Clerk's office and asked him to order some French textbooks and then explained why. 'Planning to leave us are we sir? Off to lar bell France is it? There's a war on over there you know.' He laughed kindly, 'don't you worry sir, I'll get you some nice books; no dirty postcards mind.' The other clerks grinned and chuckled as Collins winced. He went back to his office and got on with his paperwork.

Ed Collins often pondered on his eyesight problem, he was certainly feeling fit and his eyes didn't bother him. He knew that his sight was steadily improving he gave himself tests from time to time. He could now see small birds in flight two hundred yards away and read print clearly close up, even as far away as six feet. He really would like to get back to his old Squadron and start flying again.

The following day he telephoned the MO to enquire about Jeanne's progress.

'She's doing very well, off the drip and able to feed herself. Come over for a visit tomorrow afternoon, come and meet her.'

29 Years

'Righto sir, I'll be there at three o'clock.'

In the gloom, he looked in at the MO's cubicle.

'Hello Collins' he stood up, removing his spectacles 'come with me, we'll go and see how she is.' Their heavy shoes sounded loud off the concrete floor.

'Hello Jeanne, I've a visitor here to see you.' The slight figure was sitting up in bed, a mound of pillows behind her back and head. Rogers introduced Collins and explained his role then said:

'Look, I've got a heap of things to be getting on with, may I leave you two to have a chat? Collins, would you pop in before you go?' His footsteps clacked away and they looked at one another. Her gaze was clear and steady; he held it for a few moments and then smiled. Jeanne smiled back and then gave a small laugh.

'I think you should sit down, it will be more comfortable for you.'

He pulled the visitor's chair to the side of the bed and sat facing her so she only had to turn slightly to see him. She shifted a little on her pile of pillows; there was a cage over her legs holding the bedding off her wounds. 'So how are you feeling today?'

'I was feeling bored so I am very happy to have a visitor. Now, tell me, what is your name and can you explain to me where I am in England.'

Her English was good but with a charming heavy accent.

'My name is Edward Collins, my friends call me Ed.'

Pouting nicely, she interrupted 'I prefer Edouard, as we say in France.'

He grinned; 'we're near a village called Little Rissington which this station, we call it 'Rissy' is named after. The whole area is called the Cotswolds after the hills around here. Our nearest large towns are Oxford which is about twenty miles away, I mean thirty kilometres away to the east. You've probably heard of Oxford University?

Then there's Cheltenham, that's about thirty kilometres to the west. I sound like a tour guide don't I?'

'No, no, please go on I'm enjoying your tour.' She pointed at the single wing badge on his chest 'I see that you're a navigator, you speak like you know exactly where you are.'

'Thank you, you're right; well, it's a very pretty area, lots of small villages, mainly stone built houses. Many little rivers, good for fishing which I used to enjoy when I was a boy. Hills and woods but mainly farmland. There's some big country estates with very grand houses, châteaux you'd say. It was very quiet here before the war but now there are many RAF stations and lots of servicemen. I know the area quite well because I have family here and I used to come to the Cotswolds for holidays when I was a boy.'

'But what do you do now, are you still a navigator?'

'I am, I was in Bomber Command but at the moment I'm unfit to fly. My plane flew directly into a flak burst and the bright light of the explosion blinded me. I couldn't see for nearly a week. My eyesight has slowly returned but whilst I've been recovering I've been put on ground duties, which for me means hours of pushing paper and sitting at a desk. Not much fun at all. I say can you understand all this? me chattering on?'

'But of course, I can understand much better than I can speak, I do not get so much chance to speak English.'

'But how come your English is so good? I can tell you my French is pretty awful, just schoolboy stuff.'

'I was always good at English in school and I worked in the holidays as a nanny at the château in a nearby village. One of the daughters had married an Englishman. They lived in England, near London I think but they used to come with their three boys for a month every summer holiday.

29 Years

Everybody spoke a mixture of French and English so I was able to become more fluent.

They haven't been over for five years so my English is not so good now.'

He sensed that she was getting tired and said:

'I probably should be going now but I'll look in and see you tomorrow. If you're feeling up to it, maybe soon I could find a wheelchair and get you outside for some fresh air. We can look at the countryside, the views are magnificent from here because we're on top of a hill.'

She reached over and squeezed his fingers. He looked at her hand lying light as a bird's wing in his palm, he replied softly with his fingers and smiled into her eyes.

'You're very kind, that would be very nice. Au revoir, Edouard, I look forward to tomorrow.'

'Au revoir, Jeanne.' He walked down the ward to the doctor's cubicle.

'Hello sir, you said to look in before I left.'

'Yes, please call me Kit, how d'you find her?'

'Obviously pretty weak but mentally she's all there, her English is amazing. D'you think I might be allowed to take her out for a bit one day? In a wheelchair I mean.'

'I think that'll be fine, we don't want to rush things so leave it for a few days and then just ten minutes to start with. Oh and make sure she doesn't get cold.'

Ed went off feeling very cheery; Jeanne was lovely, not pretty but darkly attractive with a wonderful smile. Not hard-bitten at all, it was going to be a real pleasure to look after her. He whistled a few bars and grinned to himself.

'Oh yes, and what are you looking so bloody happy about then?' It was Jock Stewart, another Flying Officer but on the maintenance side. An Erk, he was a miserable little ginger man with a sour face.

'Lovely weather ain't it?' Collins gave him another big smile and sauntered on to the Mess for tea.

Chapter 5

Spring 2014 – The Cotswolds

'That's great Allie, I'll look forward to seeing you after lunch then.' Dave put the phone down and walked over to the angled drawing board that stood against the sidewall of his office. Clipped to it was a site plan of the area around Little Rissington dominated by the proposed development area that was hatched in red. All the roads, lanes and tracks were shown but what particularly interested him was the track that led eastwards to the A424. In order to obtain planning permission for a large number of homes he knew that access was going to be the key. There'd been strong complaints regarding the increase in traffic that would be generated by Victory Fields. He felt sure that proposing a different access would greatly improve his chances with the planning application. His thinking was that if a developer submitted a proposal that used the existing westwards access to the already over-burdened community of Little Rissington; then the Council would only grant permission for a small number of houses. If he could secure the full forty acres and had a new access to the east he could apply for three to four hundred new homes. He unrolled the cover to hide the plans then went out to the bakery to get a sandwich.

When he got to Allie's, she was standing outside the front of the house retying Clematis to the wall. She half-turned, her hands still working, as he got out and closed the car door.
'Hello Allie, great day to be doing a bit in the garden.'

29 Years

'Hello Dave, how nice to see you.'

She finished her knots and embraced him; he kissed her warmly on each cheek.

'Now' she said 'shall we go for a walk? We can chat as we go, it's far too nice a day to waste it by being inside isn't it?'

They both looked at his shoes. 'Probably best if I put my boots on then.'

At the back of his car she stood beside him as he swapped black loafers for green wellies.

'All set, where are we off to?'

'We'll go across the fields and up to the woods that you can see on top of the hill.'

'Won't the farmer mind us going across his fields?'

'I shouldn't think so' she laughed 'it's my land.'

They set off uphill, two terriers trotting with them, Allie leading towards the low sun. It haloed her fair hair and shone through her thin blue cotton skirt, outlining slim calves and thighs.

'You're pretty fit you know, sorry, err what I mean is err how do you keep so fit?' He corrected himself rather weakly.

'I ride everyday that the weather lets me. I walk the dogs, play tennis in the summer, you know, that sort of thing.'

'Tell me about the farming, I didn't know you were a farmer.'

'I'm not, not really, my father left me the land and the farmhouse when he died. My mother had no interest in farming; she lives in a townhouse in Cheltenham. I lease the land to a neighbouring farmer; we used to have this as our weekend place when we lived in London, now we live here full-time.'

'What happened, did you get fed up with London?'

'Sadly London got fed up with us, my husband had a very good job but he lost it along with many others.

He was a stockbroker, he got another job with a small private firm but over the last few years things got worse and worse. The firm wasn't making any money and so nor was he. At the same time unfortunately his social drinking became a serious habit. Eventually they had to let him go, he's very bitter about the City. We had to sell the house in Fulham and so here we are in the Cotswolds, which I must say I absolutely adore. I'd much rather be here than London any day.'

'I can't say I miss London either, I'm much happier here too.' They were side by side and smiled easily at each other. 'So tell me where does your land begin and end? Is it as far as the eye can see?' he teased.

'It's only about a hundred acres, more of a smallholding really. It used to be much larger but I sold off about two hundred acres because we needed the cash. I kept this area around the house to preserve our own little sanctuary. We used to run all the way alongside that track up to the airfield. You probably know the Merrymouth Inn?' He nodded 'Well that track comes out onto the road just near there.'

Dave stumbled in astonishment, 'are you alright?'

'Yes I'm fine thanks, just clumsy, two left feet.'

They stopped at the top of the hill and looked eastwards at the view.

'Wow, that's fabulous, wouldn't it be fantastic to have a house here, just to enjoy that every day?' They stood gazing, Dave got his breath back and said 'Now before I forget, the reason for my visit, apart from a lovely walk, is that I've been talking to an old boss of mine, a barrister. After you spoke about your son at the council dinner I gave him a call.'

'Did you? but why do I need a barrister?'

'Because this particular barrister has a daughter who's also got Crohn's disease.'

29 Years

'Oh my goodness, how terrible.'

'Yes it is but my point is that she was diagnosed six years ago and after a very rocky start she's now making good progress. I told him about you and your son and he said he'd be happy to talk to you, share his knowledge, contacts everything he's got if it can be of use to you.'

'Oh, oh, I don't know what to say. That's wonderful, just wonderful.' She choked and looked away from him. 'It's been so hard, you have no idea: James being so ill, Charlie losing his job, the debts, the lack of income, the drinking. It just seems never-ending. And Mother, she's hopeless, she's quite a drinker herself.'

Allie breathed deeply a few times then squared her shoulders. 'The thing is, the thing is you've just got to get on with it. Haven't you?'

'Well you have just got on with it, I mean, you've moved on, moved into the farmhouse. You've raised some money as well; you're doing all the right things. Is money still a problem?'

'We always need money. I'd be grateful for any bright ideas you might have on that particular topic.'

'Mmm, so would you consider selling off any more of your land?'

'No, I don't think so, I don't want anyone spoiling our space here. Why, what d'you have in mind?

They started down the hill. 'Is this track yours?'

'Yes, why?'

'What about selling this track?'

She stopped in surprise. 'Who would want the track and what would they want it for?'

'A developer might want it as an access road' he looked up and down the hill 'is it a proper track not a footpath or anything, all the way down to the main road?'

'Yes it is, it goes out onto the A424 by the pub, why?'

'Because there's a possible development site up at the airfield.'

'But won't that mean there'll be a lot of traffic? Won't it be noisy?'

They looked back at the farmhouse.

'It's about half a mile away from you so I don't think you'd really notice the traffic. They could plant a hedge as a screen, that'd cut down any noise and you wouldn't see the cars either.' They walked in silence for a bit as she weighed his words.

'Suppose I was interested, how much do you think they'd pay? And of course the farmer would still need to use the track. Who's the developer?'

'The developer would be me and I'd have to build a proper tarmac road. But, if you sold me a right of way over the track, subject to me getting the planning permission, I'd pay you two fifty to five hundred thousand pounds depending on the number of houses.'

'Five hundred thousand pounds! That's an awful lot of money.'

'Yeah but I could only pay that much if we got permission to build at least three hundred houses.'

'Three hundred, that's a huge development.'

'No bigger than Victory Fields.'

'I'll have to think about it. It's very good idea but I'm worried about the amount of traffic and noise; why don't you come back to the house, we'll have a cup of tea and talk about it a bit more?'

The terriers had run on ahead and were by the back door splashing as they drank out of their water bowl. They turned smiling and panting, catching drops of water off their whiskers with their thin pink tongues. Once they were inside, Allie lifted the lid and put the kettle on the Aga.

'I'm sorry I haven't thanked you properly.'

She turned and looked him squarely in the eyes.
'Thank you Dave, thank you very much for helping especially when I need help so badly just now.'
She put her hands on his shoulders and reaching up on tiptoes kissed him on the lips. He put his arms protectively around her and she reached up again for a further kiss. He looked into her brown eyes and pressed his lips gently to hers. Her mouth opened and he felt her tongue slide along his lips and push lightly. He let her in, his hands slipped to cup her soft bottom, she moaned into his breath.

~

John Gallen turned right opposite the gates of Sherborne House; the old car's suspension creaked down the unmade road, lurching through dry potholes. He twisted his way through the ancient cotswold stone houses, built haphazardly around the back of the village. At the very end of the lane there was a turning area in front of Brook Cottage, the house was set into the ground beside the lane. He got out of the car and saw that the land sloped towards the river about a hundred yards away across a water meadow. He went down a couple of steps and knocked at the front door.
Tom opened the door. 'Hello John, good to see you, did you find your way alright?'
'Yes fine thanks, the lane's a bit bumpy for the old girl though.'
'What a nice looking car, what age is she?'
'She was built in 1966 so, forty-eight this year, still looking good as most of that time was spent in the sun in California and Texas.'
'Uncle Ed will love it he's always been keen on old cars, come on in and say hello.'

They went into the rather cold and gloomy flagstoned hall.
'We're in here darling!' and they followed the voice on into the sitting room. The wood-burner was drawing nicely and the room was warm and sunny. Despite the warmth Ed was wearing mustard coloured corduroy trousers and a tweed jacket that was now a size too large for his diminishing frame. He was sitting in a wingback chair by the fireplace, Tom introduced his wife Denise and turned to his uncle. 'Ed, this is John, the chap I told you about who's interested in the old stories about Rissy.'
Ed pushed himself up out of the chair and stuck out his hand 'how d'you do young man?'
'Very pleased to meet you Mister Collins, I hope I'm not disturbing you.'
'No not at all, delighted to meet you, and please, do call me Ed.' He was well spoken, his voice clear and slightly gravelly. Not the voice you might expect of a ninety-four year old. 'Do sit and we'll have some tea.'
Denise got busy with the tea things, handing round cups and plates and offering cake. They all chatted about the weather saying, thank goodness the rain had finally stopped and how nice it was to see the sun again. After about half an hour of general conversation:
'So John, what was it you wanted to know about Rissy?'
Tom who'd heard all the stories many times before excused himself with jobs and chores to be done. Denise collected up some of the tea things and heading for the kitchen pushed the door open with her foot.
'I wondered if you could tell me how you came to be there and what was going on and what was it like on the airfield in the war years?'
Ed reached out and, clattering slightly, put his cup and saucer on the side table. He sat back in the high-backed chair; bony hands folded in his lap.

Ed looked at John through cloudy pupils behind thick, slightly tinted glasses. He spoke clearly and without hesitation;

'The war had been going on for a long time before I arrived at Rissy. I was at University when war broke out in 1939, however in 1943 I was a navigator in Bomber Command. In December that year we were flying missions to try and bomb the Germans into submission. Hundreds of missions, hundreds of bombers, terrible devastation. I'd been very lucky, not had a scratch in twenty-seven missions. I was stationed at RAF Melbourne in Yorkshire flying Halifaxes.

On my last mission, though I didn't know it was to be my last when we took off, our target was Berlin. The flak was terrible and as we flew through it a shell exploded directly in front of me. I was looking straight at it when it went off, the fireball seemed to burn my eyes and I was blinded.' He closed his eyes at the memory but continued to talk. 'I wasn't wearing protective goggles, I'd been looking at the map checking our position it was just bad luck that I looked up when I did. Fortunately I was the navigator; the skipper was unhurt and able to fly the Halifax on his own. We had a Flight Engineer in the crew, in fact he got me out of my seat and helped me into his so he could take over some of my duties. Of course I was no use as a navigator, not being able to see.' He laughed, a short bark.

'I was blind for a week, sitting around the hospital like a spare part or banging about with a white stick and a bandage round my head. Slowly my sight returned but they wouldn't let me go back to the squadron. I was declared unfit for flying duty and sent off to do admin work instead. That's how I ended up at a non-operational base like Rissy.' He sighed and ran a knotty forefinger around the inside of the collar of his viyella check shirt.

'It was such a wrench you know, so hard to leave a crew when you've been through so much together. I felt I'd let them down, we only had another three missions to fly then we'd have done our thirty. The rule was that after thirty we got six months off operations. I kept in touch and thank goodness they all made it.'

He lifted his chin 'it was such an intense experience for us, so many aircrew died. We didn't really think about the future. We just lived for the day; for the moment.' He was quiet for a while looking out of the window then continued speaking.

'So then I was posted, to a desk job at Rissy. The Station Commander was a chap called Pearce. A Group Captain, he was very decent to me, he'd been a pilot himself and understood what I was going through. He was bit of an eccentric; he drove an old Bugatti around the airfield. It made the most wonderful noise, he loaned it to me once or twice. Gosh I haven't thought about that for sixty years; I think he used to race it from time to time, I loved driving that car, very powerful for its time and beautifully built. Anyway, back to your question, what was going on and what was it like. Well it was a huge wind-swept airfield, high up too. Terrible weather that first winter, snow and cold all the time. Rissy was originally used for maintenance and aircraft storage; there were hundreds of aircraft dispersed around the airfield at any one time. We also had a pilot training school that ran courses for overseas pilots; there were men from all over the world passing through. Oh and there was a lot of night flying, I was often woken up by a roaring engine as some rookie pulled out of the approach and went round again. There was so much training going on that they used the relief airfields nearby at Windrush, that's the next village to here and, oh I forget their names but there were three or four others.

29 Years

It was a pretty big set-up, there must have been over a thousand permanent staff for maintenance and training plus all the pilots on courses. Of course there were many more buildings there than there are now. I tell you what, I've got some old diaries of that time; just notebooks really and quite a few old photos. Why don't you come back next Sunday and we could look at them together. I expect that'll jog a few memories.'

'Your memory is pretty amazing to me, I can hardly remember what happened yesterday let alone seventy years ago.'

Ed came to the front door to see John off. 'I say that's a nice looking motor, Porsche isn't it? An early 911 I'd say.'

'You're very close, it's a 912, the one with the four cylinder engine.'

'Oh yes I remember, I remember when they were used as Police cars in Germany in the sixties, painted green and white, I went over there once.' He nodded approvingly and peered inside, John climbed in and fired up the air-cooled engine 'yes that's it, that's the noise I remember.'

Ed leaned on his stick and gave a brief wave with his free hand as John drove slowly away.

Chapter 6

Spring 2014 – The Cotswolds

They were due to meet at six o'clock in the bar at the Lamb Hotel in Burford. Dave parked in the courtyard of the 15th century stone built inn and saw Matt looking out of the French windows. He waved and Matt crunched across the fine gravel, once again greeting Dave like a long lost brother, giving him a hug and laughing with delight. His sharp white teeth, black moustache and pointy brown face gave him the look of an amiable rodent.

'Did they fix you up with a decent room? I said that you were a very important man and needed looking after.'

'Yes of course, everyone's been very nice they've given me a great room with a four-poster bed. I never slept in a four poster before, I felt like a king!'

'Excellent; it's nice here isn't it? They turned and admired the low-beamed room, high, wood-framed settles and armchairs upholstered in a pleasing mix of tapestry and damask. Wall lights, flower arrangements and oil paintings decorated the panelled room. The fire was lit and the smell of wood smoke mingled pleasingly with the scent of spring flowers.

'Let me get you a drink, how's the family? How's your dad?' They went in to the bar 'family's all fine and send you their best, Dad's busy all the time, Mum says she hardly ever sees him, travelling all over the Middle East with his business.'

'So how is the shipping business?'

'You know him; every day's a disaster; actually I think things are going pretty well for him.

He's just bought an even bigger Sunseeker so I guess he's making money.'
'I often wondered how come you never went into the family business.'
'I did actually, for a few years after college but I found shipping a bit boring, a bit too conventional for me. But he did bankroll my first property deal in Spain and I'll always remember that.'
'Well, that's what kind, rich fathers can do for their favourite sons!'
'Oh he made money too you know, it was a business deal like any other.'
'Yeah but he trusted you, that's the main thing.'
'Could you put the drinks on my tab please? we're eating here as well.' They stepped away from the bar.
'I'm glad that you were able to come over so we can have a good discussion about this together. I've got some plans to show you, shall we go into that little lounge? We can take our drinks and sit by the fire, there's a table we can use and be quite private.'
They sat down and Dave explained the proposal for the development at RAF Little Rissington 'Rissy,' and emphasised the value of an alternative eastward access road.
'Yeah, yeah, I get it; new access equals more houses, seems pretty straightforward, what's the catch?'
Dave unrolled the site plan on the table using their glasses to hold the sides down. He pointed, 'here's the site and here's the eastward access. It's actually a farm track at the moment but as you can see it exits onto the main road over here.'
'I see, so how do we get to use this track? Who owns it? Will they let us use it?'
'I know the woman who owns it, she's interested in selling but she's worried about traffic and noise.

She won't sell us the land but I think she might sell what we call an easement or a right of way across the track, I said that we'd build a proper tarmac road and screen it with a hedge.'

'How much does she want?'

'She didn't say but I suggested two fifty to five hundred thousand pounds depending on the number of houses we get permission for. She said it sounded like a lot of money but she'd have to think about it.'

'OK, I like it. Two things: one, we don't pay anything if we don't get planning permission, two, get her to sign an exclusive agreement with us as soon as possible, we don't want another developer spotting this.' Matt looked at his phone then at his watch. 'Right, it's too late now but I want you on it first thing.' He lifted his gin and tonic and smiled, 'cheers, now, tell me, how's it going to work? How's a little firm like ours going to take on the big boys.'

'I'm good friends with the council planning officer; she's keen to support local firms in these type of developments. She doesn't want to see all the work going to the national companies, she told me so at the council dinner a few weeks ago. I've another friend who has a contact at the Ministry of Defence, the owners of the land, it's possible we might get some help from there as well.'

'What kind of help?'

'An idea of what level the opposition are bidding at.'

'Will you also get some inside information about the other developers' planning proposals?'

'It's possible but I may have to sell my body to get it!'

'No problem for a man of your many talents, I remember you seemed to be able fix almost anything when you were helping me.'

'Yeah, we'll see. I also need to hire a firm of planning consultants to put together a really professional proposal.

29 Years

By the way I've registered the company for this deal as 'Cloud Developments Ltd.'

'OK, fine, I like it. Go ahead with hiring a consultant, make sure they're blue chip and your girlfriend at the Council likes them.'

'I'm going to start needing some more money; so far I haven't had to spend much. Most of the initial capital for this project is still there. I need to pay expenses and I've been drawing from it but I'm also going to need a solicitor for the legal work and an accountant for the financial planning and budgeting. Speaking of the bid, the MoD will only accept bids from those parties that can show that they've got sufficient cash in the bank.'

'How much do you think we'll have to pay for the site?'

'If the Council give us an outline agreement for three hundred and fifty homes we should budget fifty million then we've got the building and infrastructure costs. Say forty million, allow ten million for contingencies, so call it a hundred in all. The exit value once all the houses are sold should be about one twenty. Have you got a plan for getting the first fifty million into the firm?'

'Yeah, I've got some ideas, I'll tell you when it's sorted.'

A waiter brought the menus. 'And you're both dining with us tonight gentlemen?'

'Yes, shall we go through? We can choose at the table, get in before the rush.'

The waiter led them through to the elegant dining room and once they were seated handed them weighty leather volumes.

'When I'm in England I like to eat what's in season. So different to Malta where there's not much change in the menus through the year, what d'you recommend?'

'I'd go for asparagus followed by lamb, it's all local stuff they use here.'

'That sounds good, shall we have some wine?

Have they got a nice Côtes du Rhône? And cheese, cheese afterwards, I love that English blue cheese.'
While Dave chose the wine Matt said 'what time can we visit the site tomorrow morning?'
'I'll come and collect you after I've had a chat with Allie about the track, probably around eleven.'

Dave parked in his road at midnight, the house was quiet but the hall light had been left on. He eased off his shoes and carried them upstairs; Di and the children were asleep. He lay in bed, brain buzzing, there was a lot to think about; he was excited about the development but uneasy about the capital. Matt came across as a nice guy but did he really have the money? He'd been evasive about the financing. Whose money was it? What if it was dodgy, Matt had previous, what if it was crooked? What type of crime? Did it matter if the money was clean by the time it got to Cloud Developments? What was Matt's father's shipping business involved in? He must call Allie first thing in the morning.

'Hello Dave, how are you?'
'I'm well thanks Allie, I wondered if you'd had time to think over our discussions about your track.'
'I have and I'm so glad you rang, I do want to talk to you about it, can you come over this morning?'
'Yes of course, I'll be over to see you in half an hour.'

Standing in the kitchen she was anxious and looked strained. 'Hello Allie' he smiled, reached forward and took her hand 'are you alright?'
'Oh Dave, I'm in such state, I don't know what to do.'
'Let's sit down and you can tell me what's the matter.'
She withdrew her hand and they sat opposite one another across the scrubbed oak kitchen table.

'I've had a visit from another developer.'
She reached into her apron pocket and slid a business card across the dark table. He read the title:
"James Fletcher, Director, Liberty Homes Ltd."
She looked nervously at him 'he just rang out of the blue, said he got my name and number from the manager at the inn, asked if he could come up there and then.'
'I've heard of this chap, I think I stood in for him at the Council dinner, you remember? It was where we met.'
'Oh, oh really? Well he came to talk about the track, he wanted to drive all the way up it to the top but it was so overgrown that we had to turn round. He asked me lots of questions about the land and who owned what. In fact it was a very similar conversation to the one that we had.'
She coloured slightly and looked down at her lap. 'The thing is, look, I'm so embarrassed I don't know what to say to you. I feel that you're going to think I'm behaving so badly when you've been so kind to me.'
'I'm sure it can't be that bad, I'm just sorry to see you so upset, why don't you tell me what happened.' She looked up, defensive and pink.
'He said just what you did, about access and so on, and then, and then. He was rather pushy, not very nice at all, but…'
'But what?'
'He just offered me more money, a lot more money. He said he didn't want any one else involved in our little secret. He said if I kept quiet about the deal his firm could pay up to a million pounds to use the track and make a road and all the things that you said.'
Dave was livid – this could just sink the whole bloody project before it even got started. But when he looked at Allie, his face was all concern. 'Oh you poor thing, it sounds as though he was a bit of bully.'
'He was, he was frightful, and he smelled bad.

Of course I'd love to have more money but I've been thinking about this. If I do sell, I want you to have the track and do the development. I trust you and, well, I want to help you if I can.'

'Well, that's very kind of you, so what were you thinking?'

'If you can match the offer from Liberty Homes, then I'll agree to sell to you.'

'Allie, I really appreciate you being so upfront with me but I'm not sure I can get that much money for you. A million, that really is big money. Can I call you later today? I'll let you know if I can do it or not, when do Liberty want an answer?'

'I said I'd need a week to think about it, so I expect he's going to call me in six days time. Oh, I may be out later, let me give you my mobile, I do hope you can get the money.'

It would be interesting to see how Matt reacted; in the great scheme of things another £500,000 was not a deal-breaker. If Matt's aim was to launder millions of dodgy money, the profit wasn't really relevant. It was the laundering that made the deal attractive.

He was sitting in an armchair reading the Witney Gazette in the front hall of the Lamb.

'Hello Matt, how was that four-poster? Did you sleep well?'

'Yes, very well thank you.' He folded the newspaper and stood up. 'So, how did you get on with the sorting out the track?'

'Shall we go and get in the car and I'll tell you on the way; are you all done here?'

'Yeah I've checked out and left my bag at reception.'

'Great, what time do you need to be back at Heathrow?'

'I need to be there at five, the hotel have fixed a car for me. I'll be leaving here at three-thirty.'

29 Years

As they drove over to Rissy Dave explained Allie's predicament. Matt was silent for a while, looking out of the windscreen, smoothing his moustache, tapping his lips and rubbing his smoothly shaved chin. He shifted sideways in his seat to look at Dave's profile.

'D'you think she really has had an offer of a million from Liberty? Or is she just trying to get more money out of us?'

'I thought about that, I don't think so; she seemed genuinely upset. She said she'd much rather sell to me than to Liberty. It's not really about the money for her, what's more important is being able to get the best possible treatment for her son.'

They drove round inside the airfield perimeter and stopped at a padlocked, metal five-bar gate. On the other side the track ended at the airfield security fence. In the rural silence, they could see it leading away down through the wooded slope, the tarmac was barely visible, the surface almost completely overgrown with brambles and waist-high weeds.

'That looks promising, now can we see the other end? where it joins the main road.'

They drove the four miles round to the eastern side of the airfield and turned off the A424 at the pub. They got out and looked around, Matt nodding his head approvingly.

'It's a pretty big junction already, more of a road than a track, better than I thought it would be. Good sight lines, I can't believe the landlord will object; all those nice new punters coming by his front door everyday, yeah, lovely, nice views too.' He couldn't stop smiling.

'This all works for me. You go ahead then, agree to match the million and get her to sign the exclusive. No money until we get the planning approved and our bid is accepted OK?'

'Yeah that's fine, I'm sure she'll be happy with that.'

Chapter 7

2014 – The Cotswolds

The following Sunday, John arrived at Brook Cottage for tea. Ed was standing outside to meet him, straight-backed, but leaning on a stick, he waved hello. 'How are you? how are you?' He gave John's hand a vigorous shake.

'I'm very well, you're looking good too, what've you been up to this week?'

'Come in, I've got some things together to show you, come over to my house.' They walked a few yards from the farmhouse to a green door set into the high stone wall. 'This is the way to my little home, do go in.'

They entered a grass courtyard flanked on three sides by the farmhouse, a wall and the cottage. The fourth side gave onto the view. The front door of the cottage opened into a snug little sitting room, the fire was lit and a tray of tea was waiting for them. On the side table and spilling onto the sofa was a pile of papers, notebooks, yellow newspapers and photograph albums.

'This is really nice, what a cosy place you have here, it's much warmer than my cottage. We seem to catch the wind a bit more in Fifield'

'Yes, I'm very lucky; it suits me just fine. I've got a little kitchen through there and a bedroom and bathroom upstairs.'

As they sat having tea Ed pointed to the pile;

'I started looking for stuff about Rissy and ended up just getting it all out. I haven't looked through these things for years. It brought back some memories I can tell you. I thought perhaps it would be easier if I just told you the story from the beginning.

29 Years

I've roughly arranged the papers and things into chronological order. My eyes aren't so good and I couldn't always read some of the dates so it may be a bit of a jumble, if you sit over on the sofa you'll be able to reach the papers more easily.'

So they began a slow and very enjoyable process of piecing together the story of Ed Collins.

'In 1940 I was at Leeds reading English Literature, I joined the University Air Squadron. I was mad about flying. We were trained at RAF Yeadon, it's now Leeds/Bradford Airport; very high 681 feet, not as high as Rissy but very windy. Built on top of a hill; it's still the highest commercial airport in England. I did my training as a cadet and planned to join the RAF when I graduated, in fact I joined sooner than I expected. Due to the shortage of aircrew I left after my second year and volunteered for pilot training. I was recommended for a commission, which was fine but to my dismay I didn't pass the flying aptitude tests and so was sent for Navigator training instead. After months of messing about being sent to different stations and on various courses; in 1942 I was finally posted to RAF Melbourne in Yorkshire to join a bomber squadron flying Halifaxes. There are some photos there in that green covered album.' Ed came over and they sat together looking at the pictures with Ed reminiscing over old flying pals and half-remembered places. There was an assortment of all different sizes from small box brownie photos to large posed pictures. They were mainly of his crew: outside dispersal, in front of their Halifax, in the NAAFI, on bicycles and sunbathing. 'You all look so young and so happy, you're always smiling and laughing.'

'Yes I suppose we were, there was terrific camaraderie, all the crews became very close.

There was no rank between us, except when airborne that's when the skipper was completely in charge.'

'Were you happy as a navigator?
You said that you really wanted to be a pilot.'

'Funnily enough I was, I enjoyed all the technical aspects: the meteorology, the map reading, course plotting and so on. We discovered I was quite good at it and we were often the lead aircraft due to my nav' skills. It certainly helped if we ever got separated from the rest of the Squadron, finding the way back home was my job.'

'I told you why I had to stop flying didn't I? now, look at this' he opened another album. 'Here we are at Rissy, look at the snow! Goodness it was miserable at times; thankfully I wasn't there for too long, about nine or ten months I think. I was desperate to get operational again but it just wasn't to be. So I applied for a posting overseas, the CO was very good to me and I ended up being posted to the Far East, in fact I went all over East Asia.'

They continued; John was turning the crackling pages of the album, thin tissue paper separating the leaves. There was a photo of a group in front of a grassy hillock with spades.

'What are you digging for here?'

'Oh one of the maintenance officers at Rissy had got his hands on a metal detector and he'd been prospecting around the old burial mound. All sorts of things had been dug up on the airfield when they were building it. There was always building work going on, hangars, workshops and runways. All sorts of ancient bits and pieces turned up, no one was much interested apart from Jock.

Look, here he is holding up something, it looks like a pot. It's too small for my eyes; can you see what it is? And here are some pictures of his finds, I can't make them out can you?'

29 Years

It was clear from the photo that it was taken over on the south side of the airfield near the proposed housing development site.

'No I can't either but I could get it blown up if you'd like then we could see what they are.'

'Oh you're welcome to if you like, I don't suppose it's anything much. I never had much time for Jock, he was a disagreeable fellow as I recall. Do take the photos if you're interested.' John put the photos in an old brown envelope and slipped them into his pocket.

'I will, I'll see if I can find out what they are and let you know. I'll take them along to the Ashmolean.'

John stood up and stretched, 'well that's all really interesting, I hope I'm not tiring you too much. I was thinking about what you said about your old CO and him having a Bugatti. Do you know Prescott Hill Climb? It's the home of the Bugatti Owner's Club.'

'I know the name but I've never been there, why do you ask?'

'There's a vintage sports car weekend at the beginning of August, I was thinking of going. Would you like to come with me? It might be fun to see the old cars pounding up the hill, it's a time trial on a one thousand yard tarmac road.'

'Why yes, I'd really like to see that, I wonder if I'd recognise a car like that one Pearce had.'

'Well let's do it then, I'll pick you up, we can go in my van, it'll be easier and more comfortable for you than trying to get in and out of that little Porsche.'

Ed smiled, happy at the thought of a day out with his new friend. 'Yes, I'd really like that, how thoughtful of you, I'm looking forward to it already.'

John poured more tea for them both and sat down again with the next album.

'What are these photos of this aircraft about?'

The pictures were of a high-winged monoplane with a rotary engine; the single wing was fixed into the top of the fuselage and formed part of the roof over the cockpit.

'Oh now this was interesting, that's a Lysander, I took these to remind me of one that came in in the middle of the night. Not this particular aircraft, this one came in for some training I think, or maybe it was a mechanical upgrade I forget. But I'd not seen one before so I took these snaps. People said that the one that came in in the night had been on some secret mission or other and had been shot up.'

'What happened to that one? did you know what the mission was?' Ed closed his eyes and sighed.

'Oh I don't think I ever knew, the whole secret thing, well it was probably just a rumour. There were always rumours and gossip going around the airfield. You know I was just a junior officer doing an admin job, I didn't really get involved with what happened on the flying side.'

He looked at the clock on the mantle shelf. 'Good Lord, is it six o'clock already? I think we might have earned ourselves a whisky don't you?'

Chapter 8

Early 1944 – The Cotswolds

After lunch Ed went to see the Medical Orderly and signed for a black, iron wheelchair. The rubber wheels whirred quietly along the polished concrete. Her eyes flicked open at the sound of his footsteps and she watched as he pushed it to her bedside.

'Bonjour Mamselle!'

'Bonjour Edouard!'

They smiled; pleased to see each another.

'How are you? How're you feeling today?'

'I am feeling a bit better; the kind doctor, gave me some pills for the pain and so I can sleep. I cannot move my legs very much but at last I can feel my toes again.'

'Are you able to get up if I help you or is it too painful?'

'Yes I can if we go very slowly, I must be so careful with the stitches.' She looked at the wheelchair rather doubtfully. 'So what have you got for me here today?'

'If you're feeling well enough, then this is the trip outside to see the world that I promised you last week. Major Rogers said that it's OK if you're up to it but I must make sure that you're wrapped up warm.' He pointed at a pile of clothes on the seat of the wheelchair. 'This is some stuff of mine that I brought for you; it's cold outside but not raining.'

Her face lit up. 'Oh this is marvellous and so kind of you. I think we can manage if you help me, I'm wearing a pair of men's pyjamas.'

He helped her into a sweater and then into his sheepskin flying jacket. He zipped it all the way so that the collar stood up and only her eyes were showing.

When she was sitting in the wheelchair he rolled white woollen flying socks onto her thin pale feet then wrapped a tartan rug around her legs. A silk scarf and woollen hat completed the weatherproofing. Laughing, she said; 'oh I must look terrible, what have you done to me?'
'I'm looking after you that's all, just following Doctor's orders. Now, are you ready?' She tucked her hands into the long sleeves to make a muff.
'Yes, I'm ready. You're my pilot and my navigator so I am sure you won't get us lost.'
Ed released the brake and pushed her smoothly through the quiet ward, there were no other patients to see them, the Duty Orderly nodded as they went past. The breeze was fresh outside as they looked out over the airfield.
'Look at all these planes! This is a huge place, much bigger than I imagined! What are all these different planes doing here?'
'This is mainly a training and maintenance station, there are also hundreds of planes stored here. They come from the factories and then get flown by delivery pilots out to the squadrons that need them.' Ed squatted close beside the wheelchair pointing out the different types and explaining what they were used for.
It was cold in the wind and due to the rise in the ground in front of them they could only see part of the airfield. 'If we go around the back of this building, well this big hump, we can see some of the countryside if you like. I think it'll also be a bit more sheltered, not so windy.' They wheeled slowly along the cinder track to the lee side.
'Ah yes, this is much better, much nicer. What a wonderful view, we're so high up here, we can see so far.'
They stopped and Ed pointed out the villages and valleys in a wide 180 degree sweep of the hills.

'And down in the valley there's a river and beside it runs the railway line, we can't see it now but when the trains go through we'll see their clouds of smoke and steam.'

After a few minutes she said, 'I think you should take me back inside now, I am getting a little cold and I'm sorry but I'm a bit uncomfortable.'

'Right oh, yes of course, you only have to say the word and I'll have you back in the warm in two ticks.' As they crunched along the path she said 'Ed, would you like to stay for a cup of tea?'

'Oh yes, rather! But only if you're not getting too tired'

'No, no I'm fine and when we're back inside I would like you to tell me some more about these Cotswolds.'

An hour later, as Ed was leaving the hospital he saw the doctor. 'Hello Kit, the patient seems to be improving.'

'Yes I'm pleased you're popping in to see Jeanne, she is improving but I need to take some more X-rays later today. She's in a lot of pain; I think there may be some shrapnel still embedded in her legs; if so we'll have to get in there and winkle them out. Now that she's strong enough, if I need to I'll get cracking straight away.'

'That doesn't sound too good, will she be alright? I mean, how long will it take for her to recover?'

'Don't worry Ed, she'll be fine, I'll take good care of her.' He had to be content with that but it didn't stop him worrying. He knew so little about Jeanne, she asked him questions all the time but if he asked about her past or where she was from she became evasive and asked him questions instead.

He realised it was difficult for her and that she was probably on some secret operation. Well, he'd just make the best of it; nothing was easy in wartime, even looking after pretty French girls.

'Ed, could you come and see me now?'

'Yes, sir, I'll be there directly.'

Ed strode smartly through the stiff breeze to the Station Commander's office.

'Come in, come in and close the door won't you? Now have a seat whilst I give you an update on the Jeanne situation.' Ed looked at him expectantly: 'I've had Vera Atkins on the phone.' He nodded in confirmation at the instrument, 'she wants to know when Jeanne will be well enough to move to Bennett's Farm.'

'I saw her yesterday, Major Rogers said she may need a further operation to remove some shrapnel.'

'Oh did he? Well that may delay matters a bit but never mind. The main purpose of her call was to create a cover story for Jeanne. Now she can't just appear in Sherborne as if she dropped out of the sky. Which is of course pretty much what did happen. No, what she needs is a credible background story. Atkins has come up with this: Jeanne was working at the French Embassy in London; she was hurt near her digs on the Cromwell Road when an unexploded bomb left over from the Blitz went off. She's been in hospital in London but is about to be discharged. Jeanne's mother is an old friend of Monique Smith; they met at the École des Beaux-Arts in Paris before the Great War. So, when you next see Jeanne can you develop the story? You know, expand on it, put in more names and details, then practice it together until it becomes second nature. Oh and once you've got it straight you'll have to go over and brief Monique.'

With a smile, he waved Ed away 'now go on, clear off and let me know when she's ready to be moved.'

Jeanne lay in the semi-darkness, the hospital with its thick earth walls was always quiet; sometimes she could hear the noise of aircraft engines taking-off otherwise there was little activity. It was early afternoon and she was waiting for her operation.

29 Years

After he'd reviewed the X-rays, the surgeon explained that there were some small pieces of metal deep in the back of her left thigh. He said he didn't like to leave them in case it caused more problems later. The plan was to operate at five o'clock; she'd be taken to the theatre at four for preparation and anaesthesia. She was hungry but waited calmly; the food in hospital wasn't what she was used to. Jeanne lived in a farming area where most families kept pigs, chickens at least one cow and grew vegetables. Powdered eggs and Spam were an unpleasant surprise, she'd laughed out loud when the Orderly explained what they were. She'd ask Ed what the food would be like at Bennett's Farm; she hoped it was a small farm like those she knew in France. Maybe when she was able to get up and about she could help with the animals. Jeanne liked hearing Ed talking about his country, his England, and hoped that he'd talk more about it. Her thoughts were hazy with painkillers and she drifted in and out, dozing and waking until the Orderly came to wheel her to the operating theatre.

Ed was still hoping that he might be able to return to flying duties and had decided to talk to Kit Rogers about the problem. After breakfast he cycled over to the hospital. 'Hello Ed, come to check up on your young lady? Well I can tell you she's fine. The surgeon removed a small jagged piece of metal from her thigh,' He pointed to a fragment on his desk; 'she might want to keep that as a souvenir. He had a good look around while he was in there and has given her the all clear. The X-rays picked up quite a few 'foreign objects' but I hope we're out of the woods now.'
'That's a relief, when can I see her?'
'I saw a tray going down a few minutes ago so I expect she's having tea and toast.

We haven't got coffee and croissants on the menu here yet. Anyhow, I'm sure she'll be pleased to see you.'
'Actually there's something else I wanted to ask you about.' Kit's dark eyes narrowed in concern behind black frames; 'Oh yes, what's that then?'

'My eyesight, you know I'm medically downgraded as unfit to fly.'
'Yes but I'm no eye expert, how do you think I can help?'
'I've been giving myself some basic eye tests and it seems to me that my sight is as good now as it's ever been; I was hoping you might be able to give me a chit to say that I am fit for local area flying. The Station Commander's a good egg and I think he'll go along with the idea. Then when I've done that and if it goes well, I'll make an application for a full medical and hope I get passed fit to fly.'
'Hmm, let me have a think about it; I do have the ordinary eye test equipment here but I'll request your records from the Medical Centre. When I've had a chance to review the file and do some research I'll be in a better position to advise you.'
'Oh that's splendid, thank you so much for being prepared to help, it really means so much, I feel so bad, ashamed really. I feel like I'm hiding here, not pulling my weight or doing my bit, letting my crew down you know?'
'I do understand and I'll do what I can but eyes are not my area and I can't promise anything.'
'No, no that's fine, I understand that, but it really would be wonderful if I could fly again.' He beamed 'I'll wander down and say hello shall I?'
'Yes, why don't you?' Kit smiled and shook his head at Ed's retreating back.
'Oh I say! You forgot this!'

Ed turned to see Kit holding up the piece of shrapnel, he gave a nod of thanks and the souvenir dropped into his outstretched palm.

Jeanne was sitting up in bed, wiping toast crumbs off her lips with a white napkin. Her tray was resting on the cage that kept the bedclothes off her wounded legs.

'What a lovely surprise to see you so early, have you had breakfast? Would you like some tea?'

'No thanks, I've just come from the Mess.' He pulled out the chair turning it to face her and sat down.

'So how's the leg after your operation?'

"Oh I'm fine thank you, it's a bit painful but the doctor says all is well and I'll soon be back on my feet again. I am determined to try and start walking as soon as possible. I'm glad that you'll be helping me, I can't think of anyone better to be my nurse.'

'Well that's good because I'm under strict orders to get you fit and strong again. I just popped in to see how you were so I mustn't stay long, I really should be at work but I'll come back this evening. We can have a chat, maybe play a game of something to keep you amused. I say, would you like a wireless set to listen to? I've got a spare one you can borrow if you like, I'll bring it over later. Oh, and before I go I have a present for you. First you must close your eyes and hold out your hand.' Her long dark lashes lay dutifully on her pale lower lids and she offered a slim hand, fingers together. He carefully put the fragment in her cupped hand and closed her fingers over it.

'Kit just gave me this for you, I think you should keep it, for good luck.' They waved goodbye and Ed went happily off to another day of admin' duties.

It was early evening, a week later; when Jeanne opened her eyes, in the dim light she saw a woman sitting at the desk near her bed.

Blonde hair shone faintly in the wash of a yellow desk light, she was reading some papers in a file and making notes in the margins. The woman was chewing her lower lip in concentration and didn't notice her observer.
'Hello Vera.' The woman turned on her seat.
'My dear, how nice that you're awake. I didn't like to disturb your little nap.' She folded the file and put her papers in the satchel on the floor. 'I'm hearing good reports of your progress and I hope you'll soon be able to get out of here. Now, to cheer you up I've been shopping. I've bought you some suitable country clothes, nothing too fashionable I'm afraid but at least you won't have to worry about looking like a refugee!'
'Oh Vera, how kind of you, I couldn't imagine what I was going to wear.' She sat up and Vera put some pillows behind her. 'Will you show me what you've brought for me?' Vera lifted the suitcase onto the desk and they laughed as she pretended to model Jeanne's new clothes. 'I also got you some nightwear, socks and even some stockings, no don't ask I can never reveal my suppliers! I don't have any orders for you yet but I expect that once you're up to it we'll get you on a training course and brief you on all the developments in France. Meanwhile I don't want you to think about anything, just enjoy the peace and quiet and get well.'
'Have you sent a message to my family? Do they know where I am? They'll be so worried that I haven't come back.'
'Yes we've contacted them to say you're fine but will be delayed, it's better that they don't know too much. We suggested that they tell anyone who asks that you're visiting relatives down in the south, that you are looking after a sick aunt and will return when you can. So no need to worry, all is taken care of.'
They chatted for a while until it was time for her leave.

29 Years

They embraced and Vera kissed Jeanne goodbye.

Over the weeks of Ed's daily visits Jeanne had learned a lot about England; they had played chess and cards for hours. Laughing while she teased and helped him with his dreadful grammar. She mimicked his English accented French and he loved her French accented English. During the day Jeanne worked hard at the physio' to strengthen her muscles and the purple scar tissue had been regularly massaged with Tea Tree oil to keep the skin supple. Kit came over to say that he thought Jeanne was well enough to move to Bennett's Farm to begin the next stage of her recuperation.

'That's wonderful, when can I go?' Jeanne was excited at the prospect of finally leaving the gloomy hospital and getting out to live in the countryside. 'I'm sorry Kit, you've been wonderful to me but I am really ready for a change of scenery!'

'No, don't worry. I bet you were bored out of your mind in here. Now, Ed can you arrange transport? Do you think you could wangle a loan of the Station Commander's Staff car?

'Yes of course, I'll go and ask him directly. Err, when should I say we would like to borrow it?'

'I think this afternoon; after lunch will be fine.'

So at three o'clock, having secured the Hillman and warned the Smiths of the imminent arrival of their houseguest; Ed walked Jeanne down the ward for the last time. She was slow but determined on her crutches; he put the passenger seat as far back as it would go and helped her in through the wide, rear hinged door. Ed put her suitcase on the back seat and started the engine. Kit and the Station Commander stood smiling and waved them off like a honeymoon couple.

'Now you must tell me about everything we see on the way, how far is it? Oh how beautiful the cottages are!'

As they motored steadily along the lanes Jeanne exclaimed, pointed and asked questions all the way. 'We're going to have lots of time for looking around; it'll all be part of getting you fit again. Maybe one day we'll go exploring by bike, I'll show you some of the nice towns and villages round here.'

Jeanne adored Bennett's Farm and Monique greeted her with a torrent of French, helping her out of the car and then making her comfortable in the sitting room. The Smiths clearly took to her, so once she was settled into her new home Ed drove the Hillman back to Rissy. 'Thank you for letting me borrow the car sir, Jeanne's settled in now and they're all getting on like a house on fire.'

'Excellent, now before you disappear, we need to have a chat about your wish to go flying again.

The MO's been on to me and we've decided to give you a chance to prove your eyesight. Before you go in an aircraft again he wants to run come tests on you; if he's happy I've agreed that you can do some local area familiarisation flights. Once you've got a chit from him I'll be able to sign you off. If the flying goes well, then you can put in for a full medical.'

Ed went up to his room in the Mess, part of him was excited that he might get to fly again but an even larger part was dismayed that it would mean that his time with Jeanne would be cut short. Of course he knew that she'd have to leave at some point but he wanted to stay with her for as long as possible.

He went to sleep every night thinking of her and what fun they'd have together down at Bennett's and walking and cycling together. And what did she think of him? She seemed to like him, maybe more. But now he'd gone and ruined it by wanting to fly again.

He always used to spend his time thinking about his crew and how they were managing without him. Now they barely crossed his mind. Oh shit and double shit, he'd really made a cock of it. He knew his duty was to fly if he could but that did little to lift his depression.

What if he just flunked the eye test? He sat up, yes.

No, Kit would see straight through that one, he would know exactly what Ed was up to. No that would be terrible, he might even get charged with lack of moral fibre, cowardice. No, no that'd be awful, don't even think about that. And what would Pearce say? He'd probably have him transferred to the infantry, court martialled, reduced to the ranks and sent to the front line. To a trench somewhere frightful in France, ha, that would be ironic wouldn't it? Oh bollocks. He squeezed his eyes shut and clenched his fists above his head with frustration.

In the morning there was a note from the Chief Clerk on his desk. "Report to the MO at 10.00 hrs."

His heart sank. Oh, that's just wizard! Wait for ages and then it all happens too quickly.

~

'Hello Ed, ready for the tests then?'

'Oh yes Kit, rather!'

After 15 minutes in the dark looking at lights, shapes, screens and ever-smaller letters.

'Well that all seems fine; you're definitely not blind. Actually you've got quite good eyesight.' Kit scribbled a note, signed and dated it. 'Here you are, give that to the Station Commander and you'll be up in the sky before you know it.'

~

Ed braced himself outside the door, stuck on a weak smile and knocked; 'good morning sir, the MO has given me chit saying my eyes are alright.' Ed proffered the piece of paper.
'Does he now? Well that's good isn't it?' Pearce looked enquiringly at Ed. 'Yes of course sir, can't wait.'
'Good, I'll speak to the Adjutant and he'll sort it out with the flying wing, sooner the better eh?'
At tea-time in the Mess one of Flying Training School instructors came over to Ed. 'Hello you must be the young navigator that I've been asked to look out for. I'm Dick Fisher' he eyed Ed's single wing; 'We don't see many of you clever types here so I guessed it must be you.'
'Yes sir, I'm Ed Collins, delighted to meet you.'
'Excellent, come over to the Flying Wing on Monday at ten ack emma, we'll have time for a proper chat and go on from there, toodle pip.' And the instructor wandered off, teacup in hand to pick up a newspaper.

The Smiths had invited Ed to supper; so six o'clock found him freewheeling down the long hill to Great Barrington with his heart in his throat. He hadn't seen Jeanne for four days and now he was so excited at the thought of seeing her that he could hardly breathe. Night was falling but he knew the road so well and with the yellow beam of his dynamo light it was easy to navigate.
His problem was how to tell Jeanne about the flight tomorrow; what should he say? He'd have to speak to her alone, if he let it out in front of the Smiths she might think he actually wanted to go away. How could he get her alone? They couldn't go for a stroll; she could barely walk yet. Oh God, he didn't want to upset her but he did want her to know how he felt. He wanted her to know that he didn't ever want to leave whilst she was there.

He wanted to be with her all the time, he wanted to sit beside her and hold her hand, to look into her black eyes, to listen to her beautiful voice and smell her hair and skin, involuntarily, he shivered on the bike.

Maybe he could ask Tim and Monique if he could have a few moments alone with her "Operational Matters – hush, hush you know." Yes that'd be fine, they'd be terribly nice and polite, that's just the way to do it; Jeanne wouldn't mind the subterfuge so, with his plan sorted out he pedalled on in delicious anticipation.

Jeanne was sitting by the fire in a wing back chair with her feet on a stool and a pink checked rug over her legs.

'Here he is, here he is, your knight in shining armour has come to rescue you, well not exactly rescue, just come for dinner I hope! You're not taking her away are you?'

'No, no not at all, not on my bike, anyway I don't think she's up to sitting on my crossbar quite yet.'

They sat opposite one another across the kitchen table, her eyes and hair shining black in the candlelight. Monique lifted the lid on a steaming casserole dish. 'Ah, boeuf bourguignon, it's my favourite!' cried Jeanne clapping her hands in delight, and there was wine that Ed had brought with him from the Mess wine cellar. 'Yes indeed this wonderful Gevrey-Chambertin will go beautifully with the beef' Tim theatrically inhaled the aroma from his glass.

'Ah, we could almost be in France.'

Jeanne raised her glass. 'To Tim and Monique, thank you for being so kind to me, I am, I am, I am… lost for the words, so just thank you with all my heart.' After dinner Jeanne took her crutch and limped her way back to the fireside, Ed asked Monique and Tim if he might have a quiet chat with her. 'Yes, yes, of course old boy don't you worry about us; we'll just get on with the washing-up, mum's the word and all that.'

The fire and a couple of red-shaded table lamps lighted the sitting room. Ed offered and lit their cigarettes then sat on the leather-covered fender beside her. 'I need to talk to you about something.'

'Yes of course, you look so serious, what's happened?'

'Well, nothing yet, but do you remember that I said I wanted to go flying again if I could?'

'Yes I remember, you said that you felt very bad about leaving your crew.'

'That's right, well the thing is, it looks like it might happen, going flying again. Kit gave me some eye tests that I passed and on Monday I'm going flying with an instructor to see how I get on. If that goes well then I'll have to put in for a full medical. If I pass that, then I'm sure to be posted operational straightaway; we're so short of aircrew you know.'

'But you seem upset, it's what you wanted, no?'

'Yes, well it was, it was but then you came into my life and now I don't want to lose you!'

He took her hand; 'I think of you all the time, I can't help it, I even find myself talking to you when you're not there. You're with me when I go to sleep and you're there when I wake up.' He threw his cigarette in the fire and put his hands over his face;

'Oh God, Oh God, oh I'm so sorry, I shouldn't be telling you this, I'm in pieces, I don't know what to do; you must think I'm the most awful fool. I thought of deliberately failing the eye test so I can stay with you but I know it's my duty to fly if I can.

If I pretend I can't see they might charge me with cowardice, I'd be in terrible trouble.' He knelt beside her, rested his head on her lap and slowed himself down.

'You're so strong and so brave, I feel pathetic beside you; I'm ashamed of myself.' She stroked his hair for a while and gentled him until he was calm.

He sat back on his heels and looked up as she spoke; 'now listen to me, this is war and you must understand that we can't always have what we want, you're a wonderful man and you're very special to me also but we know this moment will come to an end and we must be content with what we have.' She took his hands in hers and kissed them: 'I don't want you to go but during this time we have so much responsibility to our families and our countries, we can't let them down.'

He sighed; 'Yes, I know you're right but that doesn't make it any easier' he pressed her hands 'I L.. I L...' Unable to say the words he ran his fingers through his hair. 'I just wanted you to know how I felt, that I wasn't running off, away from you. That's the last thing I want to do. It's just that, because I've been so silly about this flying business I've brought about exactly what I don't want to happen.'

'No, I think you are quite correct in what you have done and you shouldn't upset yourself. I'll always have a very special place in my heart for you and I'll never forget you.' He reached up and held her face in his hands and marvelled at the softness of her skin on his fingertips, she looked into his eyes as he lightly kissed her lips.

'Oh my darling, I'll never forget you either.' They held each other's hands and kissed again.

'Now, you sit up here again beside me and tell me all the plans you have to get me walking and running and cycling and I don't know, climbing mountains probably.' She made him laugh and as they talked the tension ebbed, Tim came in to ask if they would like another drink or coffee. 'That's very kind but I really should be heading back to Rissy, I don't want to outstay my welcome.'

'No, not at all you know you'll always be welcome; will you be able to see alright, cycling in the dark?'

'Oh it's not too bad actually, quite light really.'

'Yes' said Jeanne, 'it's the moon period, very good for night flying, you should be quite safe.'

As Ed cycled he replayed the conversation with Jeanne, he couldn't work out what he meant to her. He'd nearly said I love you, he'd wanted to but was frightened of stepping into the abyss of her being embarrassed or affronted and saying she didn't love him. He didn't even know if she had a lover or worse a husband back in France. She definitely cared though and she had kissed him back.

Was it a lovers' kiss or had she just felt sorry for him?

Oh God it was all so mixed up and confusing, he probably shouldn't have said anything at all.

~

During the nights Monique often heard a muffled sobbing from Jeanne's room, she always waited until it subsided and eventually they'd both go back to sleep. This time it wouldn't stop, Monique was wide-awake the moon was bright. The cold grey light came through the curtains and lit the room. She slipped out of the warm bed and put on her dressing gown and slippers. It was chilly out and she tied the sash firmly round her middle to keep the draughts out.

Jeanne was curled up on one side, her body shaking with sobs. As Monique rubbed her back and stroked her arms Jeanne finally became still. 'Can you talk? Do you want to tell me what's giving you nightmares?'

She nodded and lifted the bedcovers so that Monique could get in out of the cold. They lay facing one another in the moonlight, her eyes wet and puffy with tears. They spoke softly in French; 'I often hear you but I don't like to intrude, I came tonight because you seemed worse, maybe it'll help if you talk a little.'

29 Years

Slowly, swallowing thickly on her strained throat Jeanne started to speak; 'it always starts the same way; it's the night fighter that shot my plane. This is true; it's what happened, it's how I got my wounds. I was a passenger in a little plane bringing me from France in the night.

I'm asleep in the tiny back cockpit, I wake up to see, there right behind my little plane a huge black German one. Sometimes it comes out of the clouds below, sometimes it's diving onto us. I try to warn the pilot but I can't speak, I'm screaming and screaming but he doesn't hear. Our little plane is going so slowly and this huge fighter; I know it's going to start firing.

Sometimes he waits and waits and comes so close that I can see the face of the pilot. He sees me screaming and looks straight at me as he opens fire. The bullets are pouring into my plane and still we just go on straight and slow. I feel the bullets hitting the plane then the German is past; there are bullet holes everywhere. The cockpit glass is broken, the wind is coming in and it's very cold.'

She started shaking again, Monique turned her onto her other side so she could put her arms around and hold her properly.

'I know I'm hit, I feel the bullets crashing into my body, I can feel the blood running down in my trousers and in my shoes, I can't speak, I'm helpless and I know I'll just die in the cold little plane. I'll never see my family again, I see their faces, I can see their mouths open, they're calling my name, they reach out their hands to me, they're desperate to take hold of me, to get hold of me but I can't lift my hands to catch theirs.

They get further and further away, fading as the blood runs out of me. I'm losing my vision, I can't see them, my body becomes numb and I'm so cold.'

She stopped and tried to slow her breathing and calm herself.

'I know it's just a nightmare but now I'm terrified of flying back to France, I keep seeing the German fighter that will shoot us down. My plane is so slow and so small, with no guns. It's silly, I know because I've done many dangerous things in the war. If I was caught I'd be executed but I wasn't frightened. I was working with my friends, all we could think of was how to kill Germans, blow them up, shoot them, knife them we didn't care we just wanted to get the bastards out of our country.' Monique shifted uneasily and they lay in silence for a while.

'My dear, I don't know what to say. Your nightmare is just awful, I'm so sorry that you going through such agony and all the worry about your family.' She squeezed her arm sympathetically; 'I think it's always worst in the night, I'll go down and make you a cup of tea in a minute. A hot drink will help make the dreams go away and a splash of whisky in it will do wonders for getting you back to sleep.

I think you're still in shock from your wounds, as you get stronger your mind will become quieter and when you can start walking properly and getting out in the fresh air you'll sleep much better. I'll make you a little pillow with dried lavender; the scent is very calming, it'll help relax you at night. We'll take things one day at a time; at the moment you've got too much time to think. Soon you'll be able to help us with feeding the animals and the chickens, once you start getting some exercise it will tire you out and sleep will come easier.'

'Yes, I'm sure you're right. I'm feeling calmer now with you here; thank you for listening to me, I'm sorry that I woke you.'

'Oh no, don't worry about me; I'm fine, I'll get that cup of tea and then we'll talk about happier things, maybe you can tell me about Ed.

29 Years

You two seem to be getting on very well.'
When Monique came back upstairs she switched on the bedside light and gave her the hot mug, they sat up in bed together, pillows against the headboard. Jeanne recounted Ed's anguish about how going flying would mean leaving her and how she'd jollied him out of his quandary.
'Oh the poor boy, and he's always so cheerful; I really like it when he visits it's like having my own son back home, d'you think he'll be alright? How does he feel about you?
'I think he's in love with me, I don't know if it's because I'm hurt and he feels sorry for me and likes looking after me. I don't think he really knows, he's probably never been in love before.'
'And you, how do you feel about Ed? It sounds as though you have been in love before.'
'I'm wounded, alone and far from home.' She sipped some more hot whisky tea then looked at Monique from the corner of her eye: 'It's very nice that such a handsome young man is so interested in me.'

~

In the flying wing canteen Ed talked the instructor through the incident that caused his temporary blindness and medical downgrade. Fisher said
'not something I've come across before but we'll go up this morning and see how you get on. Here's a little navigation exercise to keep us amused.' He gave Ed a list of grid references that would be their waypoints.
'The met' is on the board over there, we'll fly at eight and a half thousand feet; mark up your maps and give me a shout when you're ready.'
The day was overcast, 10/10ths cloud at 10,000 feet; light breeze from the southwest, ideal navigating weather.

The flight went smoothly, Fisher at the controls nodding appreciatively as Ed called the turns and identified the landmarks with clear, neat precision. As they came in to land his heart sank with the plane, he knew he'd done well and the next step would be a full medical.

They sat side by side in the cockpit of the Airspeed Oxford, once he had shut down the engines Fisher looked at Ed: 'You're navigation is fine, as I expected it would be with your level of experience. You could see all the landmarks, even on a dull day. However, I think we should have another sortie, on a bright day, just to be on the safe side. Makes sense don't you think?'

There was nothing for him to say. 'I'll let you know the day before, when there's a break in the weather. From the forecast I expect it won't be until next week.' They climbed down and after signing off the entry in his flying log they went their separate ways.

It was March and Jeanne was able walk without her crutches, she was using a walking stick that Tim had lent her and she was happy pottering around the farm. It was a joy to be outside, drinking in the clear air, watching the birds and talking to the animals. Ed came to visit and for their first outing they walked to the teashop in the village: 'We must remember the cover story.'

'Yes of course, I've been practicing with Monique, we're quite perfect, Tim's been testing us and asking some tricky questions!'

'I don't think we'll be meeting the Gestapo but you never know who might be listening.'

'I understand, now tell me, how did your flight go? Was it alright?'

'Yes.' He sighed; 'all went fine but as it was an overcast day they want me to go up again when the weather's fine. On a sunny day you know; just to make sure.'

29 Years

He looked sadly at Jeanne.
She took his hand and kissed the palm 'don't worry. You needn't worry about me, I'll manage, I'll be fine.'
The bell jangled on the teashop door, they sat down and the schoolgirl waitress took their order on a notepad with a thick stub of pencil on a string. 'I know you'll manage, I know you'll be fine.' He looked miserable but was determined not to spoil their moment.
'I say; shall we just not talk about it? Let's plan a proper outing, how would you like to visit Burford? It's a beautiful little town near here with the most stunning church. I'll see if I can borrow a car or a motorbike and we can go out for lunch. What d'you think?'
'I think that would be lovely, I like riding on a bike. When can we go?'
'It's supposed to be sunny next week so I'll ask for an afternoon off and come and pick you up.'
The sun was low in the clouded western sky when they went outside and set off along the wide pavement. 'Shall take we take the shortcut down here through the wood?' They turned off the lane and walked slowly under the tall pines holding hands. Ed stopped and put his arms around her; 'I must kiss you, I've been wanting to kiss you all afternoon.' She tilted her face to him; 'I want to kiss you too.' Their mouths grazed and she suckled his plump lower lip between hers while they pressed strongly together. Their bodies touching one another from thighs to mouths; their coats rustled undone to bring those yearnings closer together.

~

The phone rang; 'hello Ed, are you free for a flight this afternoon by any chance? I've got a slot at two.'
'Err, yes, yes of course'

'Excellent, see you here at one thirty for a briefing, toodle-pip.'
Right well here it was, by the time Ed got to the Mess he could hardly eat for the Sword of Damocles he felt was hanging over him.
Having been given his route and instructions Ed checked the met' and worked out the bearings and timings. When he was ready he went over to the instructor and they walked out to the aircraft.
It was warm in the cockpit of the Airspeed Oxford, the familiar smells of aviation fuel and worn, cracked leather seats. They took off into the sunny afternoon and started the exercise. It went beautifully, Ed was right on the button at each turn. They were heading Southwest, Ed called the mark and Fisher started to bank onto the new course. Ed checked his working and looked out to confirm the waypoint on the ground. As the plane straightened up the bright sun dazzled off the polished engine cover and lanced directly into his pupils. Ed cried out in pain and dropping the map put his hands to his eyes; 'oh no, oh no, not again. I can't see! I can't bloody see!

~

Spring days came green and rainy to the Windrush valley, but as the nights shortened so the sun warmed the days. Jeanne and Ed were secure in the knowledge that he wouldn't be leaving. Kit had been to visit and was happy with her progress, encouraging longer walks and suggesting climbing, swimming and when she was ready, perhaps a little running.
Ed had an aunt who lived in the Lake District; she owned a guesthouse in Ambleside and they arranged to visit for five days in the middle of May.

29 Years

Instead of going by train Ed managed to wangle a lift on a training flight that was going to Carlisle and they took the bus down to Ambleside. Aunt Betty was delighted to have them to stay, it was early in the season and she gave them a comfortable bedroom on the top floor under the eaves.

In the morning she loaned them bicycles, rucksacks and anoraks. With a picnic, they cycled along dusty white roads to Keswick at the top of Derwent Water. Bikes chained to the fence at Derwent Bank they walked up Catbells and sat beside the cairn at the top. They admired the wonderful views of the ancient volcanic landscape and looking across at the high humped hills and razor-backed ravines she said 'this must be the most beautiful place in the world.'

'And you're the most beautiful girl in the world. We're going to climb every one of these hills' he said sweeping his arm in a full circle around the world that they could see; 'and I'm going to kiss you on top of every one of them, starting right here.'

They took the path down to the lakeside for a picnic lunch and afterwards continued back to their bikes along the water's edge. As they cycled to Grasmere past the lake Jeanne called to him:

'Is that Helvellyn, the one we saw from Catbells?'

'Yes, let's go up there tomorrow.'

They knew it would be a fine day and a good challenge for Jeanne; she was determined to get to the top.

'It's a much bigger climb than today, I must warn you it's a lot further than it looks. You can't see the peak from here.'

'That's alright, I know you'll look after me, don't forget, I want my kiss at the top!'

At ten o'clock in the morning, it was getting warm as he adjusted her rucksack before they started the climb.

They wore shorts and aertex shirts, by the time they cleared the tree line Jeanne was slowing and needed a rest. 'I know I'm not very fit but my muscles are also a bit stiff from yesterday, I'll be better as I get warmed up.' They climbed steadily across the rocks and tussocks, the water of Thirlmere glittering behind them got ever smaller as they gained height. Her shirt was damp and her pale legs shiny with perspiration, the red scars and stitch marks livid on her calves and thighs. They crossed the slope where the Avro biplane landed in 1926. He pointed up the long grassy slope littered with stones, 'look, up beyond, there's the summit; we'll be up there in forty minutes. After a look around we'll start back down and find somewhere sheltered for our picnic. Actually, as there's no one here we can leave the rucksacks we'll go up quicker without them.'

They stood beside the cairn at the top; arms around each other's waists. Their shirts flapping, they shivered in the wind. They looked down across Red Tarn through the vast sweep of the lakes and mountains from Ullswater to the Irish Sea.

Ed kissed her willing mouth and led her by the hand down the slope of loose stones back to their rucksacks. They found a patch of grass sheltered by rocks on three sides, the fourth looked out over Striding Edge. Having eaten the pork pie and salad with their fingers they lay in the sun on the cloth looking up at the sky. 'Oh my feet are sore.' She took off her boots and socks and started rubbing her feet. There was a small bottle of olive oil for the salad in the picnic and she massaged her toes and heels. 'Would you like me to help? You lie down and rest.' Ed knelt below her and stroked her feet. 'How's that feel?'

'Delicious, if I lie on my front you can massage my aching legs too.'

29 Years

His hands were slick with oil as he carefully kneaded the muscles in her calves. He was close enough to see each fine dark hair shining flat in the oil. One hand on each thigh, his fingers moved up under her baggy shorts, as she sighed with pleasure; her slim legs parted slightly and he stroked higher.

'I am going to take off my shirt to enjoy the sun.' She reached behind herself to undo the brassiere strap. 'Now you can do my back as well, just a minute I don't want to get oil on my shorts.' She slid them off too and lay almost naked on the cloth. He could hardly speak, her body was so beautiful, so pale and delicate the shapes of her ribs and shoulder blades clear through the almost translucent skin. She rested her head on her arms and he could see the small tufts of black hair showing from her armpits.

He became very aroused as he massaged her back; leaning forward he moved her thick hair to kiss the nape of her neck. His erection pressed against his shorts and she lifted her bottom to feel it hard against the cleft of her buttocks.

He eased her knickers down to expose her fully to the sunshine, kissing her smooth round cheeks, running his tongue along the cleft to her furry pubes. She moaned 'make love to me now, I want you so much, right now.' She turned onto her back; the brassiere fell away showing him her hard, dark brown nipples. Jeanne reached up and pulled him down, her thighs opening to give herself to her lover.

That night as they lay in bed together in the quiet of the attic room. 'I must tell you some things; things that you should not know but I'm going to tell you anyway. You must have guessed that I do some secret work in France, I'm an agent for the SOE, I'm with the Resistance; I came to England for training in guerrilla warfare.

We do sabotage and try to kill German soldiers, will be sent back to continue my work. My section chief came to see me before we left, she wants me to report to the training camp next week, on Monday.' She lay flat on her back, 'I don't want to go but my family, my daughter and my colleagues need me, I can't let them down. I have to go, I've been here too long. It's been wonderful with you but now it must end.' She turned and resting up on one arm looked down at him, then stroking his face 'if you love me you must let me go.'

He spoke softly 'but your daughter? Are you married? Why didn't you tell me?'

'I didn't tell you because I didn't think things would go this far, I didn't expect that I'd fall for you the way that I have. In this war there are many thing we don't know, there are many things we don't need to know.' She kissed him. 'She is my beautiful girl, Hélène. She's two years old and lives with my mother.'

'Before you go, if you must go, can you at least tell me your real name?'

Chapter 9

Summer 1944 – The Cotswolds and France

Jeanne waved through the rear window of the black Riley as it lurched through the hard, dry ruts away from Bennett's Farm in the morning sun. The figures of Monique and Tim disappeared with a turn of the lane and all that remained of Jeanne's presence was a faint hanging of white dust. She rolled down the rear window and drank in the disappearing landscape trying to imprint the images on the retinas of her farewell eyes.

Once they reached the smooth road she was acutely conscious that the driver and her escort were in uniform and that she was being carried in a military vehicle. She knew that as the heavy car gathered speed she was being drawn swiftly, uncompromisingly, back to her duty, her destiny, back to the womb of war.

After four hours, having motored through Oxford, Buckingham and Bedford they arrived at the entrance to Tempsford Hall. The barrier rose beside a saluting sentry and they drove up to the red brick Victorian mansion that was to be her home for the next few weeks.

In some of her previous visits to Britain, Jeanne had undergone commando training at Arisaig in Scotland. There she learned the armed and unarmed combat skills taught by ex-police instructors Fairbairn and Sykes. She had been taught the skills of escape and evasion and then been tested on a four-day exercise. She had learned tradecraft and practiced demolition techniques using time fuses and plastic explosive.

This time she was to be trained in finding and laying out landing sites for Lysanders.

They would be bringing in supplies such as explosives, weapons, cash and wireless sets and personnel such as VIPs or agents known as 'Joes'. On their return flights they would mainly carry VIPs, Joes or escaping allied servicemen.

The Joes' task was to find suitable fields with a clear and fairly smooth area about 400 metres long without trees or power lines at either end. The field needed to be remote but accessible by vehicle for the carriage of stores or personnel. Once selected the details would be sent by Morse code wireless message to England. When the date for the landing had been set, it would be announced to the agent by a message on the BBC.

The agent would then set out the flarepath that consisted of three torches pointing skyward and arranged in an inverted L shape. A fourth torch would be used to flash a pre-arranged Morse letter. The pilot would abort the mission if the code letter was incorrect. The flights normally took place during the 'Moon Periods' when the pilots would be better able to navigate and land by moonlight. Once on the ground, the pilot could see the terrain, if necessary by using the bright landing lights mounted in the wheel covers.

In July the Allies established a bridgehead in Normandy and 'A' Flight, 161 Squadron recommenced operations.

Her training was finally over; Jeanne had been waiting for the right weather conditions for six days at Gaynes Hall. They had been driven down to near Chichester and now she stood in the makeshift Op's room at Tangmere Cottage. It was the base for SOE operations, just outside the gates of RAF Tangmere; the cottage was used as a hotel by the Joes and the pilots of 161 Squadron during moon periods.

29 Years

After supper they had sat silently while Squadron Leader Hugh Verity explained the flight details to the agents and showed them the route on a wall map of northern France. Most agents smoked, some hands trembled slightly as they lit their cigarettes. The Met' report was telephoned in, noted and pinned on the board; the flight was confirmed.

After the briefing Vera checked all the agents' clothes making sure the garments were French or made in the French style. Jeanne had a heavy suitcase containing explosives and pencil detonators; she wore a commando fighting knife in a scabbard on her belt. As on previous trips one of her buttons was a cunningly disguised suicide pill; this time it was one of the buttons on the cuff of her tailored blue jacket.

Vera had decided that because of her recent injuries it would be best for Jeanne to be landed rather than parachuted back into France. Her Lysander would put down in a field near Luzillé, a village about thirty kilometres southeast of Tours. There were four passengers with their equipment that night so two Lysanders would be flying to Luzillé.

~

After lunch Ed Collins stepped out into the little, three-sided courtyard garden at Bennett's Farmhouse and sat on the white painted bench in the sun. The house was quiet and empty, the dormer windows of Jeanne's flat above the garage looked blankly over the little garden. It was warm in the sun; he was wearing shirtsleeves and linen trousers. He leaned back, soaking in the heat and the scent of July roses. Through the birdsong and carried by the breeze he heard the first hesitant peals from the bells at Sherborne church.

The sound came and went; he turned his head to look over Sherborne Brook, to see the heron standing ankle deep in the brook, fishing in his usual place above the weeds. Ed's eyes followed the sheep angling along their worn trails through the close-cropped grass. He saw Mallards soaring and wheeling above the hill on the other bank then landing back on the water near the weir, all these things she'd watched from this seat.

As the bell ringers caught the rhythm so it became apparent from the cheerful pealing that a wedding was being celebrated. His face softened as he turned to face the breeze and listen.

Ed closed his eyes and silently the tears came. He pictured the church, the flowers the smiling faces. The ushers asking "Bride or Groom?"

From the corners of his eyelids they squeezed. Slowly at first, then an unceasing stream. So many tears that he could feel them run down past his ears to his neck. He lowered his head and his shoulders shuddered.

He brushed his wet face and reached for the cigarettes with damp fingers. Hands shaking, he couldn't strike the match. He dropped the unlit cigarette and gave way. He was twenty-four years old and wept with despair and loneliness. In his wasteland he stumbled over to the door of the flat, climbed the wooden stairs with the striped woollen runner to the bedroom and fell on the made up bed where she had slept. He pressed his face on the pillowcase vainly seeking traces of her scent. He found some clothes in a cupboard that she couldn't take with her and carried them to bed, to hug the bundle of wool and cotton. Finally he went to sleep with her in his arms.

Some hours later, Ed woke with a start; it was dark, he had to be back at Rissy by 10pm. He went into the house where the Smiths were sitting in the kitchen.

'Hello Ed, where've you sprung from?'

29 Years

'I'm sorry, I went for a lie down in the flat, I don't know what came over me. I really must head back to Rissy or I'll be late.' Monique and Tim exchanged knowing glances. 'Go carefully, come back and see us soon.'

Ed got on his bicycle and pedalled back through darkened stone villages lying still in the moonlight.

~

She got out of the big Ford station wagon beside the aircraft. 'Alright Joe?' said the pilot walking towards her. 'We'll take off in fifteen minutes; the flight will be about two and half hours. That's our kite over there; the ground crew'll help you with your kit, let's get it stowed away now and we'll climb aboard.' The suitcase was taken from her, lifted into the rear cockpit and pushed under the wooden seat.

She found her knees shaking as she mounted the short ladder to the rear cockpit. Knuckles clenched, she avoided eye contact with the crew; they helped her over the coaming, buckled her into the harness and tightened the webbing straps.

'That's you nice and snug, just relax and enjoy the ride' the Corporal said kindly. He patted her shoulder and slid the canopy shut. She wanted to scream as the humid air closed around her. She was squashed into a small space with the other passenger, both facing the tail. Her thoughts were of family and home; her daughter Hélène would be asleep in her cot. Gilles, her husband may even be at the landing site. She was desperate to see Hélène, her baby.

The engine revs increased and the plane moved forward, she was pulled towards the runway. The pilot's voice came through her headphones; 'everyone happy? Right then, we're going to taxi to the runway.

Once we're airborne keep a sharp lookout behind, you're my eyes back there.'
The plane accelerated and the memory of her last flight and fear of being shot down surged in her guts. The other Lysander followed and they took off in line astern. As they climbed to 6,000 feet the air cooled, the night was clear, the plane roared smoothly on. Her fear subsided as thoughts of the future invaded her head; she knew she must only look forward. She knew that she must clear her mind of all thoughts and memories of Edouard. She was determined to put that wonderful period of her life in a strongbox, to close the lid and throw the key into Channel. She watched the white cliffs turn grey, then dim, then disappear.

The Channel lay flat and silver below them, the sea crossing was about 100 miles and their route took them in over Cabourg. When they reached the coast the other plane banked slowly away to make its own route to Luzillé.

The sky was empty, no clouds, no planes. She could clearly see the ground: the fields, hedges, rivers and trees. She felt as if she was already in France, the very air was different; she closed her eyes and sighed with homecoming. She smelled coffee and a tap on the back indicated that a cup from the thermos was being offered by her comrade. She removed her right glove and reached over her left shoulder.

There wouldn't be any real coffee in the farmhouse, she'd heard from other Joes that rationing was strict and there were few luxuries anymore. Her family lived with her mother; her father had been killed in the Great War. Her husband, Gilles was forty this year; it was his birthday when she had been in Sherborne. He'd lost a foot in the Great War and now worked as an electrician for the railways.

His work took him all over the Indre-et-Loire department; he also worked with the Resistance. Gilles sometimes got useful information about German activities on the railways. If there was a major troop movement or large amounts of military supplies were being moved into France, the details could be transmitted by wireless to England.

If planes were available a mission could be planned for the RAF to bomb the train alternatively, resistance saboteurs could be tasked to blow up the track or de-rail the train.

She handed back the cup, waving her thanks and refusal of any more.

There had been talk amongst the Joes of recent operations. They were wary of telling each other much detail and real names were never used. There was strong evidence to suggest that information was leaking from Section F to the Gestapo in Paris. Some networks had been blown, their members shot or taken prisoner. There was a chance that her reception committee at the landing site would be German rather than French.

~

There was a clattering in the yard as the wooden gate scraped across the stones and a bicycle swung against the wall; the dog ran to the door as it burst open. 'She's coming home! Estelle's coming home!' Gustav, wearing a Basque beret and wire framed glasses beamed at them. 'They said on the BBC, there was a message after the news at six o'clock.'

'What does it mean? This is wonderful news! Sit down Gustav, tell us everything' said Gilles.

Sylvie poured a tumbler of red wine that Gustav tipped straight down his throat.

Wiped his moustache on the back of his hand and burped. 'Merci Madame, it means that she's coming in a plane tonight. It will land near Luzillé at two am.' They turned as one to the wall clock; it was 8.30.

'Who's meeting her and how will she get home?'

'I'll meet the others at the crossroads in Le Liege at one thirty; they've got a bike for her. We'll go and wait for the plane; it'll land in the field beside the road to St Quentin sur Indrois. After she lands I'll bring her back here, back to her home, back to you, her family.' He opened his arms towards them.

Gilles stood, shaking his head, 'no; no it's not right, I should be there, she's my wife, I should be there to meet her.'

'I'm sorry Gilles but you're not to come, Patrice said no. Think; what if we bump into some Boche out there? They're so jumpy after the sabotage on the railway, how can you run away? It's dangerous for us but much worse for you with your leg. Anyway, it was me who took her to the plane last time when she left, so it's right that I should be the one to bring her back to you.'

'He's right Gilles, you should stay here to look after me and Hélène; the Maquisards will bring our darling home safe.' Sylvie took his hand and looked up at him; 'I know how much you've missed her but it's not safe for you. Let Gustav and the Maquis do their work, Estelle will be here for breakfast and what a wonderful surprise for Hélène.'

She turned to Gustav; 'you must go, it's a long ride to Le Liege, do you have food? Here, take this bread and cheese.' She wrapped it in a cloth and stood to put it in his pocket. As he thanked her she kissed his bristly cheeks. 'Good luck, come back safely.'

Gilles shook Gustav's hand and patted his shoulder

'Merci mon vieux, à bientôt.'

29 Years

~

'That's Caen on your left; we keep away from there, they'll send up some heavy flak if they spot us. We'll see the Loire in about forty minutes and should land ten or twelve minutes after that. It's all quiet ahead, we might be in for an easy run tonight. Are you both comfortable? There's brandy in the metal flask under the rear seat if you'd like some. D'you see anything behind?'

'No, it's all quiet here too.'

She scanned the empty sky; having got used to the noise it was almost peaceful in the plane, her mind wandered, she caught her eyes closing and jerked awake. The horizon tilted as they turned onto the last heading, the Loire so familiar but quite strange from above, passed underneath.

'There's the lights, that's the landing field. Recognition signal correct. We'll be landing in one minute, brace yourselves.'

Throttle closed, nose slightly up, the plane sank into the darkness, stick back; she hit the ground with a bump and jolted past the torches across the hard grass field. A sharp left turn and they stopped, a smiling face at the canopy and eager hands helping her out. Suitcases were tugged free and passed down, passengers for the return flight climbed in. They stood back to wave the plane off. The pilot returned to beginning of the runway, held the aircraft on the brakes and ran up the engine until the slipstream lifted the tail. Released, it shot away and was airborne in sixty metres. The whole process had taken less than four minutes.

The heavy cases were carried to an old van waiting in the moon shadow beside the hedge. Gustav held a bicycle for Estelle; 'let's go before the Boche come snooping around.'

She followed his square body in the moonlight, thick legs pumping along the deserted road. After an hour they reached a forest, he stopped and walked his bike into the woods. He passed her a bottle of water then they sat down and ate the bread and cheese. 'Can you manage the journey? We're about a third of the way now, we really must get you home before dawn.'

Jeanne made it home; she staggered into the kitchen and fell onto the sofa. Her legs ached, her backside was burning and she was very tired. Sylvie brought her a glass of water and sat in a chair beside her, stroking her hair with motherly fingers. All was calm; all was unchanged.

'Where is Gilles?'

'I made him go to bed at midnight, he wanted to stay up but he's so busy at the moment. He needs his sleep but he'll be up in an hour and Hélène will wake up when she hears him. I'll look after them, you go back to sleep'.

In her dream she heard a child's voice; 'Mama, Mama!' and opened her eyes to see her daughter's shining, excited face beside her.

'Mama' she said happily and pulled herself up onto the sofa and put her short arms around Estelle.

'My darling, my baby I'm so happy to see you, you're so beautiful'.

Gilles crouched down his arms around them both, he kissed Estelle; 'and you're so beautiful too, I'm so happy to see you'.

They sat in the kitchen while Sylvie prepared breakfast; smiling and laughing, delighted to be a complete family again.

'I'm so glad I was here when you returned, have you heard the Maquis has made so much trouble for the Boche? I'm often called away, travelling to different sectors of the railway that have been damaged. How was it in England? What happened to you?

Why were you away for so long?'
And Estelle talked until it was time for Gilles to go to work.
That night as they lay in bed, the house quiet around them, windows open for a faint breeze to move the humid air. Gilles wanted her, she was tired, her legs hurt, she was too hot. She was his wife and so he took her anyway. She had never loved him but everyone said he was a good man, much older than her but so many men had perished or been badly wounded in the Great War. Some said she was lucky to have a husband at all. He, still in his vest, finished, rolled off and lay on his back; 'you didn't come back for me, you care nothing for me, what am I to think?' She said nothing; they pretended it would all go away, that somehow things would work out. It was the war; everything would be alright when the war was over. She lay on her side at the edge of the bed staring out at the darkness and tried not think of Ed.

~

Just as in many of their previous meetings, the members of the Valençay réseau were sitting round a table in the back room behind the bar of the Café de la Paix.
Patrice spoke low and quickly:
'Our orders are to blow up the railway line south of Tours in as many places as possible, the Germans are moving troops north towards Paris because of the Allied invasion. I've selected some possible areas where we can plant explosives.' He pointed to the map 'Eloise and Max I want you to put plastique at these two places, Sophie and François at these two; make sure you don't attract suspicion. Estelle and I will look at these areas here. We'll set the explosives to go off on Saturday night; the Boche will be out drinking and will be slow to react.

Set delay detonators to go off when you'll be at home asleep, understood? Your equipment is here, take a suitcase each and make your plans.'

She met Patrice at the barrier. The train was full of German soldiers and travellers; there weren't any seats available so they sat on their suitcases in the corridor. The heat disguised their sweat of fear; the corridor was packed with people. There was a faint draft of air from the open windows but the train moved slowly, the incoming air was hot and gave no relief. After a tense stop start journey of about forty minutes the train wheezed to a halt at their station and they got off to plant the first bomb. A wide dirt path ran alongside the line and they walked along side by side, looking for a culvert to hide her suitcase. There was a dip in the surface and a large pipe ran under the railway. 'This looks good, let's set it in here.' Patrice armed the twelve-hour pencil detonator and tried to push it into the plastique. His fingers were slippery with sweat; he dried them on his shirt and tried again. 'Ça va.' He closed the lid and carefully slid the case into the pipe, stood back and smiled at her. 'Good, now for the next one.'

He picked up his case and they walked back to the station to wait for the southbound train. As they stood on the platform a Wehrmacht patrol pulled up outside. The soldiers got out of the open back truck and immediately began asking for identity papers and tickets. Patrice stood beside her and held out his documents.

'What's in the suitcase? Where are you going?'

'Just some clothes, we're going to visit my mother.' The soldier looked disbelieving 'Why is it so heavy? Do you have some black market cheese or a nice farmer's ham in there?' joked the soldier. The Sergeant came over, 'yeah, I'm hungry, what's inside?'

29 Years

Patrice froze, his face was grey and strained he tried to speak, his mouth moved but no words came out, a sheen of sweat covered his skin. He looked at her and looked at the Germans, she thought Patrice was going to vomit. He dropped the suitcase and ran: 'Halte! Hande hoch! Halte!' He kept running, hoping to dodge in front of the incoming train before they opened fire. He stumbled on the loose stones under the rails and fell forward. The train couldn't stop; the steel wheels ran over his arms and chest crushing and killing him instantly. She fell to her knees on the concrete and felt a rifle muzzle drilling into her spine.

'Hande hoch!'

She was handcuffed, put in the back of a troop carrier and taken to the Wehrmacht Headquarters in Tours.

~

Gilles sat at the kitchen table with his hands over his face. 'They've arrested Estelle, taken her prisoner. Patrice is dead, oh my God what shall we do? What shall we say? They're going to come here and ask questions.'

'You must carry on as normal, if the Boche come here you must say you thought she was going to see her aunt in Bordeaux, we mustn't give her away.' Sylvie turned from the sink with wet hands; 'You must be strong, you know how dangerous it is now.'

'But tomorrow I have to go away, probably for three or four days, maybe longer. I've been told to work on the main railway line from Paris to Bordeaux. Just south of Tours there's a small village called Sainte Moure de Touraine; Maillé is the next station. They've a lot of work for me to do at each place after the sabotage, the Germans are furious. They know they've lost, how long can it be before they retreat? How will the Maquis like that?

There's going to be terrible trouble, I know it, it's all going to go wrong.'

~

'Feld Kommandant Stenger speaking.'
'Good evening Herr Oberstleutnant, this is Leutnant Schlueter, local area commander at Sainte Moure de Touraine.
'Yes Schleuter.'
'Sir, I have to report an attack by the Resistance on two of my vehicles. Three of my men are dead and five badly wounded.'
'What? What's going on in your area? Why are you having these constant attacks? Can't you keep control down there?'
'The Resistance are very strong in this area sir, particularly in Maillé, we know they're receiving weapons and ammunition by parachute from the RAF.'
'Well you had better do something about it, we can't allow any more of this terrorist activity. Sort it out, sort it out tomorrow. I expect a full report.'
'Yes Herr Oberstleutnant, I understand, I shall attend to it immediately.'

The following morning at 8 am, on 25th August, the same day that Paris was liberated by the Allies, the soldiers of the 17th SS Panzer Division advanced on the outskirts of Maillé.
With rifles and bayonets they murdered every man, woman, child, baby, horse and cow that they found. With flamethrowers they set fire to every farmhouse and farm building. As the noise and smoke reached the village centre, Gilles and the family he was staying with took cover downstairs in the cellar beneath the house.

29 Years

They heard the heavy boots and hoarse German shouts in bad French:
'Come out, everyone come out of your houses and hiding places! You must leave the village.' The command was repeated all around the sixty houses. Gilles and his friends decided it was safer to stay hidden. There was the occasional shot and sometimes the sound of running feet. They waited in the cool dark silence underground.
At noon a military train carrying an 88mm gun and an anti-aircraft flak canon arrived. They started firing, the shells were landing in the village, houses exploded and collapsed. Those still in hiding were crushed, suffocated or burnt alive, their village was utterly destroyed, obliterated and wiped off the map.

~

Sylvie was in the kitchen and Hélène was having her afternoon sleep when he arrived.
'Oh Gustav, Gustav come in, come in and tell me what's happening. I thought we were saved, the Allies have liberated Paris, when will we be safe?' He closed the door and leaned against it.
'I think it'll soon be over, the Germans must retreat soon or be cut off.'
'But what of Estelle, she's been gone for two weeks and where is Gilles? Why hasn't he returned.'
'Let's sit down and I can tell you what I know.' She poured him a tumbler of wine then sat and waited.
'Well the good news is that Estelle is alright, she was seen in Tours, being put in a car with two others. I was told that they've been taken to Paris. My guess is that she'll be sent to the Gestapo headquarters.'
'Oh my God! My baby. What will the Gestapo do to her?'

'I'm sorry I don't know any more but look, the Allies are in Paris, it can't be long before they find her. I'm sure we'll hear something soon.'

She wrung her hands, she was a strong woman but he could see her blinking back the tears.

'So what can you tell me about Gilles?'

'He was staying in Maillé, I heard there's been an attack on the village by the Germans, they left notes behind to saying it was a punishment for terrorists.'

'Is it for the sabotage? The sabotage that Patrice and Estelle had organised?

'I don't think so; I'm told it was a reprisal because of an ambush on some German military vehicles.'

'But is he hurt? Is he alright? Is he at work?' She looked beseechingly at him.

'He's not yet been found among the survivors.'

'What do you mean survivors? What on earth has happened?'

He told her and added 'only eight houses remain, the rest are ruined. There are over one hundred dead, they're still searching in the cellars for possible survivors'.

She broke down; 'both gone, both of them. I can't bear it, what about little Hélène? No Maman, no Papa.' She ran upstairs, apron over her face to hide her grief.

~

Estelle stood on the carpet in her dusty, scuffed shoes, she hadn't washed for three days. The floor length windows in 84 Avenue Foch looked out across sunlit trees bordering the wide Paris boulevard. She was in the office of Sturmbannfuehrer Kieffer of the Sicherheitsdienst, he was known as, the spycatcher.

He was powerful looking man wearing a light grey suit; 'please sit down.'

He indicated the armchair for her and sat on the sofa. He studied her for a while in silence with her papers in his hand.

'Tell me Madame Levavasseur, what were you doing at the railway station?'

'I was going to visit my aunt in Bordeaux.'

'Ha, ha, ha' he burst out laughing; 'what! with a suitcase full of plastique? I don't think so'.

There was another silence while he just looked at her.

'Now; why don't you tell me the truth? That way we'll get on so much better together.'

'I have nothing to say.'

'Ah but I'm sure you do Estelle, may I call you Estelle? My name is Hans Josef Kieffer.'

Silence. She looked past him, out of the window.

'Or should I call you Jeanne?' She swallowed.

'Why would you call me Jeanne?' She said hesitantly.

'Because that's what your friends call you, your English friends.'

'I don't know what you're talking about, what English friends?

'Well, let's start with your friends Colonel Maurice Buckmaster and Flying Officer Vera Atkins.' She was stunned, her mouth moved but no words came.

'You seem surprised,' he laughed again. 'This is my job; I'm here in France responsible for counter intelligence, don't think that I've been wasting my time. Come and look at this,' he walked over to a chart on the wall.

'Look, here they all are, your name will go in here.' The chart was an almost complete list of all the commanders and networks of the SOE in France. She thought she'd faint and held onto the back of a chair.

'Would you like some coffee? Are you hungry? I think you should go to your rooms, have a bath and some food. We can have a proper chat afterwards.'

'How, how do you know all, all this.' She pointed a trembling finger, unbelievingly at the chart.
'I know everything, Claude tells me everything.'
She shut her eyes and breathed heavily, it couldn't be true. Claude? Claude was Henri Dericourt, she knew him; he'd organized all the landings and parachute drops.
'I have nothing to say.' She repeated mechanically.
Kieffer stared at her then smiled and opened the door 'take her upstairs.'

Chapter 10

2014 – Malta and The Cotswolds

'Hello' Tumas Nasim answered his phone.
'Hi Dad, if you're free today can I drag you away from your desk and buy you a nice lunch?'
'Hello Matt, that sounds good, what's up?
'Let's talk when we meet, how about the Phoenicia Hotel, in the bar at twelve o'clock?'
'Perfect, see you later.'
Matt sauntered through the gates and along the palm shaded drive to the grand art deco hotel, lengthened his stride to the columned portico and took the wide marble steps one at a time.
Father and son kissed cheeks and hugged each other in the bar.
'You're looking well my son, keeping busy I hope; and keeping out of trouble too.'
Oh, you know me, always got things to do. How's the new boat?'
'Fantastic but I've only been out in her twice. You must come, bring Latifa and the kids, we'll have a nice day out, waterskiing, windsurfing we've got all the toys on board.'
After lunch they walked into the gardens, dark green grass edged with a white stone balustrade that underscored the view over Valetta harbour. They sat in the shade of a palm tree for cigars and coffee.
'So tell me my boy, what d'you want talk about?' Tumas leaned back making the wicker chair creak.

'It's a property deal. Residential property, a housing development.'

'Hmm, I think that bubble's burst, I keep reading there's unsold property everywhere.'
'Yeah but not in England, the market's really strong there.'
'England? I thought you weren't very popular with the authorities at the moment, not allowed to be a company director or something?'
'I've got some temporary difficulties but meantime I've put some money into a small company. It's managed by a very loyal friend who helped me a lot in the past, it's all very clean and above board.'
'What are you doing with this small company?'
'It's a real estate firm, mainly building new homes, it's been trading for eighteen months.'
'OK' he eased his jacket and blew out a thick stream of blue smoke 'So how can I help you?'
'We've got a new opportunity; it's potentially quite a big development. I need more capital to finance the land purchase and the construction of up to four hundred homes.'
'How much capital?'
'Fifty million pounds for the land and up to fifty million pounds for the construction and infrastructure, we expect to sell the houses for one hundred and twenty million.'
The corners of Tumas's mouth turned down, he looked impressed and doubtful at the same time.
'You're talking about a lot of money here, how d'you think I can help?'
Matt leaned forward 'I know you've got contacts who've got a lot of money, some of it might need to be; how shall we say, made cleaner?'
'Be very careful.' He looked around the gardens and lowered his voice; 'be very careful what you're saying, it's not for discussion here. This is not an easy business, there are many…. no, let's leave it there.

29 Years

I understand what you want, I'll make some enquiries then I'll call you when I've got some news.'

~

Dave sat at his desk; in the file was Allie's signed agreement to sell the Right of Way and he'd engaged the planning consultants that had succeeded with the Victory Fields development. They'd have an outline proposal ready for review in four weeks' time. He'd also hired Armin Patel, a small but well-respected firm of accountants in Witney to prepare the finance and bid documentation.

The next job was to find a solicitor suitable for the legal process and they needed to be well-in with the County Council. Easy, it was probably time for a chat with Jo about the planning application, she said she wanted to know about anything big coming up. She'd recommend the right firm; he picked up the phone and invited her for lunch the following day.

The escrow account was a different matter he wanted to keep that away from the other advisers, he certainly didn't want any awkward questions about the origin of the funds. Carson de Salis had been a very successful solicitor until he had overstepped the guidelines and started to think of his clients' money as being his own. In fact he didn't just think about it, he spent it. For a bright man he had been very foolish, after running into debt, he thought he could borrow from the firm and put it back some time in the future without anyone noticing. There'd been a snap internal audit, he was discovered and sacked; he was lucky not to have been struck off.

De Salis had been very decent to Dave when he had started as a clerk in Oxford and this would be a nice way to repay the kindness.

Here was a straightforward piece of work and there'd be a decent fee in it for the solicitor. Dave knew Carson was working for a 'consultancy only' firm of solicitors on a business park near Witney; he looked them up on the internet and started dialing.

~

They were sitting on the sofa at Ed's cottage; John had his laptop open, showing Ed the photos he'd taken at Prescott, they'd had a great day out. The sun was shining and the sheer number and variety of cars was amazing, there'd been about ten or twelve Bugattis and many other famous marques: Alvis, Bentley, BMW and ERA, there was so much to see. They'd wandered around the paddock in amongst the heady smell of Castrol R and the ripping blasts of racing exhausts. The highly tuned sports cars had smoked their tyres off the start line and stormed up the narrow tarmac track. The fastest could cover the one thousand yard climb in forty two seconds, the driver working furiously in the high open cockpit.

They had slowly made their way up the hill from vantage point to vantage point watching the cars skidding round the corners and listening to the snatched and sometimes missed gearchanges. Ed pointed at the photo of a Bugatti, taken as it had braked into the hairpin below them. 'I'm pretty sure my old CO had one like that. I remember it was blue and I do remember the horseshoe-shaped brass radiator surround; it had that little red enamel badge at the top.'

'That's a Type 35, probably the most famous; they were very successful Grand Prix racers in the 1920's.'

'You know, I think he got it for a song, people just didn't want these cars in the war, petrol was so hard to come by they practically gave them away.

I don't think I ever drove it on the roads, just had a bit of fun, you know, tearing around the perimeter track.' He smiled at the reminiscence and rested his head back in the chair to look at ceiling, after a few moments silence:

'Let me tell you a story. You remember we were looking at a photograph of a Lysander the last time you were here? There's actually quite a tale involving one of those aircraft. One morning in early 1944, I saw one of them sitting out on the airfield. It had come in during the night having been shot up over the Channel. I went over and took a good look at it there were a lot of bullet holes in the fabric and canopy and bloodstains in the rear cockpit. A few days later I was called to see the CO, he told me that a French secret agent had been the passenger and she was now in the base hospital.' He smiled at John's look of surprise. 'Yes the agent was a woman and after her surgery I was to act as liaison officer and help her get fit again to rejoin the Resistance in France. Well one thing led to another and during the months of recuperation we fell in love. Of course it all had to end and when she left she made it pretty clear that that was the end of it. She was going back to a very dangerous job, she was in the SOE; mainly sabotage work, in German occupied northern France. She was incredibly brave but wonderful and charming; she was such fun and very modest.'

'What was her name?'

'She was called Jeanne, that was her cover. She never told me her real name.' He opened a brown manila envelope; 'Here's some photos.' He passed them over; small, black and white snaps. 'Gosh, she's very striking, beautiful, all that thick black hair and she's got a lovely smile' John returned them to Ed's shaky hands.

'She went off to do her training somewhere in England and then back to France. I was in a bit of state, I'd never been in love before and it shook me up pretty badly.

It was autumn, the Allies were advancing into Germany; life at Rissy was very dull, all I could think about was Jeanne and worry about her. At a dinner party one evening I was sitting next to the CO's wife, she knew some of the story about Jeanne and had put two and two together. Anyway she was very kind and did her best to cheer me up. A few days later I was called to see the CO. "Look Ed, I think the best thing for you is a change of scenery so I've arranged for you to be posted to the Far East. India in fact, winter's coming and it can be pretty bloody here so I propose some action, sunshine and spicy food for you. Go and see the Adjutant he'll fill you in on all the details. You'll be going as Second in Command to an old chum of mine who's commanding RAF Alipore at Calcutta. So there's a promotion for you as well!" To say I was surprised would be a bit of an understatement but anything was better than moping around at Rissy so after much thanks I went to find out about my new posting. The Adjutant told me to come back the following week once my travel warrants had been produced. The days suddenly passed a lot more quickly, the Chief Clerk gave me the lowdown on Alipore and there were many chaps at Rissy who had been to India at one time or another who were happy to tell me their stories. By the time I saw the Adjutant I was all ready to go. I can see him now, he had a file on his desk and a travel warrant in his hand. "Yes Ed, do sit down. Now about your posting to India, well there's a slight delay and we'd like you to do something else before you go." This sounded ominous, I said "yes, of course sir, what would that be?' He looked through his notes, thin lips pursed.

"You're to go to northern France, err' he peered at the document more closely 'near Orléans, to assist in airfield security as a liaison officer; the CO says you speak French pretty well.

The situation is that airfields are being used as dumps for arms, ammunition and other war materiel. There's kit everywhere; the problem is that the Frogs nick anything. They seem to think that once the stuff is in France it's theirs. Mr Churchill wants all war materiel secured, the concern is that there's more trouble coming. We need to transfer our efforts, that means men and equipment, to the war in the Far East. This job in France should only be for six to eight weeks and then you'll be on your way to India."

Once again I was lost for words. The complete change of direction seemed enormous. Of course I thought that maybe if I was in France I'd try and find Jeanne, I remember being nervous and very excited. So off I went, winter came, it got colder and colder and the work was tedious. I got involved with some of the investigations; sometimes acting as an expert having to identify certain military equipment so I spent a bit of time with their police, the Gendarmerie. There was a lot of blackmarket traffic going on which was very murky. You couldn't always be sure whose side the Gendarmerie were on. All the time I was thinking about finding Jeanne, I thought about asking one of the Gendarmes but the trouble was it was impossible for me to know if they were sympathetic to the Resistance. I knew there'd been purges against collaborationists but my French wasn't good enough to understand the nuances of the situation and I was concerned that I might blow her cover.

I did meet one man, a Judge, "Procurer" they say in French. We talked about the Resistance, he was friendly but more important he didn't seem to trust the Gendarmerie and was often sceptical of their arrests and charges. Possibly cases where old scores were being settled. We met for a drink after work one evening and became more comfortable with one another.

I just had to ask him; he explained about the Resistance and why the Police were so cagey. I asked if there was anyone he knew in the Resistance who might talk to me. The Judge agreed to help and said he'd try and set up a meeting for me.

A few days later he said he'd found someone who had been trained in England and arranged a date. You can't imagine how elated I was. I was going to meet someone who knew Jeanne, from the inside as it were, someone who might be able to lead me to her. However, there always seems to be a however in these stories, two days before the meeting was due to take place, a signal arrived to say my posting to Calcutta was confirmed.

I was to report to Rissy on Monday morning at 08.00 for a debrief on the French airfield situation, it meant I'd have to leave the following morning. I went to see the Judge to explain but he was in court all day, so all I could do was leave a message. I was devastated, so close to tracing Jeanne but the chance was lost at the last minute The war or the RAF was determined that I should never find her.

I went back to Rissy and then on to India, the journey took weeks, I went by troop ship from Liverpool and then through the Med' and the Suez canal to Bombay. From there I went by train about twelve hundred miles east to Calcutta. It was all very exotic for a young man, I was about twenty-four years old, the heat and sights and smells were astonishing.

The train journey took two weeks, can you believe it. Sleeping in the luggage racks, buying food and tea on the platforms. I loved all of it, I was still there in 1945 when the Americans dropped the atomic bomb on Hiroshima and the Japanese surrendered.

I liked Calcutta very much and stayed on there after the war ended.

29 Years

I didn't fancy going back to England, you know what with rationing and I hadn't any professional qualifications to get a job. I applied to stay on for a year in the RAF, still at Alipore, it was a big aerodrome where Air Command, South East Asia was based. All sorts of dignitaries came visiting, I saw Lord Mountbatten once. He had a very pretty RAF girl as his Personal Assistant. He arrived in his own plane, a Dakota DC3, an American built cargo plane. We managed to sneak a look inside, it was all fitted out like an airliner; it even had a cabin with a double bed. We were very impressed I can tell you, how the other half lived!'

'Here's an odd little story: I went with some other officers one evening to a dinner dance at Firpo's which was the top Italian restaurant on the Chowringhee Road. The food was wonderful, the whole place very European, we were looking smart in uniform and many of the local Indians and Chinese were in western clothes.

The band played all those famous American big band numbers, you know Count Basie, Duke Ellington, Glen Miller. I heard 'In the mood' so often that I got rather fed up with it. Anyway, there was a large family party of Chinese at a nearby table including a very beautiful girl. I kept catching her eye and after a while went over to ask her father if I might have the pleasure of dancing with his daughter. He was very polite, spoke perfect English and was wearing a very nice suit.

Quite slowly and deliberately he thanked me for my invitation and said, without consulting her, that "his daughter preferred not to dance with me." He shook his head and smiled.

'Anyway, I digress, the Japanese surrendered in 1945 and Hong Kong became a British Colony again. Everything was in complete disarray and I was looking for a permanent job by then.

I heard that the Hong Kong Police force was going to be rebuilt so I applied and was accepted for training as a Police Officer.

Whilst I was in Hong Kong I saw 'School for Danger' a film made by the RAF about secret missions of British and French agents behind enemy lines in France during the war. The film even had two real agents as actors. I forget their names but they acted out the roles that they'd played for real in 1944. Of course I quickly cottoned on to exactly what Jeanne had been up to.

I came back home on leave in 1947 and my parents introduced me to a local girl named Mary Timms, she was a teacher and had lost her husband who was a pilot in the war. I invited her out to Hong Kong, she liked it, we got on well, and so we decided to get married. After the children were born she went back to teaching and got a job at the old British Central School; it became King George V School on the Tin Kwong Road. When they were older, Mary wanted the children to go to school in England but couldn't bear to be parted from them. So she brought them back to the Cotswolds in 1960 and they started at Burford Grammar School. Shortly after they arrived there was a junior teaching vacancy that Mary was offered and so everyone settled in very well. After a year or two I got a job with the Gloucestershire Constabulary at Cheltenham and came back home to join my family, at that time we lived in Northleach. Time went on and we both steadily rose through our respective career paths. By 1973 both children had left home and gone to work abroad, my older son to Mexico and the younger to Australia.

29 Years

Sorry, I'm forgetting myself, have you got time for a drink? Shall we have a whisky?' John got up and while he was making the drinks Ed kept talking.

'I was very interested in France and what had happened there in the war, I watched a television series called "The World at War" during which I first heard about the massacre at a village named Oradour-sur-Glane.'

John shook his head never having heard of the event. 'It was the opening sequence of the first episode; one of those awful atrocities which came to light some time after the war ended but it absolutely gripped me and Jeanne came vividly back into mind. I watched the television dumbstruck, it catapulted me back through the years, straight back into the war. This massacre was one of many carried out by the German Army in reprisal for acts of sabotage by the Resistance. The Germans took the view that the Resistance was a terrorist organization and under the Geneva Convention that was in force at the time they were entitled to carry out reprisals to deter further terrorist activity. Of course my head was suddenly swamped with the memories of Jeanne and I felt that I had to know what had become of her.'

Chapter 11

Spring 1973 - England

'What's the matter? you look as if you've seen a ghost; are you alright Ed?' Mary took two steps across the sitting room and touched her husband's shoulder in concern. They were watching "The World at War" on TV, it opened with a film about the massacre at a village named Oradour-sur-Glane. He pointed at the screen 'that's terrible it just brings it all back. We won but there were so many tragedies, you lost Jamie which was awful for you and there were so many other families that lost sons and daughters but this, this is cold-blooded murder.

Wiping out a village as a reprisal for acts carried out by the Resistance? God but they were bastards those Germans, how could they do it? How could anyone, in cold blood, just march into a village one morning and kill defenceless people?

I can't believe the numbers, they got everyone in the village market place for an identity check then took the men, a hundred and ninety men, took them to barns where machine guns had been set up and shot them in the legs. Then when the men couldn't move the bastards set fire to the barns and burned all the wounded.

The two hundred and forty seven women and two hundred and five children were locked in the church. Once again the SS set fire to the building and as the women and children tried to escape through the doors and windows the soldiers shot them. Dead. Unbelievable, just unbelievable and this was all as a reprisal for the Resistance capturing one German officer.'

29 Years

He shook his head, lost in wartime memories and buried, erupting emotions. He began slowly 'I knew someone in the Resistance, she was an agent, in the War.' Mary pulled up the footstool beside his armchair and took his hand. 'You never mentioned this before, do you want to tell me about it?'

And so he did; he took off his glasses and as the words started to come and then tumbled out he pinched the bridge of his nose to help control his breathing. The feelings that he'd buried for so many years burst out as sharp and painful as the day she'd left.

'So what became of her? What happened to Jeanne?'

'I don't know.' He gestured at the TV 'Maybe she was killed in a reprisal; maybe she was caught by the Gestapo and tortured to death, she could even still be alive, I just don't know.'

They had an unsettled night and the atmosphere was rather strained between them for the next few days, the buried memories had come into the light and hung between them.

It was Saturday morning. 'Look' said Mary, 'I think we need to have a talk about Jeanne, I know you've been thinking about her and I can see that you're upset. What do you want to do about it?' He sat at the kitchen table; 'I'd just like to know what happened to her, to know that she's alright. I mean the reality is that she's probably dead you know, but it's just to set my mind at rest.'

'How will you do that? You don't even know her real name, or where she lived.'

'You're right; I don't have a lot to go on. I've been thinking about her too, thinking about what I can do, where to start. I could go to Rissy; it's the Central Flying School now. They may have a record of a Lysander coming in from RAF Tangmere.

That's where her plane came from; if they've got a note in the aerodrome log, I may be able to find out the name of the pilot.'

'What will you do then?'

'I guess I'll follow it up and see where it takes me.'

'Well if you must, then you must but you might be opening up a real can of worms. I think you should also prepare yourself for disappointments.'

'Do you mind me doing this?'

'Not really but I can see that you've become fixated by it so I don't see that I've got much choice in the matter.'

'Thank you.' He gave her a hug. 'Thank you for being so understanding.'

'Hmmph' she got up and went to her study.

On Monday he rang the Central Flying School, the operator put him through to the Station Warrant Officer, the Senior NCO responsible for discipline and administration.

'Mr Martin' answered the phone, Ed explained who he was and that he was trying to trace a Lysander from RAF Tangmere that had landed at Rissy in February 1944.

'That's not Flight Lieutenant Ed Collins, the navigator?'

'Yes it is.'

'This is Bill Martin, I was one of your clerks in 1944, here at Rissy.'

They both burst out laughing; 'what a wonderful surprise, you've done well Bill.'

'Thank you sir and what are you up to these days?'

'I'm a Police Officer, Chief Superintendent.'

'So you've done well too, I'm glad to hear it, now tell me again what it is you're after and I'll see if I can help.' He explained in more detail.

'Is this to do with that French bird then?'

'What! What do you know about that?'

'Not much remains secret in the clerks' room sir.'

'Well yes it is, I'm trying to find out what happened to her, if I can discover who the pilot was, maybe I can track him down and find out where he picked her up from.'

'There's a fair bit of water under the bridge since then sir. I know it was 161 Squadron that operated the Lysanders. We've got a lot of records here but that was a covert mission so it might not be logged. Mind you, we've got a few instructors here that might have known someone in 161, I'll ask round. Tell you what; would you like to come up to the Mess on Thursday evening for a drink? We can have a laugh about the old days and I'll let you know what I've found out.'

'That would be marvellous, I'm really looking forward to seeing you.'

'Me too sir, see on Thursday at six o'clock, I'll leave your name with the Guardroom; they'll be expecting you.' It was strange to be back, he hadn't been on the airfield since he left in '44. As he drove, he looked around, the place was covered in aircraft of all types; he knew the Red Arrows were based there because he often saw them in the skies above the Cotswolds. There were many other training aircraft, lots that he didn't recognize and some helicopters. He was shown to the Sergeants' and Warrant Officers' Mess and found Bill at the bar. Bill soon introduced him to many of his friends; there was much banter and laughter.

'Now sir, let's go and have a quiet chat over by the window and I'll do my best not to breach the Official Secrets Act.'

They sat down and looked at each other expectantly 'Oh, before you get started, please call me Ed, I think we know each other well enough don't you?'

'Righto Ed, now I've made a bit of progress but after this I think you're probably on your own.

Some of the stuff that I came across is still classified, those boys at 161 kept things very quiet you know. I couldn't find any record of a Lysander landing here, however one of the instructors here knew a few of their pilots, he was in 138 Squadron flying Halifaxes, they provided the heavy drop capability for the agents. He told me that the boss of 161 at the time you're interested in was a Squadron Leader Hugh Verity.'

'Yes, this is quite exciting, do go on.'

'I looked him up, he retired in 1965 as a Group Captain, and then joined the Industrial Training Board.' He passed a slip of paper across the table. 'That's their phone number.'

'That's amazing, wonderful, can I get another round Bill?'

'Unfortunately not, you're in my Mess, I'm delighted to help and all the drinks are on me. I should say though I'd rather you didn't ever mention my part in any of this, err investigation.' Returning with fresh pints, Bill quizzed Ed about "The French bird" and over more beer they swapped stories of their different postings, cheerily parting as best of friends, Ed promised to let Bill know how he got on.

~

Back in his office at the station he smoothed Bill's piece of paper between his fingers, laid it on the desk and dialed the number, the operator put him through straight away.

'Verity' Ed apologized for telephoning out of the blue and explained his request.

'No, no, not all don't worry about that. Look as a matter of fact I've been collecting a lot of information about that period during the war.

I thought it might be of interest to a few people and here you are. Now then, the best thing you can do is come and visit me at home, I've got all the papers and log books and photos, oh all sorts of stuff that might interest you. Come on Sunday afternoon, what's the period you're interested in again? Yes, Lysander, shot up, landed at Rissy in February '44, fine I should be able to find that, come at three, stay for tea.'

Ed motored over in his Ford Cortina to see Hugh on Sunday.

'How very nice to meet you, do come in, lets go through to my study.' The tables and bookshelves were filled with files, papers and letters. 'It's all a bit of a shambles at the moment but I am getting it together. I've been contacting as many of the 161 members as I can and they've been sending me all sorts of information, anecdotes, notes and reminiscences, utterly fascinating stuff. Not always relevant but fascinating anyway.'

'What is it you're compiling?'

'I want to put together a record of all the amazing pilots that flew the pick-up sorties into northern France and tell some of the stories of the agents, "Joes" we called them, that we carried and also those that we trained to find landing sites for us.'

'It looks like you've had a good response.'

'Yes, I'm very pleased but of course a good many of the people were lost but even so.' He looked around the room. 'Yes you're right it has been a good response; we were all very close you know, very close friends.' He went to the desk and picked up a bundle of papers.

'Now, here's the period you're interested in, I've been looking for a reference to that flight you told me about. I've got some letters from the Fitters who had to go and collect that Lizzie in February so we roughly know the date. Ah here, look the aircraft was 'G' George.

Now let's see if anyone mentions which pilots flew George.' He reached for another file. 'I know all this might seem a bit haphazard to you but do remember that because the operations were secret we didn't really put anything in our log books and we were told not to keep diaries.

I've started to put together a summary of all the pick-ups that we flew in France; here, you can see these are the sorties in February 1944. January was a washout due to the poor weather, in February there were eleven of which four were carried out in Hudsons. That's a much bigger plane, could carry ten passengers with a two-man crew. Now of the seven Lizzie flights, three failed due to bad weather and one crashed in France; that leaves us with three possibles.

One had no return passengers so we're left with two sorties one of which was a double – that's two planes going to the same landing ground. The three pilots were Flight Lieutenant Stebbings, Flight Lieutenant Booth and Flight Lieutenant Knowles.'

He turned to a ledger and opened it. 'I know Stebbings died in 1945, I'm in contact with Booth but I don't remember anything from Knowles, I've logged all the correspondence so we can see if I've had anything back from Graham.'

He flipped through the pages and rubbed his chin. 'Hmm, I wrote to him last year at an address in Yorkshire but I can't trace a reply. Well there we are, I think you've got two leads, that's what you chaps say isn't it?

'That's terrific, may I copy their addresses?'

'Yes indeed, I hope you do better with Graham than I did, do give them my best wishes when you speak to them won't you?'

He came from behind the desk pointing at his chair.

'You sit here and here's some paper, ah you've got your notebook' he smiled, 'am I err, helping you with your enquiries?'

Ed laughed; 'you certainly are and this is very much personal not business.'

'I can hear tea-time noises next door, when you're ready, let's go and have some and I can't wait to hear your side of the story.'

They sat in the drawing room and over Earl Grey and Victoria sponge exchanged wartime and peacetime career stories. They were about the same age and quickly found experiences and comrades in common. Their ease and trust in one another grew as Ed explained his quest for an agent named Jeanne who returned to France sometime after mid-July in 1944.

'Well if it's a girl then that narrows it down somewhat, I'd say more than half the Joes that we flew were women, can you remember anything about her that might help to distinguish her from the others?'

'She'd been badly wounded in the legs on the outward flight; I expect she'd have been landed rather than parachuted in. Regarding area, I got the impression that she lived near the Loire so possibly she was taken back to that region.'

'OK, so it could be a Lysander or a Hudson. Thinking about dates, let's say she had two weeks training that takes us to the beginning of August. More tea?'

Ed looked at his watch; 'Do you think we might have another look?' He inclined his head to the study. 'See if we might be able to come up with a few more possibles?'

Hugh grinned; 'Yes, let's get at it; I do enjoy a detective story. Actually it sounds more like a detective love-story, a bit of cherchez la femme!'

They pored over more letters looking for mentions of flights in August and setting them to one side.

After an hour they had finished sifting the papers.
'Good, let's make a list of what we've got; there's twelve in all so we'll take them by area. We used to reference the landing sites by "Départment" you know the French equivalent of an English County.
So along the Loire we're looking at:' He checked the map on the wall which was marked up with black felt tip pen:

'Cher, Indre-et-Loire, Loire-et-Cher, Loiret and Maine-et-Loire. We then cross-check against the flights: of the twelve flights only two Départments are near the Loire that's Cher and Indre.' He went back to the pile of letters 'the flights to Cher were Hudsons, the one to Indre-et-Loire was a Lizzie. And I can also tell you who flew them, the pilots were Squadron Leader Jamieson, Flight Lieutenant Swayne and Flying Officer Heffens.'
'That's fantastic may I..."
'Be my guest.' Ed sat at the desk, made some notes and copied the addresses.
'Now what you'll need are the locations of the landing sites.' He picked up a wooden pointer. 'We had code names for each of them, the one in Cher was named "Carpe" it's here between Bourges and Chavannes and the one in Indre-et-Loire was named Planête.' He tapped another red circle on the map 'it's between Tours and Luzillé.'
'I can't imagine how I could have made such progress without you.'
'Not at all, it's a pleasure. Now there are some other people you should try, obvious really should've mentioned it straightaway.' Ed looked at him, eyebrows raised in enquiry.
'The chap who knew everybody was Henri Dericourt, he was in the SOE, very involved with moving Joes back and forth from France to England.

He would probably have known your Jeanne.' Ed's pulse raced. 'Yes, that sounds promising, where is he now? What's he up to?'

'I'm sorry to say he's dropped out of the picture, the last I'd heard was that he was seriously hurt in a flying accident somewhere in Laos. No, the person I was really thinking of is Flying Officer Vera Atkins; she looked after all the Joes, she was their handler if you like. She was often with us at Tempsford and Tangmere. Always there before the Joes flew out, you should talk to her. I've got her number here somewhere.' He found a brown leather telephone book.

'Here you are' he read out the number 'she's pretty cagey and very clever but I'm sure you'll get along fine with her.' It was time to wrap up and go home. They tidied up the papers and walked to the front door where they shook hands. Ed shut the car door and wound down the window to say goodbye.

'I really wish you all the best, do give me a ring if you think I can be of any further help.' Hugh patted the Cortina's vinyl roof in a good luck sort of way.

On the drive home his brain boiled with information and emotion; excitement that he was making progress and concern at Mary's reaction. He took some deep breaths and settled back in the velour covered seat. He told himself to look at it objectively; the only thing to do was to treat it as a police-type missing persons enquiry, try and be emotionally detached. Just be methodical and follow up the leads. If he got somewhere then fine, if not, well that's just the way it was going to be. He grunted to himself in approval and switched on the car radio. He tapped his fingers on the steering wheel listening to 'Pick of the Pops' with Alan Freeman.

Over their usual Sunday night scrambled egg supper Mary asked how his visit had gone.

'It was really helpful, Hugh's working on a book about his wartime squadron, he had a lot of useful information. He's given me some contacts too, you know, names of pilots who might have brought Jeanne over from France or taken her back.' She looked over her glasses at him.
'How will that help?'
'Well, I might be able to get a better idea of where she lived. I'm pretty sure it was south of the Loire but not too far from the river. Obviously I need to fine it down a lot better than that before I start searching. He also gave me the locations of the landing sites, oh and the name of the SOE woman who looked after the agents, she might also be prepared to help.'
'I know all this was a long time ago but are you sure people are allowed to give out this type of information? Isn't it all still secret?'
'Hugh doesn't seem to have a problem; after all he's writing a book about it so it can't be that secret. Anyway d'you remember me telling you there was a film about it that I saw during the war, so no, I think it should be alright.'
'So what's next in your, err, investigation.' She said wryly.
'I'll try and make contact with the five pilots and the Atkins woman, just treat it like any other missing persons enquiry. You know follow the leads, knock on doors, see what turns up.'
'You sound like Dixon of Dock Green, have you ever done any of this kind of police work? I thought you were more of a management type.'
'Well I know the basics and I know where to get expert advice if I need it, thank you.'

~

Ed cleared his in-tray and had the rest of Monday afternoon to himself, after closing the office door he took off his jacket, pulled a foolscap pad towards him and opened his notebook on the desk.

By the time the tea lady knocked he'd filled several pages. Stebbings had been at home and answered the phone straightaway; he sent his best wishes back to Hugh Verity but didn't know anything about a plane being diverted to Little Rissington.

Ed couldn't find a phone number for Knowles so he rang the York and North East Yorkshire Police to find out if there was a local police station in Coxwold, they promised to call back with the information.

Next he spoke to Jamieson, the man was a pompous ass who refused to help him adding that he had no intention of sharing state secrets with a "flatfoot".

He dialed the numbers for Swayn and Heffens but they were both at work and their wives suggested he ring back in the evening.

Later, after supper when Mary had gone back into to her study; she was now Deputy Headmistress and always had pressing issues to deal with, Ed rang Swayn.

The conversation went well enough but Swayn was reticent, he didn't remember much, he didn't seem to want to get involved. He was still serving in the RAF as a retired officer and was looking forward to his pension. The only thing he was sure of was that he had never carried a female Joe out to France, so at least he could be taken off the list.

Heffens was delighted to hear from him; in fact he had been talking to Verity and was expecting Ed's call. He remembered the flight:

'Yes' he said, 'there were two Joes, look I started making some notes about all this when I got Hugh's letter asking for reminiscences.

Of course some things take longer to come back than others but once I started thinking back, all sorts of memories sprang up. It was a completely uneventful trip that night, I knew the landing site "Planête" pretty well and the local agent was a reliable man so all went smoothly.'

'Was there anyone else there that you spoke to or recognised that night?' 'No, I don't think so; a good turnaround time was less than five minutes.

They put some packages in and there were two passengers coming back. We always kept the engine running when we were on the ground you know, in case of Jerry turning up and we took off as soon as they were on board. I'm looking through my notes here but I don't think I've got anything else that would be much use for you.'

He promised to call Ed back if he remembered any more which might give a clue to finding Jeanne.

The light was still showing under Mary's study door, she didn't turn as he looked in. 'I'm going up now' 'right oh, won't be long, don't wait up.' As usual, Ed went up to bed alone.

In the morning there was a message on his desk from the York and North East Yorkshire Police with the details of the Coxwold Station.

The local Bobby said he knew Mister Knowles and yes he would pop in later that morning to see if he was alright and find out if he had a telephone. 'Oh if he hasn't got one would you be good enough to ask him to ring me from a phone box?' The Bobby slowly reassured him that he knew what the Superintendent wanted and he himself would ring back in a few minutes; 'as it were only a step or two along t' lane t' Manor."

Sure enough about ten minutes later the Constable was on the line.

'He's there right enough, all on 'is own. I give him yer message but he's phone, it's not workin' so he'll be ringin' yer back later from call box alright?'
Shortly before lunch the call came in from Knowles, their conversation was stilted, he was hesitant and occasionally there were long pauses between his words. Ed couldn't work out if the pilot was evasive, drunk or ill. He was friendly enough and understood what the enquiry was about, he didn't want to talk on the phone and suggested that Ed come and visit.
'When would be convenient?' 'Oh anytime, I'm here all the time, come anytime that suits you.'
They arranged for that weekend, on Saturday evening. Ed was to go up to the Manor when he was ready.
Further discussion with the Constable provided Ed with the number of the village inn, The Fauconberg Arms, where he booked a room and a table for dinner.
'Would I like to go to North Yorkshire for the weekend on your wild goose chase? I'm sorry Ed I'm really far too busy to come with you at the moment. There's such a lot going on at the school, what with the new curriculum and the possibility of an inspection, I really can't get away. You go, go ahead, don't worry about me.'

After changing trains at Oxford and London, Ed arrived at Thirsk and took a taxi to the pub in Coxwold. It was about four o'clock by the time he was unpacked in his room. After tea and biscuits in the lounge bar he set out to explore the village before his meeting with Knowles. Up the hill past the church he walked past Shandy Hall, the notice outside explained that it was once the home of the Reverend Laurence Sterne, author of "Tristram Shandy."
On the way back he spotted the entrance to Graham Knowles' house, Turnwell Manor and continued past it to visit the village church.

It had a surprisingly magnificent interior that belied the somewhat forbidding exterior. The ceiling was intricately vaulted and below it there was a beautifully made and unique tongue-shaped altar rail. On the opposing walls either side of the choir were beautiful carved reliefs of ancient notables, it was altogether a charming and very peaceful place.

At seven o'clock Ed went over to the Manor and collected Graham for supper. He was ready, wearing a blazer and white shirt, a small man with thin sandy hair and dandruff on his shoulders.

They ordered at the bar and sat down at one of the brown varnished tables. Both had Lancashire hot pot and they shared a bottle of Mateus Rosé. Conversation was slow at first; Ed had to do most of the talking, even with prompting, Knowles still seemed distracted and somewhat vacant at times. Each time Ed raised the topic of flights to exfiltrate Joes from France, Graham went silent. Instead, Ed slowly pieced together what the pilot had been up to since flying for 161 Squadron. Knowles had stayed on in the RAF after the war and flown Austers as spotting aircraft for the artillery in the Korean War in the early 1950's.

He became even more hesitant as he related the stories of life in remote forward area outposts. Rough landing strips in the jungle, cockroaches, bugs, mosquitoes and the constant fear of a surprise attack. After about six months Knowles had been shot down by enemy ground fire, he crash landed in a paddy field and was taken prisoner by the North Korean Army.

'They kept me for nearly two years, chained up in huts in the jungle, I became very weak with dysentery, there was only poor food, rice and dirty water. I didn't wash for months; I didn't think I'd make it. I was too weak to escape and no idea where I was or where to run to.

They kept moving me; it was very disorientating and confusing. I didn't see another European for nearly a year, I was released after the war ended in 1953 and finally came back to England in early '54.'

'You poor chap that sounds like a dreadful experience.'

'I haven't got over it I'm afraid. I must seem like a very odd sort to you, I didn't used to be like this but now I'm just all over the place. I can't get a job, I'm always ill with either malaria or some sort of jungle fever and my pension is tiny. I don't really have any family, I lived at Turnwell with my mother when I came back; she left it to me when she died. I'm sorry I'm such lousy company, would you like to come over tomorrow morning before you leave? I've started making some notes for Hugh. I'm sure there will be something there that will be of interest to you. And I've got some old diaries; just brief jottings but we can have a look at those as well. Perhaps I'll feel better after a sleep.' He finally looked Ed in the eye and grimaced weakly at his poor showing 'thanks for the dinner by the way.'

Ed went back with Graham to his house and wished him a good night. As he walked back down the wide main street of the village in the faint moonlight, Ed wondered if he'd done the right thing. He'd clearly upset Graham bringing back horrible memories. He felt uncomfortable and selfish as he let himself back in to the almost empty lounge. Ed stood glumly at the bar and ordered a large whisky and soda to reflect over. He was excited that Graham might have information that would bring him closer to finding Jeanne but was concerned that he was stirring up unhappy memories for the troubled man. Well, he'd come this far he might as well finish the job; he tipped up his glass and savoured the last swallow.

In the morning, having checked out, he left his bag at reception and retraced his steps to Turnwell Manor.

The big wooden front door opened almost immediately, Graham was ready for him and this time seemed almost cheerful. 'Thank you so much for dinner last night, I'm so sorry I was such a bore, do come in I've got some bits and pieces ready for you.' Graham led the way into the rambling old house; they entered a small dining room where there were various papers spread on the table.

'I've collected all my RAF stuff here, Flying Log Book and so on and tried to recreate some details of the flights when I was at 161 Squadron. I also found some photos from that period.'

They sat on either side of the table in the paneled room. 'You must think I'm a bit barmy, I know exactly why you're here but I couldn't talk about it last night. The thing is, that on that night, when I eventually got back to my squadron there was some bad news waiting for me.' He stopped and picked up a black and white wedding photograph. 'This is my wedding, that's Tizzy my wife. At that time she was heavily pregnant with our first child, I didn't know it of course but he was to be born prematurely, on that very night in fact. There were complications.' He stayed looking at the photograph. 'At the time I was flying the wounded Joe back and was so concerned for her safety, my wife was dying in hospital. She'd had a massive haemorrhage and there just wasn't enough blood available to keep her alive. She just kept bleeding and bleeding, and there was nothing they could do to stop it.'

'Oh no, that's just so sad, I'm so sorry for you, what a dreadful thing to happen. The poor girl, how awful.' They sat in silence for a minute or two. 'Yes, unfortunately, well possibly fortunately looking at me now, our baby didn't make it either. It was terribly bad luck for Tizzy, I felt so responsible, you know for not being there when she needed me.

By the time I got to the hospital they were both gone.' He put the photo down sadly; 'it was such a long time ago, I should be over it but it's just the memories of that flight and Tizzy and the baby's death are so closely linked in my mind that it just sets me off.' He closed his eyes and took a few breaths in through his nose, visibly trying to pull himself together. Looking up, Graham smiled ruefully, 'I'm sorry once again; now shall I make us some coffee? will you have a cup? Let's go into the kitchen and I'll put the kettle on.' While waiting for it to boil Graham related some of the history of his ancient house.

Back in the dining room, 'here's a photo of my Lizzie, fabulous plane I loved her, more fun to fly than an Auster. God I tell you one felt very vulnerable in the Auster, all fabric you know, like the Lizzie but rather more frail.'

They could smell delicious wafts of a roast being cooked; 'I say, would you like to stay for lunch?' Ed looked at him quizzically not having noticed any cooking going on in the kitchen. 'Not here, with my neighbours, well my tenants actually. The house is so big that I've sort of divided it up and they have that part.' He pointed at the wall 'that's the main part of the house, the rooms are much too big for me and I can't afford to heat it; what do you say? They very kindly always get me over on Sundays, they're really only there at weekends so it's jolly decent of them. I have asked and they said they'd be delighted if you could join us. Do come, they're jolly nice, good fun.'

'That's really kind and I must say whatever it is, it smells very good, I'd be delighted.'

'Excellent, now don't be surprised but it's two chaps actually; Crispin and Mountjoy they're a little bit camp but they're very good to me.' Ed wondered what he was letting himself in for and laughed, a bit nervously.

'No, no that's fine.' He cleared this throat; 'Absolutely

fine, lovely.'

'Good, that's settled; now about that eventful flight, here it is.' He picked up a sheet of paper 'I took off for Planête at about ten pm, two male Joes, straightforward flight I suppose. I don't have any specific memory of the outbound. I'd been to Planête before and found it easily, just south of the Loire. Err, clear night but cloud later. Yes that's right we had to run for cover from the 110. I was fine but the girl; your girl, she was hurt. We got shot up, attacked from behind and she got the worst of it.

I didn't think she was going to make it but you tell me she did and you looked after her?'

'Yes we spent a lot of time together whilst she was recuperating, I helped her get fit and we became very close. The truth is, we fell in love but once she was ready she had to back, to rejoin the Resistance, I thought I'd never see her again so I buried the memories and got on with life without her.'

'Then what happened, I mean why the sudden interest now?'

'I have this feeling that she needs me and I must find her, I need to know if she's alright. I'm sure it sounds a bit ridiculous but I have such a strong sense of her that I can't leave it alone.'

Graham nodded in understanding,

'Yes I can understand and no it doesn't sound ridiculous, I'm sure I'd feel the same. How do you think I can help other than you knowing it was me who flew her out of France that night?'

'Can you remember anything about the landing, I mean who was there on the ground? You see I'm trying to get some idea of where she lived at the time to at least give a start point for my search in France.'

'Maybe Dericourt was there.

It was his area, there were other men too, let me think.'

29 Years

He picked through the papers. 'I think it was Henri and there was this big guy there. He said, oh he said.... remember I'm in the cockpit, she's saying goodbye and he's shouting at her over the noise of the engine something about "It's a long way back to Valençay and they must hurry." My French isn't brilliant but I'm pretty sure he said Valençay, the name stuck in my mind because I'd flown all over that area and I'd studied the maps very closely.' He stood up and went to the bookcase. 'Here's a map' Graham unfolded it; 'this is the route we used to take.'

He traced his finger along the map from the coast to Le Mans then Tours then Luzillé. He pointed; 'That's Planête, where we landed and here.' He tracked eastwards; ' Yes, here it is, there's Valençay. It looks about thirty miles, that's a fair distance. Certainly possible, it would take about three or four hours, I suppose they could have made it before dawn.'

'Oh my God, I didn't think it would ever really happen, I didn't think I'd get this close. Do you really remember it that clearly, I mean about Valençay?'

'Yes, yes I do and I saw the big chap in my landing lights. Big black moustache and beret, just a typical looking Frenchie, straight out of central casting.'

He looked at his watch, 'now I must go and find a decent bottle of wine, Crispin is very keen on his vino and Mountjoy does the cooking, if you know what I mean.' He winked and disappeared.

Crispin, elegant in corduroy and a tweed hacking jacket with a silk scarf poured champagne into crystal flutes. Mountjoy wearing an apron brought a silver chafing dish of warm curry puffs. The drawing room was a splendor of velvet, candles and gilt-framed oil paintings.

They had a marvelous time, Crispin was in advertising in

Soho and Mountjoy had an interior design business in Walton Street. Their hosts were riveted with the story of Ed's quest, Mountjoy was a francophile and knew the Loire valley well and was sure he had visited the château at Valençay as a boy. Once the beef was carved and admired and Graham's claret appreciated he started to tell the story:

'If it's the same place it must have been thirty years ago, no nearer forty, well anyway I was about ten years old. My father knew the people at the Château; one of his best friends from school had married one of the daughters. Father knew them in England, they lived somewhere near us at Oxted in Surrey and I suppose they'd invited us to stay in France.'

'Do you keep in touch? Do you still see these people?' Mountjoy smiled at Ed's excitement but shook his head.

'No, you see they were Father's friends; I was an only child. I didn't see them in England the children were much younger than me. I mean they were probably six or seven but at that age of course it seems such a gulf, in fact' he laughed 'I remember I was furious because I was sent to play in the nursery for the day with these other kids that I didn't know and even though they were younger they made me feel foolish. Well, because they kept speaking in French and pretending not to understand when I spoke in English and then when I tried to speak French they pretended not to understand me either.' The table roared with laughter, 'So who was supposed to be looking after you, weren't there any parents around?'

'No, there was a crowd of adults, no one I knew but they went off for the day together and left me with the evil French kids. Oh there was a nanny, as sort of child minder, yes she spoke English to me, she was nice to me.'

'I say Ed could that have been your girl?
You said she mentioned working at a château nearby.'

29 Years

He was struck dumb, the roast potato caught in his throat, his gullet was in spasm, he couldn't swallow and then he couldn't breathe. He tried to choke it out and started attempting to stand. Crispin whipped round behind him put his arms around his chest and lifted him from the chair, simultaneously, smartly performing the Heimlich manoeuvre.

'Cough!' The no-longer crispy potato shot out of his mouth and made a mark on the white linen tablecloth, air poured in and out of his lungs and Ed held weakly onto the back of his chair.

When he was able to stand, he hugged his rescuer.

'Golly, I thought I was a goner there, you saved my life.' Ed emptied his water glass and took a few deep breaths.

'You need wine after a shock like that.' Ed obediently put down the water and emptied his wine glass.

'Oh I was so worried' said Mountjoy, 'I often get things stuck in my throat; thank goodness you were here Crispin.' He looked up admiringly, stroking and patting the manly saviour's sleeve.

'Apologies Mountjoy, it was the shock, the surprise, the idea that you might have actually met Jeanne all those years ago.'

'Jeanne? Is that the name of your girl? I don't remember anyone called Jeanne but then I don't remember any of the other names. My pa was a keen photographer I've still got his albums, sadly both my parents are no longer with us; shall we look after lunch and see if there are any snaps of that holiday?'

Back in the drawing room with coffee and liqueurs, Mountjoy pulled down his father's albums. They were all bound in red leather with the year stamped in gold on the spines. 'Let's start with 1933.'

He laid it on a sofa and quickly paged through the card

and tissue paper interleaves to the summer snaps but there were none of a French château. He then opened 1934 and after a few pages; 'here it is look!' In white ink on the black card page was written "With Temperlys at Valençay."

'So you were there! Are there any other photos? Where are you? Is there one of the nanny? Can you take them out so we can see if there's anything written on the backs?'

The excitement was infectious, everyone was laughing and backslapping and cheering Mountjoy. He turned the page, there was a single large photo that had been posed.

The house party was gathered on a wide flight of stone steps leading from the terrace to the lawn, children on the grass, adults sitting on the steps.

'Who d'you recognise?'

'I think I'm going to need some more light and a magnifying glass.' He carefully eased the picture out of its corner frames and took it to a library table where there was a reading lamp. They crowded round as he sat down and slipped a magnifying glass out of the drawer. He leant forward with the glass and switched on the lamp. 'Oh look, there's me, I'm sure I must have seen this photo before but I don't remember it. There's Father and Mother, these are the poisonous French kids. These adults, hmm I remember Mr Temperly as being smooth and shiny that's possibly him with the slicked down dark hair.' He turned the photo over, 'there's some pencil writing.' He angled the photo toward the light, 'yes it's a list of names, well surnames, family names of those in the picture. Sagan, Temperly, Ossington - that's my family and de Richelieu, I suppose that was the other French family.' At the bottom it's been signed, probably by the photographer.'

'Where's Ed's girl, you know, Jeanne?'

'I don't see her, could you bring the album over and we can have a look at the other photos.' They were able to cross-reference and identify all the people from the house-party photo and match them with their appearance in other pictures. Other than one photograph that included a side view of a previously unseen young girl who looked about fifteen years old, Ed pointed at her with a biro 'who's that Mountjoy?'
'That's her, that's the nanny! I think that might be your girl you know.'
Ed picked up the photo 'may I?'
He took the offered magnifying glass with a shaky hand and bent forward under the light, after a few moments of close study he shook his head. They looked at him expectantly;
'I'm not sure, it could be but I just can't be sure.'
'Would it help if I got it blown up?' said Crispin; 'we've got some very clever chaps at the agency they're wizards with photographs, maybe they could make it clearer, give you a better idea. I could get all of these copied if you like and post them to you.'
'That would be marvellous, very helpful if you wouldn't mind.'
'No, not at all, we'd be happy to help you if we can, I'll take them in tomorrow and you'll have them by the end of the week.' They exchanged phone numbers and Mountjoy promised to call if he found anything useful amongst the old family papers.
Back down south at his office on Tuesday afternoon, Ed looked through his notes that he had made with Hugh Verity. He found her number and telephoned Vera Atkins at her home on the south coast in the ancient small town of Winchelsea. He introduced himself, explaining what he was interested in and asked if he could visit her.
When he'd finished putting his case there was a silence

then she replied in a cool, precise voice:
'I don't know you, why should I help you. You seem to presume that because your request is romantic it automatically gives you the right to the information that you seek. Why, is love always right? Is the half-remembered youthful passion that you seek to rekindle justification in itself?

What about the other lives that you'll affect, this is not simply satisfying a need to put your mind at rest as you so disingenuously put it. Your making contact out of the blue will be most disturbing.

And to what end? What about Jeanne's life and circumstances? Have you considered that she may be very happy never to see you again? That she may have forgotten you as soon as she left Sherborne?

You expect me to ask myself these questions and to respond positively to each one. As presumably you have asked yourself otherwise you wouldn't be asking me. You say you're a policeman; surely logic is your strong suit. You expect me to judge your situation and to find you deserving of the information that you seek. Why should I be your judge? Why should the responsibility be mine? I'm not the judge who should decide on the shape of your future. It may be that I've had to decide too many futures that have not ended happily. Maybe I don't want to decide another one.

In this instance the matter is taken out of my hands, the information that you seek is still classified. You will no doubt go to the records office and check. I'm afraid that I do not belong to the "old boy" network that may have helped you thus far.

You are barking up at the wrong tree today, good-bye.'
She replaced the receiver.

Ed was stunned, chastened and upset, he didn't enjoy

being forced to confront the reality of his actions in such a cold light. The warm rosy hue of his imaginings seemed naive when exposed to Vera's harsh examination of his motives.

Chapter 12

Spring 1973 - England

'Hello Mary, are you planning a trip somewhere?' The tweed-skirted Headmistress came briskly into the room and saw the map on Mary's desk. 'Oh France, I love France, where are you off to?' Mary looked at her with a pained expression. 'What's the matter? You don't look too happy at the prospect.'
'No it's not that, it's Ed.'
The Headmistress clicked the door shut and sat down. 'Tell me.'
And Mary explained Ed's sudden infatuation with a wartime girlfriend and his proposal the previous evening to go and look for Jeanne at Valençay.
'How do you feel about it?'
'I don't know, it's so out of character. He's normally so solid, so reliable. It's..' She waved her hands in frustration 'it's so unsettling.'
'So what will you do?'
'I can't think straight, there's so much to do here and maybe I've been neglecting him and it's so distracting, I'm not sleeping, I'm imagining all sorts of things. It's not fair. I've never been in this sort of situation before and I just don't know what to do for the best.'
'Let me have a think, come and see me before you go this evening and we'll make a plan, sort out what you might want to do.'
Feeling like one of the pupils, she straightened her skirt and knocked on the Head's door at six o'clock.
'Come!' She let herself in.
'Ah, Mary, let's sit over there by the window. Now, how best to proceed?

First of all, can you tell me how are you and Ed getting on these days?'

'We're fine; happy I thought. We seem to get along pretty well you know, we've been married for twenty-five years. The children left home a while ago they're both working abroad and we're both here, both busy with our jobs.'

'My suggestion is that I think you should work with Ed on his search, stay close to him, be a help and support to him. Be his confidante; get involved, I imagine he's probably finding it difficult to deal with this spectre that's raised itself. If you don't help him lay this ghost to rest it may not go away and it may become be a source of friction and anxiety for both of you.'

'Golly, mmm;' she nodded slowly 'well, I think that's a really good idea, that's what I'll do then.'

She turned the proposal over in her mind for a few minutes while the headmistress looked kindly at her.

'Yes, I'll cook us a nice dinner and get started tonight.'

'Good, and while you're at it, you might consider planning that trip to France in the summer holidays.'

'That smells good, what're we having?' Ed kissed Mary on the cheek.

'Liver and onions and there's chocolate steamed pudding afterwards, be a dear and pour us each a glass of sherry would you?'

Ed poured the Harveys Bristol Cream and put a glass on the dresser near Mary then sat at the table. 'You seem cheery, had a good day?'

'Yes, yes I have thank you and all thanks to you.'

'Oh, how so?'

'I've been thinking about your missing persons enquiry' she smiled over her shoulder 'and I think we should go to the next stage.' He raised his eyebrows enquiringly.

'We should plan a trip to France, to Valençay.

Let's see if we can track her down.'

'We? You're saying we should go together?'

'Yes, it'll be fun. There'll be lots to see, I'm told the Loire is gorgeous and I can help you with your sleuthing. I can speak a bit of French and read the map and you can teach me about the police work and, and we'll work as a team.'

Ed was astonished and babbled to cover his surprise.

'That's marvellous, what a good idea, when can you get away? When were you thinking of? In the summer holidays? That's quite soon isn't it?'

'Yes, the end of next month, we can take the car, get the ferry over and have a bit of a touring holiday.'

Ed took a large swallow 'whatever made you think of all this then?'

'I decided that I need to support you, I want you to find this woman and I want to help. I can see that it's bothering you and it's important so I think we should do it together.'

To his amazement, they started making plans as they ate their supper in the kitchen.

By the end of the week the dining room looked like a police incident room, Ed had borrowed two large easels from HQ. One carried Michelin maps of the area; a small-scale map of northern France and a large-scale map of the area around Valençay. The other carried copies of Mountjoy's photos; the group pictures with captions and notes identifying the people.

There was only one portrait, the enlarged side view of the girl who might be Jeanne.

His notes and correspondence lay on the dining table, the chairs stood by the walls out of the way so they could move easily around the room.

He set out two work places with blotters, foolscap pads, pens and pencils on opposite sides of the table.

29 Years

On Saturday morning after breakfast they went into the dining room and got started. Mary pulled the curtains open a bit wider to let some more light into the room. 'Well this is all looking very efficient, where do I sit and what would you like me to do?'

'If you sit there I can explain everything to you, point out the various people, places and documents and once you've got it clear then we can discuss what the next steps should be.'

She pulled the pad towards her, picked up a pencil and grinned up at him 'I'm all ears.'

Sometime later:

'Before we stop for coffee shall we have a brief round-up?' He nodded. She looked at her notes and began 'so it seems to me that this is what we have to go on: Jeanne was born between 1918-20 so about fifty-three to fifty-five now. In 1944 she said she had a young daughter named Hélène, let's say the girl was about two years old then so born in 1942. That makes her thirty-one now. You've also got your useful contacts being Verity, Knowles and Mountjoy. Not forgetting the unhelpful Vera Atkins, I wonder why she was so off with you?

And then there's these other people to trace; the Temperlys of Oxted or thereabouts and the pilot for the return flight, it looks like that could be either Swayn or Heffens.

Can we also do some touristy things? When we start to plan our trip we should try and fit in some places that would be interesting to visit.' She stood and looked at the map. 'Valençay.' Traced her finger up, 'Blois, Amboise, Chambord all wonderful châteaux. Orléans, I've always wanted to go there. That's where Joan of Arc came from isn't it the Maid of Orléans?'

'Of course! How did I forget? I've been to Orléans, I was sent to France for an utterly miserable two months.

Did I ever tell you? It was before I was posted to Calcutta. God, airfield security, all the Allies kit going missing, I was sent as a liaison officer, the Allies were stockpiling all sorts of equipment, our own, captured stuff, unneeded stuff. Tons and tons of it. Well a lot of it was dumped at Clastres, north of Paris and I spent most of my time there but there was also a case near Orléans. I forget where, but, but... I know; there was a judge, a nice man, we became quite friendly. He wasn't very impressed with the behavior of some of the Gendarmerie. You know there'd been a lot of collaboration problems. The Judge thought there might have been some old scores being settled.' Ed picked up an old blue RAF notebook. 'These are some notes that I made at the time.'

'I'll put the kettle on while you're looking.' He paged through the notebook and called through to the kitchen. 'Here he is, Monsieur le Juge, err, Boileau. Here he is again, ah Etienne. That's it Etienne Boileau. Now, golly where did he live, well I guess it was near Saint-Quentin, that was the main town next to Clastres, yes that was where his court was, where he sat. We could try and find him, he might be able to help, I'll put him on the list.'

They put together an itinerary of places to visit and the towns where they'd like to stay. Mary volunteered to book hotels and started working through the Red Michelin Guide; Ed made a list of the jobs he had to do.

He rang Directory Enquiries to trace the Temperly family near Oxted. 'We have got one but they're ex-directory I'm afraid.' So he called the Surrey Constabulary and obtained the number for the police station at Oxted. The desk Sergeant agreed to assist. 'Leave that one with me sir and I'll get back to you.'

Swayn was home and answered the phone. 'Yes I thought you might call, Collins is it? Yes the missus said you rang, how can I help?'

'Ed explained his enquiry and said 'could you check your Flying Log Book and see if you flew a female Joe into Planête in a Lysander in August '44?'

'I can, I'll just put the phone down, hang on a minute' it clunked onto a tabletop; faint footsteps and a while later. 'Right, August '44, yes, yes. Now, are you there? right, here it is, on the 6th August, Lysander, took off 11.30 pm flying time 5hrs 20 minutes for the return trip, I've a note that there were two packages, that normally meant two passengers.'

'Can you remember anything else? was one of them a woman?'

'Yes, I'm pretty sure it was a man and a woman.'

'What about at the landing site at Planête was there anybody there that you knew or any conversation that you remember?'

'There was a group of men but I didn't know any of them.'

'Was one a large chap with a beret and a thick black moustache?'

'Yes, now you say it yes, he came to the cockpit and gave me a big garlic kiss! He didn't say anything but he was clearly a very happy chap; oh, and he was wheeling a bicycle. Does that help you at all? It does? Well good luck, do call again if you need me.'

The phone rang, it was the Desk Sergeant, 'About the Temperlys sir, they live at Forest Manor and I have their phone number if you'd like it.'

A slightly querulous voice answered, quite high-pitched and hard to tell if it was male or female. 'Hello Temperly here.' Ed explained the reason for his call. 'Valençay yes, Sagan yes, holiday yes, oh 1934 with the Ossingtons. I do remember, what was it you wanted to know? The nanny's name? Goodness, I can't imagine, let me ask my wife.

Hold on would you?' There was some indistinct conversation in the background, then; 'She thinks it could have been Esther or maybe Estelle something like that, amazing memory my wife has, does that help? Sorry not to be more precise.'

Esther, Estelle. Ed couldn't sleep; his conscience was bothering him. He was pleased that Mary was helping and seemed to be enjoying the challenge of finding Jeanne. He realised that it was her way of keeping an eye on what was going on but his conscience kept telling him that he wasn't being truthful with her. In his heart Ed knew that he wanted to find Jeanne not just to make sure she was alright and to put his mind at rest but because he was still in love with her. And there were Vera Atkins' questions that had upset him; they kept going around in his mind and he felt uncomfortable, selfish and a fraud to his wife. Once again he decided that he must just treat this as a routine enquiry and whatever might happen would happen.

The Cortina was packed for the seven-day trip, they were to take the ferry from Dover to Calais; it wasn't far from there to Saint-Quentin where they'd start the search for M. Le Juge Boileau.

On Monday morning they went to the Palais de Justice which was a very grand building in the centre of town. 'I remember this square very well it was so cold here, the wind never stopped blowing but this building was always warm.'

The Palais Clerk was a helpful little chap with round glasses and an almost completely bald head. Ed was soon able to establish that the Clerk had worked in the Palais before the war and had returned after his service in the French Navy. He was sure that he remembered Boileau; he suggested that they return after lunch when he should have some news for them.

29 Years

Sure enough, he had tracked the judge down, now working in Paris and the Clerk proudly handed over a card with Boileau's phone number on it. 'Let's ring him, let's call straightaway!' The Clerk, smiling at Mary's enthusiasm gestured to a row of public telephones across the hall.

'Etienne was delighted to hear Ed's voice and remembered him immediately. 'Yes of course, where are you now? The Palais de Justice! Can we meet for dinner? You can, excellent!' They arranged to meet later at a bar in the square and go on to eat afterwards.

Boileau looked just as Ed recalled him, his hair had gone grey but the straight back, hooked nose and penetrating gaze were just the same. With Ed translating occasionally where Mary couldn't follow, they swapped stories about the intervening years. Etienne asked about their holiday plans, Ed explained that it was a touring holiday to the Loire including a search for an old friend who was in the Resistance. Etienne caught on immediately.

'La Resistance, the girl, I remember; you looked for her when you were here before no?' He had spoken very quickly and Mary hadn't understood, Ed didn't translate. 'We think she lived near Valençay, near Orléans. Can you think of a way that we might find her?'

Etienne burst out laughing; he'd seen it all now, an Englishman taking his wife on holiday to find his old French girlfriend! He covered his amusement by apologising for his laughter and explaining that it wasn't a good idea to talk about the Resistance these days. There were still some nasty memories.

Some awful reprisals had been carried out by the Maquis against those they accused of collaboration. Thousands of people had been summarily tried and lynched after the war. It had been a bad time for France and they were keen to forget it.

'Now Valençay, you must understand this is in the heartland of the Resistance and there were many agents operating near there. They performed lot of sabotage and murders and there were reprisals by the Germans. Oh yes it was not a nice area.' He shook his head solemnly. 'You had better go carefully my friend.'

'Can you help? How do suggest we do this?'

'I think you should go and have a nice holiday looking at the châteaux and I'll find her for you. In Paris we have the best access to records, you can telephone me in a few days and I'll tell you my progress. Is that OK? Well then, let's drink to your holiday.'

Ed rang Etienne from Chambord. 'Yes I've made some enquiries and received some answers for you. The woman who you are looking for is named Estelle Levavasseur she was born in 1919 and was married to Gilles Levavasseur in 1941; they had a daughter named Hélène. Estelle's mother was named Sylvie; she died in 1971. There aren't any records for Gilles since the end of the war so he may be dead also. I haven't found an address for Estelle but her daughter is married and lives in Valençay; would you like the details?'

'That's amazing thank you yes.' Ed noted it down. Etienne continued hesitantly; 'there's some information on Estelle, from the war, I don't know if it will help you but she was arrested in July or August 1944 and taken to Gestapo HQ in Paris. Umm it is not clear but possibly she was taken to Germany. It happened to quite a few Resistance members. I err, I know many were taken to concentration camps.'

Ed was shocked; this wasn't what he'd expected, he immediately thought the worst, gas chambers, torture and starvation. Visions of all the dreadful photographs and newsreels that he'd seen of starving prisoners in the camps filled his mind.

29 Years

The skeletons in rags, just skin and bone and those were the ones who had managed to survive.

Oh God, oh Estelle, did she get out alive? Was she still alive? He was stunned; he thanked Etienne and put down the phone. Mary saw his distress and put her arms around him. 'We don't know what's happened to her, let's go and visit Hélène, we'll find out from her if she knows what happened to her mother.'

The next day they drove to Valençay and checked in at the Hotel Lion d'Or. There were two teenage English schoolboys working there, improving their French during the summer holidays. Chris took the bags up to their room whilst Robin lurked behind the bar. It was a soft sunny evening and the Estaminet looked out over the modest town square, so there they sat having a Pastis before dinner. M. Le Patron was very much in evidence, a choleric overweight individual in a bulging stained shirt. A yellow Gauloise hung from the corner of his mouth as he spoke with some old black-jacketed regulars. He was sharing his strong opinions from behind the zinc counter top. As he became more voluble and agitated the ash dropped onto his paunch. Unconsciously he would brush the ash away, revealing the habit causing that particular grey mark.

M. Le Patron was also the Town Magistrate and a new law had just come into force making crash helmets compulsory. The young men of Valençay didn't appear to be aware of the new edict and it was the Magistrate's duty, as he saw it, to apprise them of the rule. To the infectious amusement of the English boys, his ear was cocked for the sound of a moped engine. Hearing one he looked out of the full-length plate glass windows. On spotting a regular offender he would start swearing and reach for the till where he kept a small shiny revolver.

To the onlookers' delight he would then dash out into the street waving the weapon and threaten the jeering youth with dire punishments. His language was lurid with a string of obscenities, references to the mother's probable profession and the likelihood that they did not know who their fathers were. The disappearing youth would be followed with advice on adopting sexual practices that were certainly illegal and some that were physically impossible.

In the morning Ed woke early and left Mary sleeping, he decided to walk around the slowly stirring village to find Hélène's address. He crossed the market square, his heart was beating fast and his throat was dry as he approached number 25; rather than go past, he stopped and retraced his steps.

'Have you had breakfast?' 'Yes' he lied; in fact he couldn't eat anything. Once Mary was ready they set off with Ed leading the way, the grimy metal-famed glass front door of number 25 opened directly onto the narrow grey street. They watched a distorted figure come along the short hall towards them in answer to the knock.

A young woman opened the door and looked at them with surprise. ' Yes, can I help you?'

'Are you Hélène?'

'Yes' she looked at them curiously, 'what do you want?'

'We are looking for Estelle Levavasseur, do you know where we might find her?'

'Yes of course, she's my mother; she lives here with us. Why do you want to see her?'

'Oh my goodness, I had no idea.' He could hardly speak.

'She, she's an old friend from many years ago in the war. My name is Edouard Collins, this my wife Mary.'

'You are English?' Her eyes flickered from one to another.

'Yes I knew Estelle in England.'

'England? I didn't know that Maman had been in England.' She collected herself and smiled in welcome, then pushing back her hair and undoing her apron; 'come in, she's here, she'll be so surprised, I'll fetch her for you, come into the sitting room, I'll tell her she has visitors from England.'

Chapter 13

2014 – The Cotswolds and the City of London

'Hi Allie, it's Dave, how are you?'

'Very well thanks, how are you getting on with our housing estate project?'

'Yes, fine thank you, it's sort of because of that that I'm ringing, I'm going to Florida next week to look into their house-building techniques, there's a Trade Fair in Tampa that I'm attending.'

'That sounds err quite fascinating.'

'You know business, just business but I wondered if I might be able to help you. I could pick up some medication for your boy if you like, you said it's cheaper in the States.'

'Oh yes, that'd be wonderful, I'll get a prescription for you from our GP, he'll be able to fill in all the details so we get it exactly right. I can drop it in at your office later today if you'll be there.'

'Yes that's fine I'm around all day, see you later.'

She bounced in full of smiles, I've been shopping, I do like Moreton don't you?' She put the shiny carrier bags down in the corner and came over to hug him and kiss his cheek. 'Here's the prescription for James; oh and here's one for me If you wouldn't mind awfully?' He shook his head; 'No, not at all, so long as I can fit it in my bag.'

She laughed 'it's just some pills for me, they're no longer available on the NHS and they're rather expensive on private prescription. They're just HRT but super-low dose. This is so kind of you, we really are so grateful for all that you're doing for us. Charlie, you met my husband Charlie didn't you at that Council dinner?

He's so excited at the thought of all that money; he can talk of little else actually. Here's a cheque, that should cover everything but you must tell me if it doesn't. Now, you said you're going to Tampa? Well my sister married an American and they live near there, you might be able to meet, friendly face and all that.'
She took another piece of paper from her handbag.
'These are their contact details, I seem to remember he's in construction of some kind, engineering I think, anyway, they're both nice, good company and I'm sure they'd love to see you.'
'Yes that's very kind I'd be delighted.'
'Great I'll email Sue and cc you. What's your email Dave?'

~

John Gallen walked up the familiar white stone steps and through the pillars of the Ashmolean Museum in Oxford. He'd visited the place many times: on school trips, university lectures and for the pure pleasure of spending time at a fabulous museum with extensive collections from all over the world. In his briefcase were blown-up copies of the photos that he'd borrowed from Ed. He asked the receptionist for the department of Ancient British Archeology. She telephoned to find out who was available then put the phone down and directed John to Dr. Fanshawe's office.
'Hello Mr Gallen, what've you got for me?'
'These are some photos taken during the war by a friend of mine. He was in the RAF and one of his colleagues had a metal detector, they did some prospecting and digging around on the airfield. I wondered what the artefacts that they'd found might be, I thought maybe you could help me to identify them.'

Fanshawe put a photo under his illuminated magnifying glass.

'Hmm' he adjusted his spectacles. 'This one appears to be Roman, probably a piece of a brooch. About 1st century I'd say.' He spread the others on his desk and arranged them in order to work through.

'Do sit.' After further examination: 'this is an amulet, snake-shaped and these are ceremonial rings. These finds are interesting, from what you've shown me; the jewellery and artefacts, this was originally a Bronze Age burial site. I don't suppose they dug very deep as they were amateurs just passing the time.' He looked enquiringly at John who said 'I think you're right.'

'So I'd be very interested to know exactly where the site is so I could have a look. Where are these artefacts now?' He tapped the photos, John shrugged, 'I'm afraid I've no idea.' 'Hmm, well then, if you could find out and it looked promising we could carry out a proper investigation. Dig some trenches, map it out and see what else there might be.' He raised his eyebrows encouraging John to share some more information.

'Thank you for looking, I'm pleased it's of interest, my friend was stationed at various airfields but he wasn't sure where these photos were taken. I'll ask him to have another think. Do you have any idea where it might be?'

'Strangely enough I do, this photo shows quite a panoramic view in the background so I think it's high up, say on a hill or edge of a hilly area. There were a lot of wartime airfields in the Cotswolds; it could be one of them. See if your friend has some more photos and we might be able to identify which one. Better yet, you could also ask him if he was stationed in the Cotswolds; that would narrow the search down.'

~

Charlie Shiffton nodded to the barman who smiled politely 'another vodka and tonic sir? Large?' Charlie nodded again. He felt marvellous, back at the City Club, a couple of drinks before lunch with his old chum Reggie Carter de Pole. 'Reggie! What can I get you? Reggie rocked up to the bar immaculate in hand made suit and glossy tasselled loafers.
'A glass of Chablis please Godfrey.'
'Certainly sir.' Godfrey placed a small square of white linen on the bar in front of each man then stood the wine on one and the vodka on the other. Between them he sat one silver dish of cashew nuts and another of plain crisps. They raised their glasses to one another and each took a long drink. Reggie turned and leaned his back on the bar, resting on it with his elbows, pink socked ankles languidly crossed, allowing the members a chance to admire a fellow still very much in his prime. He lifted his chin slightly so as not to spoil Charlie's view of an otherwise perfect profile. Charlie did admire Reggie very much; 'Very good to see you old boy, it's been a while stuck down in the country looking after things you know.' He spoke without looking at Charlie. 'So what are you up to these days?'
'Oh this and that, there's always stuff to do on the farm and James isn't that well at the moment. I'm always running around I can't imagine how I found the time to do any of it when I was working.'
'Probably 'because you were always on the piss and did sod all leaving lovely Allie to do everything I expect.' He turned and smiled to rob the words of any offence. 'Cheerio.' They emptied their glasses.
'Shall we go in and have some lunch?' They climbed the wide stone staircase in the hall and each nodded at various friends as they entered the dining room.

'Good turn out.'
'Yes it's still pretty popular but membership's on the decline, clubs just don't seem to have the same appeal nowadays. What'll you have? Fish? Good.' Reggie noted their order on a chit, the waitress picked it up; 'Oh and a bottle of Chablis please.'
'Tell me, how's Allie?' Allie was a cousin of Reggie's and they had been fond of one another since they were kids. They chatted of mutual friends and life in the City. 'How's it going with you at Menards?'
'You know the fund management business, it's all about confidence, fashion and popularity. If the punters want in, they come in droves; they fly out just as quick though. My investment managers are pretty cute and they're very much in vogue at the moment. I'm in charge of sales and we've got a great team, the cash just keeps rolling in. We're up to about seven billion now.' 'Is that pounds or dollars?' 'With that amount to invest it doesn't really matter.' He called for another bottle. 'Actually I think I'm a bit of a fraud, I'm almost embarrassed to take Menards' money, they do all the work, I just have to turn up and keep an eye on things.' He adjusted his cuff to cover the heavy gold watch.
'You're looking pretty well, are you managing alright?' He did hope that Charlie wasn't going to ask him for a job again.
The dining room was almost empty; there was no one near them. 'We've had a bit of luck actually. Allie's been approached by a property developer interested in buying a right of way across our track. You know they built a housing estate on the airfield? Well the plan is to build another one on the south side.'
Reggie nodded in understanding. 'Sounds good, will it affect your property?'
'No it's far enough away that we won't see or hear it.'

'So what's the deal?'
'When they get the planning permission we get the cash.'
'It's Allie's farm isn't it, so she gets the cash, right?'
'Yes, she might need to talk to you about what to do with it, there'll still be a lot left after we've cleared our debts.'
'Who's the developer?'
'I don't know him, Allie's been dealing with him. A bit of a barrow boy named Dave Chatham but heart in the right place apparently.' They strolled back down the stairs and into the bar for a brandy. Sitting comfortably in the red leather club chairs 'so how much money are we talking about?' Charlie had been waiting for the question and savoured his response.
'They've agreed to pay a million.'
'Proper money then.'
'Yes they're called Cloud Developments, they hope to build three to four hundred homes; it's a major property deal.' Reggie looked thoughtful. 'And where exactly does the money come from? I mean a project that size is going to require tens of millions of capital. Where does your kind-hearted barrow boy get that kind of money?'
'We don't know, I guess this chap has the backing from somewhere.'
'Do you want me to look into it? We're very hot on money coming from unusual places. We use an agency that looks into money laundering and so on.'
'No, no thanks, not at the moment best not to upset the apple cart.'
'Fine, you just let me know if you need any help.'
They parted on the steps, Reggie to his high-rent sanctum, Charlie to catch the last train permitted on a super-saver return

Reggie decided to leave it a few days and if Allie hadn't called he'd give her a ring.

He didn't trust Charlie's judgment and was uncomfortable that Allie might be getting into a situation with people she didn't know.

Dave was with the planning consultant going through the drawings, diagrams and photographs that made up the presentation; he looked up from the wide table.
'This looks great, how'd you come up with the layout?'
'The other estate, Victory Fields was constrained by the existing roadways and a requirement that some buildings be retained in order to maintain the World War II heritage aspect. Here we can be a bit more creative so we've pretty much copied the layouts of several nice Cotswold villages and produced a modern take on the old styles. Market square, village hall, shop, primary school etc. We may not be able to afford all of it but it'll give the Council a good idea of what we're proposing. Not a standard dormitory-type estate but a proper village with a sense of community. The purpose with this development is to bring new working people to the area, not just recycle the existing population. There'll be enough low-cost homes for those honest grafters that want a perfect Cotswold cottage but have been priced out of the market by the weekenders from London.'
'I love it, that's exactly the right approach, have you got some copies that I can have?'
'Yeah, sure and I'll email you a presentation, it includes the artist's impressions of the houses, showing the architectural styles and materials that we propose.'
Dave rang Jo and made an appointment to discuss planning for the following morning.

~

29 Years

The boys had left for school, Liz was clearing breakfast away and Dave was getting ready for his meeting.
'That planning consultant's a genius; he knows just what buttons to push at the Council. What d'you think? you know Jo better than me.' She came and put her arm around his shoulders as he sat looking at the presentation on his laptop.
'I think it looks lovely, I can't imagine why nobody's thought of this before. I know Jo'll love it, she's always going on about that village that Prince Charles created you know err, Dorset somewhere. Let's look it up, google it.' She reached over and opened a new tab 'here it is, Poundbury. You might say that you're basing your ideas on that. Oh, you're so clever my darling.' She switched back to the presentation and clicked through the slides.
'Wow, there's a lot here, how many houses are you thinking of? I thought you said like, twenty or thirty.'
'Err we've moved on a bit.'
'How many?'
'We're going to apply for three fifty to four hundred.'
'Moved on a bit! I'll say, how d'you think you'll manage? You've never done anything as big as this before.'
'Yeah, well Matt's done a few huge estates in Spain and he'll be guiding me. Then we'll sub-contract the building work, it's pretty much a virtual operation. Once we've got the Outline Planning agreed, I'll put the bid in for the site. The money's on it's way so we're looking good.'
'Yeah that's another thing I wanted to ask, who is it that's actually lending you the money? Did you go to the bank?' She pointed at the artist's aerial impression of the Cotswold idyll. 'How much is all this going to cost? I mean it looks like it's millions doesn't it?'
'Yeah, the site alone probably fifty and another fifty to build.'

'God, you didn't tell me. It's huge.
So, a hundred million.' She sat down, numb.
'One. Hundred. Million.' She shook her head slowly in disbelief. Patiently. 'Where the fuck did that kind of money appear from?'
'Matt and his dad, Tumas Nasim.'
'Matt and his dad? Matt and his dad? Where the hell do they get that kind of money?'
'It's alright, they've got some business contacts that want to invest in UK property. The Nasim's are the fixers, the masterminds, businessmen from Malta.'
He shut down the laptop and packed his briefcase.
'Look I must go; Jo's waiting for me, see you tonight, I'll be back around five or six.' He kissed the top of her head and went out through the front door to his car.

Liz was right; Jo absolutely loved the village idea and she was sure the other members of the Planning Committee would too.
'You remember the Deputy Leader of the Council, Dick Marris? You met him at the council dinner, he was on our table, he likes you, in fact you're in his good books.'
'Oh, how'd I manage that? I hardly spoke to him.'
'Ah, that's because you danced with his wife Sylvia, he hates dancing and was so pleased that you'd taken the pressure off, that was a good move.' She nodded to confirm her words.
'Now, tell me about numbers? How many units are you thinking of?'
'Well, I'm aware of the access issues but I've taken into account being able to use this track.' He unrolled the site plan on the table and traced the route. She shook her head; 'I don't think so, I had Liberty Homes in last week, they say they've an understanding with the owner of that track.'

'Maybe they think they do but I can tell you that I've got a signed agreement on my desk from the owner to sell the right of way to my company.'

She smiled, 'You're a shrewd operator Mister Chatham.'

He dipped his head in thanks. 'So you sweet-talked Allie did you? Yes I remember you two had your heads together rather a lot that evening. You sure didn't let the grass grow; a last minute invite and you've walked off with crown jewels. You obviously charmed the pants off her, well done you.'

'Numbers' said Dave, you asked about the numbers. We're looking for your thoughts on us applying for about three hundred and fifty to four hundred homes. It needs to be enough to make a viable village. Big enough to support a school, one or two shops a doctor's part-time surgery and allow for say twenty-five percent affordable homes. What d'you think?'

'I think that we'd be very happy, you know we're behind on the new housing requirement, this'll keep everyone off our backs and allow us to be a bit more err thoughtful in our stance on other developers' proposals. So yes, I think you're onto a winner with this scheme. Let me run it past Dick, if he says yes I'll drop you a line to confirm our position and you can get on with preparing a full submission. We like your planning consultant by the way, he's a good sensible guy, won't lead you astray.'

'I'm delighted, you'll let me know if you need anything else won't you?'

When Dave got back to his office he rang Matt with the good news. 'That's bloody fantastic, well done, you've got a real result there Dave, what's the next step?'

'Before we go any further I need to know if you've got the finance in place, is that sorted yet?'

'Yeah, I've got the hundred and ten mill' available, the first fifty's ready when you need it.'
'Great, so who's our backer then?'
'He's a friend of my dad's, a guy named Arman; he's the agent who put the cash together. There's a lot of money floating around in the Middle East looking for safe investments in the UK. It's all sound, don't worry the money side is all fixed.

Later that evening when Dave got home Liz was in the kitchen. 'How'd it go? No, tell me everything after the boys have gone to bed and I can give you my full attention.' When the house was quiet they sat in the living room with a bottle of red wine; Liz listened as Dave recounted the meeting with Jo. 'So they agreed the full three fifty to four hundred?'
'Yeah, she really went for the village idea. She was in favour of all of it, she's going to recommend the proposal to Dick Marris.'
'That's fantastic, wonderful you've done a great job.' She sat beside him on the sofa. 'Now I'd like to talk about a completely different subject. I need to tell you something and I want you to promise not to be upset or fly off the handle or get cross or anything.' She willed him to obey with her eyes. 'I just want you to be you, calm considered and thoughtful.'
'Yeah, of course, you can tell me anything you know that. What've they done now?'
'No it's not about the twins, it's about me.'
'Go on.' He waited. She took his hand and looked him in the eye.
'When I was first in London, ages before we met, I was young, a girl, about nineteen.' She shut her eyes, 'me and my girlfriends used to go to a bar, a sort of nightclub in South Ken.

29 Years

One night a couple of Araby looking guys came and chatted us up, that was normal enough, we were a fun group of girls. Well they wouldn't leave us alone, buying us drinks and we all got a bit pissed, I hadn't eaten since lunch and was probably feeling it more than most. All of sudden I couldn't stand, my legs went from under me, these guys said they'd look after me, put me in a taxi home you know. Well, they put me in a taxi and came with me. I could see it all happening but I was stoned, drugged, I had no control of my legs and arms or my voice. They took me to a hotel on Park Lane.' Her voice started quivering 'they walked me into the lift, no one noticed. They took me into the bedroom and stripped me, then they held me down Dave.' She started to cry 'I was so out of it that I couldn't resist, they held me down and they took it in turns to rape me.' Her voice wobbled 'They took it in turns.' She buried her head in his shoulder. 'I'm so ashamed, I've never told anyone apart from my sister, I'm so ashamed that I never told you. I've been living a lie ever since. I'm not worthy of your love, your trust; your children. Whenever I think of it I'm disgusted with myself. I'm so sorry, I'm so sorry. I had to tell you.'

'My darling, I love you; I'll always love you. It makes no difference to me what happened in the past. I'm just so sad that you had such a terrible thing happen to you.' He held her quietly, stroking her hair and murmuring endearments.

'So you did nothing about it? Not pregnant or anything?' She wiped her eyes on a cushion.

'No, thank God, no, I did nothing, what could I do? Girls out drinking, we never get believed in court they say you were asking for it.'

'Who were they, these men, what's their names?'

Very quietly she said. 'You know them.

They're your backers: The Nasims.'

He threw his head back against the sofa 'oh my God, those fucking bastards. Those fuckers. Shit!

That's why you had to tell me now. I'll kill 'em, I'll fucking kill 'em, those filthy fucking Arab bastards!'

He drew in a big breath, and exhaled heavily, mouth open, ready for a fight.

'Right then, you tell me, just tell me what you want me to do to them and I'll do it.'

'What can you do? You're in this too deep. They don't know you're married to me, they probably don't even remember my name.'

'Christ what can I do? I can't just do nothing. Help me darling; I don't know what to do, I'm floundering here. I feel so bad for you, I feel dirty for dealing with those, those bastards.' She took both his hands in hers.

'Thank you for being so kind, thank you for being angry for me but I've thought about this, I've thought of nothing else all day. What can we do? It was a long time ago, twenty years ago, we're just normal, ordinary people. We're not gangsters who can have people, I dunno, murdered or beaten up or something, that's just not us. Let's be realistic; look, I can live with this if you can. Just do what you're doing, do the deal, get your bonus, you know your dividend when the development's all done. Then just walk away, just use them like they used me.'

'Oh Liz I don't know if I can do this. How can I speak to that bastard Nasim? Can we think about it some more? Not decide now, leave it a few days, let it settle, you know what I'm like. Sleep on it for a couple of nights and things'll be clearer.'

He poured some more wine for them both and sat quiet for a while. He sighed and said 'now, how about you tell me what my terrible twins have been up to today.'

Chapter 14

2014 - Cotswolds

John let himself in through the garden door to Ed's little house.
'Hello, anyone about? Hello, Ed?'
He saw the back of Ed's head through the sunroom glass, he didn't like to catch the old man by surprise; the head had turned at his call.
'Over here, is that you John?'
They sat having coffee together in the warm room, the door open to the garden.
'These photos Ed, the one's you had of the digging at Rissy, the old Roman bits and pieces. I spoke to an archaeologist at the Ashmolean, showed him the photos, he's quite interested and asked if you can remember any more about it.'
'What does he want to know?'
'He asked where are the artefacts are now.'
'Golly well, it would be that little ginger fellow you'd need to ask, he was the one who always ended up with the stuff. If any one else found anything he'd always wangle it off them, saying it was for the collection. "That the collection had to be kept complete." I'm not sure he got everything though.'
'Oh really, what d'you mean?'
Ed smiled at the memory.
'I'll tell you another little story; one of the clerks was very stuck on a beautiful local girl, daughter of the pub landlord. All the lads were keen on her, especially the Americans. You know there were thousands of Yanks here in the war? Yes, about six thousand engineer troops in Great Barrington Park alone.

There were miles of tents and hundreds of vehicles of all types. Funny thing was, they were all white men but they had to be segregated from the coloureds. The coloureds were all stationed up at Ashton Under Wychwood. They couldn't meet you know. The regiments had to be kept apart otherwise they fought, the fighting could be awful. Very strange to us now but that's how it was then, they were all here to build runways on our airfields.

Anyway this clerk, wanted to give the girl a present that would knock her socks off. He'd got involved in the digging and found a piece of jewellery; ginger whatshisname wasn't around so he kept it. I remember him showing it in the clerks' room one morning. He asked me what I thought it was; I said I thought it was a torc, a type of Roman necklace or neck ornament, I said it had probably belonged to a princess; he liked that idea. It was yellow and had coloured gemstones embedded in it, very striking it looked almost alive. It had been in the ground for hundreds, probably thousands of years but it looked as if it had just been made. He was delighted; he was going to give it to this girl. Well I never heard anymore about it, maybe she's still got it.'

'Do you remember exactly where on the airfield that the digging was done?'

'Maybe but it's so long ago, my memory plays tricks on me. I couldn't be sure but I think it was around the area of the hospital that was also used as an air raid shelter. It was a big grass-covered hump.'

'What if we went up there, had a little drive around, would that help?'

'I'm not promising anything but I'd love a drive, it's a grand day for it.'

'OK great, I came in the van today, shall we whip up there now and take a look around, see if anything jogs your memory?'

Dave reread the letter from the Council. Jo had been as good as her word; it was signed by her and Dick Marris, they were minded to approve the proposal and looked forward to the full submission. He rang the planning consultant and read it out to him. 'I'll scan it and send you a copy, I'd like you to get started on the detailed plans as soon as possible.'

He called the accountants, Armin Patel and said he'd like to ahead and submit the bid to MoD, he'd confirm it in writing; they'd offer fifty million and had outline planning approval for a minimum of three hundred and fifty dwellings.

'OK, but you know that you've got to transfer funds to their escrow account within ten days of them receiving the bid documents.'

'Yeah, that's fine I'll advise the solicitor who's handling the transfer.'

He rang Carson and brought him up to date.

'No problem, the money's here and it's all set up, just let me know when you want me to press the tit, I'll need the instruction in writing, an email will be fine.'

The last item to deal with was a letter from Her Majesty's Revenue and Customs; they wanted to carry out a routine visit before the end of the month. He sighed and rang to fix a date. His mobile buzzed, it was Matt. He steeled himself to be normal.

'Hi Dave how's it all going? How was the States?' Dave took him through the recent developments as Matt grunted in approval. 'And the American construction techniques for prefab housing, what d'you think?'

'It's certainly quick but I don't know if we can use it. We're going for the traditional stone-built look. I'll have to talk to the architect about how we could clad a timber frame with stone. It's not something that the yanks have tried so we'll have to do a bit of research.

Regarding the money; it's all set up Carson's just waiting on an email instruction from you to make the transfer. I'll check and sign the bid documentation next week and submit it on Friday morning. I suggest you transfer the money on the Friday as well. If that's alright with you I'll tell Carson what to expect.'

'Yeah that's fine. Great, that all sounds good, you're doing great, this is exactly as we planned, how come you don't sound very happy?'

'Oh it's nothing really, I just got a letter from the bloody HMRC saying that they want to carry out a "routine visit."

'Hah, you want to be careful of those guys, that's how they started with me remember? You have to be very nice to them and they'll leave you alone.' He laughed again at Dave's obvious discomfort; 'you get the books nice and tidy, I'm going for lunch!' Matt rang off.

'Twat' he muttered at the silent phone.

~

'Hi Allie, it's Dave, I've got some packages for you!'

'Oh wonderful, when can you come over? Can you come for lunch tomorrow?'

Dave went to the wine merchant in Moreton who recommended a chilled bottle of Puligny-Montrachet. It was a beautiful day and he was looking forward to lunch.

Allie opened the door looking great; years younger and happy, she was a changed woman from the one he had met at the Council dinner. She was cheerful and chatty;

'How lovely to see you and thank you so much for getting the medication. Are you sure I don't owe you anything? What would you like to drink? Thank you so much for this lovely bottle, let's save it to have with our lunch, would you like a drink?

29 Years

I've got white or red or beer or how about a Bloody Mary? I know you're driving but we can walk it off after lunch. We're celebrating, a bit early I know but I can't help it. Charlie had a word with a big fund manager, Menhards in the City, it's my cousin actually; he's going to help us with the investment side of things. Yes I'd simply adore a Bloody Mary, I'll have one if you make them.'

Allie opened cupboards collecting the ingredients and Dave got busy with the cocktail.

'Just taste that for me,' she dipped her finger in the mix and sucked it appreciatively.

'Yummy, you try' she stuck her finger in the jug again and gave it to him to suck.

'Lunch is antipasti and charcuterie with salad from my veg garden and hot ciabatta.' Don't know quite what we'll have afterwards, what do you fancy?

Dave relaxed, Allie looked after him, the house was full of sunshine and the summer came in from the garden. They ate and told each other stories of their youth and golden years. She laughed a lot at his stories of clerking; the Montrachet was delicious with beads of condensation jewelling the glasses.

She stood to clear the table her thin blouse outlining her still firm breasts. She stretched forward over the central island and as he passed behind her, pushed slightly back and bumped against him. 'Thank you for helping.' He leaned over and kissed her cheek. 'Thank you for a wonderful lunch.' She turned and kissed him properly; he ran his hands across her back and along her bare brown arms. She pressed against him and he cupped her buttocks.

'I want to hold your naked bum while I kiss you.' He lifted her skirt and pushed her panties down. They were loose french knickers that fell easily to the floor.

She lifted her feet out of them, her tongue in his mouth, his fingertips slipping up the inside of her thighs. She undid the mother of pearl buttons on her pale blue blouse 'I want you to kiss my breasts' they were white with a flush of pink and red desire flaring between them to her throat. Allie leant back, raising her breasts to him 'oh suck my nipples' he undid her bra, lifting and guiding one hard brown teat into his mouth whilst he massaged the other. Her breasts were small enough that he could take each one in turn entirely into his mouth.

'Take me Dave, darling Dave take me now, right here.' She turned and held onto the worktop, resting her forearms on the warm wooden surface. Her mouth was half-open in delicious anticipation of the first enormous intake of breath that would accompany his entrance. He held her hips as she involuntarily bucked against him. 'Put it in, put it in now' she reached back behind her with grasping, eager fingers to guide him in, panting, as he slowly, thickly filled her warm wetness.

~

The next morning: 'Hello John, how's things?'
Gallen came into Dave's office and sat down. 'All fine thanks, how're you getting on with the Rissy deal?'
'Pretty good I think, you never know until it's all signed but we're making progress. What've you been up to?'
'I've been thinking about the site and possible landscaping works. I'd like to get some ideas from you of what you might need so I can give you some costings.'
'Oh I'm not sure we've got that far, once we get the bids in from the building contractors we can see what they'll offer as part of a package.'
That was exactly what John did not want.

'Hmm, I thought it was all agreed that I'd be getting the landscaping contract for the entire development?'

'I'm sure we'll be able to sort something out, it's not all down to me you know but I'll make sure you do OK.'

John didn't look happy, Dave was surprised, he thought John would back down pretty quickly.

'There's something else I've come across at the airfield site.'

'Oh yeah been doing another one of your field studies then?'

'Sort of, you remember I mentioned there was a Long Barrow on the airfield?'

'Yeah, it was broken down or dug up or something, no traces left, we couldn't see anything right?'

'We couldn't see anything but an archaeologist would.'

Is he trying to threaten me with something? He squinted at John.

'Why would an archaeologist be looking at the airfield?'

'Because there were some important discoveries made there in the war which were never reported. If someone did decide to report them then the archaeologist at the Ashmolean said he'd be very interested to carry out a full survey, dig trenches, map out the area that sort of thing.'

They stared expressionlessly at one another.

'So how do you know about all these important discoveries?'

John gave him a file containing photocopies of Ed's photographs.

'These were taken at Rissy in 1943/44, that's a piece of a Roman brooch. That's a snake-shaped amulet, and those are ceremonial rings. The jewellery and artefacts, mean this is a Bronze Age burial site.'

'This could be anywhere.'

'It could be, but it so happens that I was given those by a man who was there at the time.

'He can identify the location as Rissy.'
'So what d'you want?'
'I want the landscaping contract.'
'Yeah well, I want to know how much Liberty Homes are going to bid for the site, contact your man at the ministry and find out what's going on.'
'Yeah, then what?'
'Then I want the original photos and full details of where you got them, everyone you've been talking to, dates, times, places everything. Fair enough?'
'I'll draw up an exclusive contract for the landscaping works and once you and anyone else who has to, has signed it, I'll give you the photos and the other stuff.'
John paused sensing agreement then continued
'You send me your outline plans and I'll get on with drafting the landscaping and maintenance contract.'
Dave looked out of the window, little shit, trying to blackmail him. We'll see. He turned back and grinned at John.
'OK, John, yeah that's fine. When you tell me what the Liberty bid is I'll email you the plans, thanks for coming by, good to see you.'
John felt uneasy, was there something he'd missed, still, he was holding the aces no doubt about that.

~

Thursday afternoon, Dave's mobile buzzed, it was Matt.
'Hello finished lunch yet?' he opened sarcastically.
'Ha, Ha, no time for lunch today; too busy, how's it going with you, are we all set to submit the bid?'
'Yeah all fine, Liberty's going to offer fifty million as well but they've got subjectivities on planning permissions and they haven't got the track so they're pretty much stuffed. I reckon we're in the box seat.

I've signed the papers and the courier took them just now.'

'Fantastic, I'll email Carson today, have you had the HMRC round yet?'

'They're coming on Tuesday; I'm all ready for them. Yeah and I need the million to pay for the right of way over the track.'

'No problem, I'll transfer that today as well, have you got someone sorted for the conveyancing?'

'Yeah, there's a good firm in Burford, I'll use them.'

~

'Ed, you know the torc that you mentioned last week, did it look like any one of these?'

John had taken photos of all the torcs in the Ashmolean and all those that he could find in their reference books. They sat on the sofa and swiped through the images on John's ipad.

'Yes that's the sort of thing, just like that but with coloured stones.' A few minutes later - 'There it is! That's it or something very similar, isn't that beautiful?'

'That one comes from a dig in Suffolk, it was declared a Treasure Trove, blimey they paid thousands for it. I don't suppose you can remember anymore about the clerk or the girl or the name of the pub can you? I'd really like to find that wonderful torc.'

'They're probably all dead by now John; I don't think many of us get past ninety you know. Hang on though, just a thought, maybe; could you pass me that address book beside you? I wonder if Bill Martin's still with us.'

'Who's Bill Martin?'

'He was one of the clerks in '44, I saw him again in '73 he'd done well, Station Warrant Officer, we kept in touch and exchanged Christmas cards.

I'm sure his address is in here. M, M, Martin, there you are, there's a phone number too.' He looked up eyes twinkling with excitement, 'let's give him a call.'
Bill picked up and was delighted to hear Ed's voice.
'I do remember that girl as it happens; she worked in the pub in Cold Aston. I think I went to the wedding, she married Dick Torrance, nice chap, dead now I'm sorry to say. Why do you want to know? The Roman torc? You mean the necklace thing? Yeah I'm pretty sure she wore it on the wedding day. Where is it now? Goodness knows, you could try her daughter Janice though.' There was sound of pages being turned. 'She's somewhere in the Midlands, I've got her number here if you like.'

'Ed this is amazing, shall we call her too? I think we're on a roll.' He dialled again:

'Yes this is Janice, you're Ed Collins, friend of my dad? Yes, Mum's wedding necklace? Yeah, yeah I've got it, it's in my drawer upstairs, d'you want to see it? You do.'
And so they arranged a date to visit.

~

'What's going on Matt?'
'What d'you mean Dave? What's going on?'
'With the money! The effing HMRC were all over me, it wasn't a routine visit at all, they're after me for money laundering! You said this money was from proper investors.'
'Yeah it is.'
'So why's HMRC saying it's proceeds of crime? They've been watching it; they know where it comes from. They said I'm part of a money laundering syndicate and I'll go to prison. What the fuck's going on? Have you set me up?

'Calm down, calm down, no one's going to prison.'
'Yeah well you're fine aren't you? You're out of the country they can't get you. When they find out you're behind all this I'm in deep shit. I don't want any more to do with this. I'm out of it.'
'No, no you can't drop it; let's find out what they know and see if we can work something out.'
'Don't you understand, they told me not to leave the country. They took my passport. I'm under a criminal investigation, I'm going to be charged; I'm in big trouble. It's all falling apart. Shit. Why did I trust you? What the fuck have you done to me? What about my wife and kids? How can they manage if I'm in the sodding Scrubs? You stupid twat, who've you got mixed up with?'
'Hold on, hold on. How do they know anything about the money?'
'The woman who agreed to sell us the right of way over the track, Allie Shiffton, remember? Her idiot husband was blabbing about the deal to some investment bloke in the City. He, being a nosey git asked his money-laundering investigation agency if they knew anything about it. They did some digging and set off an alert at HMRC. What an arsehole, he's dropped us right in it!'
'What are you going to do?'
'I'm leaving, right now; they'll be back with an arrest warrant next and I'm not going to be here. You better do some fast thinking or you're going down with me.'
'No, don't do anything hasty.'
'You better believe I'm going to be hasty. I'm not hanging around for the four o'clock knock. If I'm banged up I can't do anything to help myself. At least if I'm out of the country they can't get me.'
'How can you leave the country without a passport?...'
The phone went dead.

Chapter 15

Summer 1973 – France

'Hello, Edouard?' She came in through the door to the sitting room. They stood up. 'Is it really you?' She lifted her hand to her mouth. 'Mon Dieu! Vraiment. It's you.' Dropping her stick, she took his hands. They kissed cheeks French style. 'How wonderful to see you, how did you find me, why are you here?'
'Estelle, this is my wife, Mary.'
'Aha, Estelle, not Jeanne.' Smiling she shook her head at his detective work.
'Mary, enchanté.' They shook hands.
'Tell me everything; what brings you here? How did you find me? Would you like some coffee or tea? Yes, English tea. Heléne will bring us some. Let me look at you, still so handsome, he is a handsome man no? Mary? Won't you please sit down.' She eased herself onto an upright chair.
'Are you OK, your leg...'
'Oh it is nothing Edouard, I have suffered much worse.'
'So Mary, what brings you to our house like a..' She gestured at the ceiling 'like a something from the sky.'
As Mary talked Ed looked at Estelle. Her once black hair was white. She was beautiful, her eyes shone with excitement; she nodded with swift comprehension as the story unfolded. She would reach out and pat Ed's arm with affectionate propriety of his skill as each stage of the missing persons enquiry was explained.
'You are so clever, both of you. I'm so pleased to see you and to meet you Mary. I can't believe that you have gone to so much trouble to find me. Can you stay and have dinner with us? Yes? Have you visited the Château where I was once a nanny?

No, well then I propose you tour the Chateau de Valençay and then return to us at 6.30 for dinner. Heléne and I will go shopping and cook something special for us.' They protested, suggesting going out for dinner instead but she was unyielding.
'No, no I insist, it will be a pleasure for me.'

~

'Why did these people come to find you Maman?'
'I am not sure yet.'
'The man, he was in love in love with you in the war?'
'I think so.'
'Did you love him?'
'Yes, very much.'
'But what about papa?'
'You know at that time none of us knew how long we would live, we just took each day one at a time, it seems so unreal now. Can you imagine this village was very busy with resistance activities; we were always plotting together. Often in the restaurant at the back of the Lion d'Or.'
'Where was I when you went to England?'
'At the farmhouse, Grandmére and Papa looked after you. We all lived there together until Grandmére died.' Hélène gently put her arms around her mother and hugged her.
'I'm a bit worried about you Maman, all this excitement. I think you should sit down for a while, I'll go and do the shopping.'
'No, no I want to chose, let's go to the market now, I can have a rest later.'

~

They walked up to the chateau, the narrow dusty road

leaked out of the corner of the village over the level crossing. The heat was dense, the road was lined with plane trees, walking in the shade gave some relief from the bright sun. Ed took off his jacket. There was no traffic; the road was deserted, silent between the baking fields of maize. There was no wind, no breeze to stir the hot leaves, sweat patches showed on their clothes. Then there was a slight gradient, a little more effort required to reach the chateau. The huge ornate building standing in its grand park was partly visible through the high iron gates. There was a glass-covered noticeboard on the wall.
'Horaires d'ouverture'
'Well the timetable says it's ouvert.'
The gate swung open as he pushed it, they looked conspiratorially at one another, then as if into another land they entered the grounds, the loose gravel surface of the drive crunched unnaturally loudly under their shoes as the cream stone castle steadily revealed itself.
An old woman took the 20 francs entrance fee and gave them each a small, flimsy paper leaflet describing the history of the chateau.
It was ancient, dim and cool inside, the smell of old wood and tapestries hung faintly in the corners of the shuttered rooms. Huge stone chimneypieces with ornate crests and coats of arms underpinned with family mottoes in Latin dominated the galleries.
They toured the formal gardens, Ed reprised Mountjoy's photo scene in his mind he pictured the family group on the steps and looked around for the living stairs. He found them, balustraded in stone and took a photo for Mountjoy, of Mary, sitting on the steps, chateau behind.

'What did you think of her?'
'She's very charming, very pleased to see you.'
'Yes, she likes you too, I could see that.'

29 Years

'She looks rather old.'
'I think her life's been pretty tough, I think that's why I wanted to see her, to see how she was.'
'And?'
'And I don't really know, they don't seem very well off, and that awful limp she has, she looked in pain.'
'I wonder what happened to her husband.'

After a tense and unrestorative lie down in their stuffy bedroom they each had a tepid shower before dinner. 'I'm just going to pop across the square to the wine shop and get a couple of bottles for dinner.'

The front door was open, 'Come in, come through, we're in the garden.' There was a small stone-flagged courtyard, the brick walls splashed with white jasmine flowers and clothed in climbing greenery. There was a vine on the pergola and a table laid in the shade.
Heléne introduced her husband Jacques and their three children. Eight of them sat at the table, delicious smells came from the kitchen; Jacques roughly sliced a fresh baguette. 'Thank you for the lovely wine,' Estelle looked at the label and looked back at him 'Gevrey-Chambertin; you remembered.'
He inhaled the delicious scent 'Boeuf Bourguignon, you remembered too.' She touched his hand, enjoying the shared memory.

Everyone was cheerful at dinner, Jacques was charming and funny and as the sun set Heléne took the children up to bed. When they settled in the candlelight and jasmine scent Mary asked Estelle what had happened after she left Sherborne.
'I went to a training camp in the South of England; I don't think I ever knew the name of the place.

After a few weeks training I was flown back to France.'
Ed jumped in

'That's right, it was in a Lysander flown by a pilot called Swayn and you were met by a man, a big man with a big black moustache!'

'Yes it's true, how do you know where you there? That was Gustav, he always wanted to look after me; he was very kind and very brave. He's still here, he lives not far away, still with the moustache.' They laughed.

After a few moments the smiles faded and she continued, 'I was captured by the Germans at a railway station with a suitcase full of plastique; I thought they'd shoot me on the spot, my colleague ran and tried to escape around a moving train but he tripped in its path, he fell across the rail and the train ran over him. He died in front of us.' She took a sip of water.

'They took me to Tours and then to the Gestapo in Paris, I was treated well, the man in charge was named Kieffer, he knew all about our network of the Resistance. He had a map, on the wall it showed all the resaux, all the agents' names, the English commanders, everything. I was so shocked it seemed all our work was in vain; I didn't know anything that he didn't know already. It seemed another SOE man who I knew, Henri Dericourt, had betrayed all our secrets. Kieffer kept us in separate rooms in 84 Avenue Foch; sometimes he had me brought down for questions, not interrogation, merely to confirm information that he already had. The Allies were very close and the Germans were getting ready to leave Paris, we were taken by truck one night in August to Pantin; it's a railway station northeast of Paris. There were hundreds of French prisoners. I heard after the war that there were over 2,000 men and about 500 women, some Resistance, some political prisoners. We were taken to Germany, to Buchenwald concentration camp, near Leipzig.

I heard later that it was the last convoy out of Paris.'
'But how did you survive, how did you manage?'
'We were fortunate; it was not a death camp like the ones the Jews were sent to. Many died of heat and exhaustion on the train; we were packed into cattle trucks. Hardly any food, very little water it was August and very hot in the day. I was lucky, I was young and quite strong; the older people did not live very long.

The American army liberated the camp in 1945, soon afterwards the Red Cross came to help us; we had to prove our identity, quite difficult when you have no papers I can tell you. It all took quite a long time but finally I was sent to Sweden and then by boat to England.

Thankfully Vera Atkins was searching for all the SOE agents to try and help them, I was very fortunate she collected me and arranged for me to get back home to Heléne.' She smiled at her daughter who put her arm around her mother's shoulders and kissed her cheek.

'When I returned to Valençay, my mother hardly recognised me. My hair was white, as you can see and I was so thin and crippled, walking on crutches. She told me that my husband Gilles had been killed in the war. He was one of those murdered in the massacre at Maillé on 25th August, at the same time that I was on the train to Buchenwald, I thanked God that my mother and my little girl were still alive.'

Ed and Mary looked at her in the silence and then looked at one another.

Chapter 16

Summer 1973 – France and The Cotswolds

'So is your mind at rest, now you've seen her?'
They were in the Cortina, nearing Calais on the way home. He could feel the wrench of leaving France as a physical force. 'Hmm?' he played for time.
'Have you set your mind at ease, like you said, having seen Estelle?'
'I don't know, I think so.'
'I hope so, turn onto the A16' she pointed through the windscreen 'see the sign for Calais.'
Mary went straight back to work in her study. She was keen for the school to do well and she knew her part in it would be recognised; she was not without ambition. Their lives quickly reassumed their mundane pattern; work, supper, he to the TV she to the study, he to bed, she still working. The summer faded and the autumn term began. Estelle was always on his mind, he went to sleep thinking of her; he woke up thinking of her. He talked to her in the car as he commuted to work; she came to him in dreams, calling his name, reaching out her hands to him.

~

'We need to talk.'
'Is this about that woman?'
'Yes, it's about Estelle, I need to see her again.'
'Why?'
'Because she needs me.'
Mary started breathing deeply trying to control her suddenly racing heart.

'She's managed perfectly well without you for all this time, why now?'
Her composure was breaking; she had known this was coming. Determinedly she continued 'Is it because you want her? You want her more than you want me? Am I to be cast off so you can go and look after your bloody French invalid?' she gulped; 'are you just going to walk away? Walk away and leave me, just leave me?'
She was fighting to stop the tears. He went to put his arms around her 'No, get off, get off. Go; you go then.' She pushed him away.
'Please listen to me, let's just be practical for a minute.'
'No, let's not be fucking practical, let's be emotional, you're doing this because you're still in love with her, you don't love me any more do you?
Her face was hard and ugly with anger. 'Just be honest, don't hide behind practical.' She was quivering with rage. He nodded in agreement. 'Yes' he said simply, 'yes that's about it.' They stood for a minute looking at each other as their marriage disappeared around them. He stepped out of the void 'I'd better go and pack.'
Three hours later he was filling up with petrol near Oxford, it was midnight, he didn't want to stop, he couldn't resist the pull from Estelle; she needed him. He slept in the car at Dover, waiting for the first ferry. A full English breakfast on board set him up for the drive to Valençay. It was rush hour as he hit the outskirts of Paris; the Périphérique was choked and slow moving. He stopped only for petrol and a sandwich; even so it was late afternoon when he arrived at the Lion d'Or. He parked in the courtyard went in and asked for a room.
After a shower and a clean shirt, he squared his shoulders and heart in mouth walked to number 25.
The glass front door was still grimy; Jacques answered his knock.

'Edouard, what a surprise, what are you doing here?' He didn't look pleased.
'May I come in?'
He shrugged and half-stood aside.
'Is Hélène here?'
'She's at the hospital.'
'Oh dear, is she alright?'
'It's not Hélène; it's Estelle, she's very ill.'
'Oh no! What's wrong?'
'Maybe you should go to see her.'
'Why won't you tell me what's wrong?'
'It's better that you see her, today. You should go now, she's at Tours hospital, ward twelve, ask at reception, they'll direct you.'
He ran back to the Lion d'Or and drove fast to the hospital. Less than an hour later he was in the Emergency Ward approaching her bedside. She was so small, so slight, Hélène turned at his approach. She closed her eyes and raised her face to the ceiling. 'Thank God you're here.' Opening her eyes again:
'I don't know what you can do but she nearly died.'
The figure in the bed was still and silent.
'She's asleep or in a coma, they don't know.'
'What happened?' He pulled up a chair and took Estelle's small hand in his.
Hélène shook her head; 'you won't believe it,' looking around 'where's Mary?'
'She's not with me.' Hélène compressed her lips in brief comprehension. 'I thought not.'
Hélène fussed around her mother's bed for a few moments then:
'She loves you very much; in fact it seems she loves you more than her own life, more than me.
Maman was so pleased when you visited, she knew, she told me, she knew that one day you'd come.

29 Years

It's why she never remarried; she wanted only you.

She could never tell anyone. She didn't know where you were but she felt that somewhere, somehow you'd find her. Over the years those feelings slowly softened, became less frequent, the pain of loss became more bearable. She said that it was you, the thought of you that kept her alive at Buchenwald, her love for you. When you came, when you came to my house it was a dream come true for her. She knew.

At dinner we all knew, we could see it in your eyes and hers; we saw how much she loved you. And yet you left, with your wife.' She paused to look at her mother. 'Maman was sure you'd ring, sure that you'd write, she was so happy, she sang all the time, she was laughing, smiling, so happy. She told me the story of your time together, how precious it was in the war. But the weeks went by and nothing, nothing from you.'

Hélène was having trouble keeping her self-control.

'How could you be so cruel? She had such a hard, hard life and you were so special, so important for her. What did you imagine she was thinking?'

He shook his head dumbly.

'Two days ago I went to her room when she didn't come down for breakfast. I couldn't wake her, she'd been sick, vomit on the bedclothes; it stank. She looked red; her face and hands were red. I ran for the doctor, to his office in the square.

When he examined her he said, he said she'd taken poison. How could she have poison? Why would she have poison? He said it looks like cyanide poisoning. He asked if she was in the war, in the Resistance. He said maybe she had kept her suicide pills.' Ed squeezed the limp, cold hand.

'Oh God. Oh Christ. Oh Estelle what have I done? What have I made you do?'

Chapter 17

2014 – The Cotswolds, Malta and Amsterdam

Dave locked the panniers on his BMW GS 1200 motorbike and swung into the saddle.
'I'll be back in couple of days, call you later.'
He pressed the starter, the big, flat twin caught and the Akrapovic exhaust crackled; he revved gently, easing the clutch as the heavy bike rolled out into the road. In his jacket was the ferry ticket to Holland, paid for in cash. At the main road he slid down the full-face visor and powered up through the gears.

~

'Yeah, who is it?'
'Mister Nasim this Arman, what is happening with my money?'
'Everything's fine, we're proceeding as planned.'
'Mister Nasim, we have decided that we do not wish to continue with this project, we wish you to return the money immediately.'
'But I can't do that.'
'Why not? Where is the money?'
'It's been transferred to the British Ministry of Defence to buy land for a housing project, that's what you agreed.'
'Our plans have changed; we are no longer interested in this project. Return the funds immediately, I will call you tomorrow, you will have it arranged.'

~

29 Years

'Mathias? Get round to my office now.'

Tumas Nasim was furious with his son. 'What? What? The HMRC! What's going on?' Matt explained and repeated the phone call from the previous day with Dave.

'So you're telling me:' he ticked the items off on his brown fingers:

'The money's locked up in an escrow account. The HMRC have accused Dave of money laundering. Dave's going on the run. Arman wants the money back.

How are we going to explain this to Arman? He's going to be very unhappy.' He paced the office, sweating.

'I thought this was too good to be true, too easy. You made it all sound so easy.' He stopped and turned.

'Right', he pointed at his son 'you fix this, you get hold of Dave and you sort it out.'

'He won't answer his mobile. I don't know where he is.'

'Well he can't go far without a passport can he? Where's the money now?'

'I emailed the lawyer last week, Friday. Dave said it'd be transferred it to the MoD straightaway.'

'So get it back. Call the lawyer, now.' He pointed at the phone. Matt dialled Carson's mobile.

'Carson it's Matt Nasim. Yeah, I know, I know that but I want it back.'

'Why not?'

'HMRC's been to your office, you're suspended.' He slumped in the chair listening and repeating Carson's words:

'Pending enquiries.'

'Who's your boss?'

'Why won't he speak to me?'

'HMRC said no contact without authorisation.'

'Have you given them my name?'

'They took a copy of the email; with my name on it!'

'Oh Jesus.' He sat stunned, his chin dropped.
'We're in trouble Dad. HMRC have blocked the money, the lawyer's been sent home. We can't get the money back.'
'You need to speak to Dave right now. Send him a text, tell him to call back straightaway.'
Matt texted but Dave didn't call. Neither of the Nasims slept that night.
'Mister Nasim, can you confirm that you have transferred the money?' Tumas confessed that he hadn't.
'Why not?' Tumas blustered for while.
'This is not my concern. But I am concerned that you are not being honest with me. Why should the British tax authorities be interested in a legitimate transaction? I think you're hiding something from me. Are you thinking of taking this money for your own purposes? Don't play with me Mister Nasim, it would not be a good idea for you.'
'I haven't got your money, Dave Chatham has got it.'
'Who is this Dave?'
Nasim explained.
'You find him and you sort out your problems. I'll call you tomorrow; I expect answers. I expect correct answers.'

~

'Matt, it's Dave.'
'Where are you?'
'That's nice, not even a "how are you?"'
'Don't be a tosser. Where are you now?'
'Somewhere safe.'
'Where's that?'
'Are you prepared to help me?'
'If you help me. What do you want?'

'I need ID. ID to get me back into England, a driver's licence and cash.'
'OK, text me a selfie, take it in a passport photo booth. How much cash d'you want?'
'Ten thousand Euros, OK?'
'No, not OK, I can't help unless you get the money back.'
'Yeah but obviously I need to get back to England to sort it out.'
'Where are you?'
'Amsterdam.'
'How'd you get there without a passport? Hide in a Dutch caravan?'
'No, I went on my bike, they never check the bikers going out but I need ID to get back into UK. I'll meet Carson in London, we'll figure a way for him to straighten things out with HMRC and go ahead as planned.'
''fraid not, the investors want the money back, the deal's off.'
'Oh bollocks, who are these people? You can't just duck in and out of deals like this.'
'These people can.'
'Oh yeah, what people? Who is this Arman guy anyway, why's he want to pull out?'
'He's a heavy-duty middleman for untraceable money. He's very well connected to all sorts of people you don't want to meet.'
'Who are these people then?'
'Kazakhstanis. These are serious people Dave; they don't wanna do the deal. We need to give their money back.'
'Kazakhstanis, shit how'd you get mixed up with them? No, don't tell me.'
They were both silent for a while.
'So where shall I send this stuff? What's your hotel?'
'The Ibis; it's near the central railway station. Put the stuff in a left luggage locker at the station.

Leave the ticket at hotel reception in the name of Herr Schmidt, when will it be ready.'
'Give me three days; it'll be there on Friday afternoon.'

~

'Mister Nasim, what are your answers?'
'Dave's going back to England on Friday to sort it out with the lawyer and HMRC.'
'How's he going to get back into England?'
'We're getting him ID and money.'
'Where is this Dave now?'
Nasim explained how the ID and money were to be delivered on Friday afternoon.
'Maybe I should speak to Dave.'
'Here's his mobile number.'
'Maybe I'll call him.'

~

On Friday at 6pm a tall slim blonde escort girl collected the envelope for Herr Schmidt. She walked back to the Victoria Hotel next door, went into the bar and handed it to Dave.
'There you are Herr Schmidt, shall we go upstairs now?'
'No thanks, I've changed my mind.' She looked cross. 'Don't worry; I'll still pay you. He gave her €150. 'That's not bad for two minutes is it?'
She slipped the notes into the zip-up side pocket in her handbag 'best sex I never had.'
She sashayed off and slid back onto her barstool with the other girls.
Dave picked up the Adidas holdall and went to the station; he pulled up his hoodie and walked down the slope into the hall past the left luggage lockers.

Other than two hard looking men with poor skin and dark complexions wearing square cut leather-look jackets hanging around at each end of the tunnel, the area was deserted. There was no CCTV.
'Yeah, thought you might be here', he muttered to himself.
He went to the bench of homeless at the front of the station and chose a fairly clean, normal looking man.
'D'you want to make some money? it won't take long.'
'Money; ja.'
Close up the man looked a bit vacant, not the full shilling.
'Take this bag and put in this number locker, here's the key. He pointed at the clock on the concourse. 'At 6.15 not before?'
'Yes, 6.15' he stood looking at the clock.
'I'm going to buy my ticket, I'll see you back here later.'
He took out €50 note and tore it in two and gave half to the man.
'What's your name?'
'Ludo.'
'OK Ludo, when I come back, I give you this other half, understand?'
'Other half, understand.'
Dave walked off leaving Ludo looking at the clock and then at the key.
At the railway police booth he slipped the hood off and called to the uniform on duty.
'Excuse me but I think I should tell you.'
The armed policeman came to the door.
'Yes' he said pleasantly 'tell me what?'
'Erm it's none of my business but I just heard a man talking on his mobile.'
The policeman looked puzzled 'mobile?'
'They were talking about drugs.'
'Drugs?'

'Yes, the man was to hand over the drugs in the luggage hall at 6.15'
'6.15? what man?'
'That one, standing near the clock in the grey anorak.
'OK, wait here.' He got on the radio and called back-up.
'You wait here' he repeated.
Dave ignored the command and followed, watching with interest.
At 6.15 the grey anorak started to open the locker and was immediately grabbed by two of the hard-men. To their surprise four armed policemen, pistols drawn ran towards them shouting a warning. The Kazaks put their hands up and let go their captive. Dave walked swiftly away.
They were all handcuffed and questioned. The Kazaks, had weapons but no permits, their IDs was dubious. The homeless man had no idea what was going on, he kept showing them half of a €50 note as his explanation for events.
The sports bag was opened, it was full of clear plastic bags containing fine white powder. Each bag bore a Chinese character and the numbers 99.9%. A blue van came and took them all to the city police station. The detective on duty looked at the bags of powder 'what's all this then?' He cut one open, dabbed, tasted and made a puzzled face. 'Sugar? Caster sugar?' He looked at the packaging again.
'And what's this Chinese character and numbers mean?' He went to the desk, clicked on his PC and tapped in google translate 'Chinese'.
 'An upside down letter Y with three horizontal lines' He scanned the options, 'sweet, it means sweet. 99.9% pure. That's funny.'
He laughed at the uncomprehending Kazaks.
'You've been done boys, well and truly done.'

He shook his head in amused disbelief as they were led away to the holding cells.

~

Dave's mobile buzzed, it was a text. "Call me" followed by a country code and number that he didn't recognize. He looked up the country code on his ipad. Kazakhstan.
'Dah.'
'You texted me to call.'
'Yes. Yes Mister Chatham, how are you? Thank you for calling me, can you tell me where you are now?'
'You know where I am, Amsterdam.'
'Yes, that's nice, now when do you go to London?'
'Tonight.'
'Do you have your papers, your ID?'
'You know I haven't.'
'Mister Chatham, why is Mister Nasim not cooperating with me?'
'He's not cooperating with me either; he's got me into serious trouble with your money. Money that HMRC says is the proceeds of crime.'
'I cannot speak about the origin of the money, the transfer from Turks and Caicos to your lawyer was legitimate transaction.'
'Yeah well somehow I need to get myself out this situation and get your money back to you.'
'So, our interests are the same. How will you get back to England tonight without ID? Do you need help?'
'No thanks, I'll think of something, what's your name anyway?'
'You should call me Arman; telephone me when you have a plan.'

~

'Mister Nasim why did you tell the Dutch Police that my men were waiting in the luggage hall?'
'What? What? What are you talking about?
'Mister Nasim, why are you making so much trouble for me? Are you trying to stop me from getting my money back?
'What?! What?!'
Why have you set my men up in some sort of drugs crime? The Dutch police are very confused and my men are in jail.'
What?! What?!'
'Stop saying "what" Mr Nasim. You are making my life difficult; you are being stupid. You make another mistake if you think I am stupid. Do you think I am so rich that I don't care about fifty million pounds? Where is this Dave?'
'I don't know where he is and I don't know what you're talking about.'
'I don't believe you Mister Nasim, if you want me to believe you, give me back the money.'

~

Dave rode the big BMW back to the ferryport at Antwerp, at UK Customs and Immigration he showed his British passport. A few days later Dave was back in Amsterdam. At the hotel he called Arman.
'Dah.'
'Arman, I know where your money's gone.'
'Yes I know too, it's with your MoD.'
'No it's not, it never went to the MoD.'
'I'm listening Mister Chatham.'
'Matt Nasim sent instructions to transfer it to a different account.'

'This is very interesting, what is this other account?'
'The lawyer gave me a copy of the email instruction from Matt Nasim, it shows the sort code and account number; he's used a money transfer facility named Freedom Reserve. I don't have the name of the bank yet but I'll find it and tell you.'
'Can you take photo of this email with your mobile and attach it to a text for me please?'
Arman sat at his desk in a deserted office block in Almaty looking at the email from Matt Nasim. He was not happy, he flicked to contacts, scrolled, tapped and lifted the mobile to his ear:
'Mister Nasim, listen carefully, I know where you have sent the money and I will get it back. I can also tell you that the money isn't mine. It belongs to clients of mine. It's not my money, I am acting as their agent, they trust me; do you understand? They are very demanding clients and they expect the best service.
This money belongs to ISIL; they are violent men, ISIL fighters liberated this money from the Bank of Iraq. Can you imagine how this money came across the desert? Yes I think so, with great difficulty. You have caused me a lot of problems Mister Nasim.'
'Listen I don't know what you're talking about, I'm trying to get your money but Dave won't talk to me, the lawyer won't talk to me, I'm doing everything I can.'
'You are doing nothing, I am not interested in your excuses.'

~

'Dah.'
'It's Dave; your money is in EncipBank, Cyprus.
In Turkish Northern Cyprus, I've got a plan how to get it out but it'll take some time.'

'This is good, how long time?'
'Six, maybe nine months.'
'That is no good to me, I need it now.'
'I understand but what I can do is clean it for you so your clients can have access to the money any where they want in the international markets.'
'That is interesting, how will you do this?'
'I'll move it by road in small amounts and deposit it in banks in southern Cyprus, I'll say it's the proceeds of selling assets in Northern Cyprus, like villas, hotels, small businesses.'
'Tell me, I'm interested how do you travel without your passport?'
'I borrowed one from a friend who looks like me.'
Silence.
'I like that, simple; you are indeed a resourceful man. OK, I am in agreement; you may proceed with this plan. Afterwards, will you be in trouble with tax authorities in UK?'
'Yeah. Normally, if you've not personally profited from money laundering then the penalty is a suspended sentence and banned from being a director of a UK company for five to ten years.'
'Maybe you could be director of one of my companies here in Almaty.' They both chuckled. 'Mister Chatham, Dave, you have been very great help to me, is there something I can do for you?
'I'm sure I'll think of something, I'll let you know.'

Chapter 18

2014 - Malta

It was nearly midnight; Matt and his dad were sitting in sweaty shirtsleeves in the study at Matt's apartment, they were angry, confused and drinking. Wordlessly Matt leaned over with the bottle, his dad lifted the glass; another large slug of Remy Martin slid into the crystal balloon.

'That bloody Arman, he gives me the creeps with his "Hello Meester Naseem" he swallowed and belched

'And where the fuck is Dave? He started all this panic about HMRC, now Arman says the money's not at MoD. You said it was transferred last Friday, so where the bollocks is it? Fifty million, that's a shit load of cash, it can't just disappear.'

'I sent the lawyer an email telling him to do the transfer to the MoD account, it can't have gone missing.'

'Alright let's go through this step by step; show me this email.'

Matt opened gmail on the widescreen iMac and swivelled it so they both could see the screen, he moved the mouse and clicked on Sent Mail.

'There it is.'

'Is everything correct?' Matt checked against a paper on his desk.

'Yeah the sort code and account number are correct.'

'So what's gone wrong? How can the money have gone to a different account?

Did you receive an acknowledgement to this instruction from the lawyer?'

'No I didn't, I didn't really expect one, Dave set it all up; the email was just a formality.'

'Yeah but you know lawyers, they like to make work to charge money. One letter two hundred pounds, one phone call one hundred pounds, one email fifty pounds, why is there no confirmation?'
Matt checked his inbox and the trash and the spam, no confirmation.
'Look at your sent email again.'
'Is the email address correct?'
Matt opened his contacts and crosschecked.
'Yeah, it's correct.' He clicked around on various other emails for a few minutes.
'I dunno Dad, it's late and I've got school run tomorrow, do you want to stay the night or go home?'
'I'll walk home; it's only fifteen minutes, the exercise will do me good.'
Tumas walked through Valetta to the old town from his son's new apartment block. He slung his jacket over his shoulder and lit a cigarette, his head filled with the confusion of the past few days. The exercise did nothing to help solve his problems.

'You were up late last night boozing with your dad, you stank of brandy when you came to bed.'
'I thought you were asleep.'
'I didn't want you getting any ideas.'
'Am I taking Ella to school?' He smiled at the six-year old girl who was eating her breakfast.
'Only if you're sober.'
'I'm fine, another coffee and I'm ready.'
He slipped a capsule into the Nespresso machine, levered it into position and watched the short stream of hot brown liquid, two sugar lumps mashed, nectar.
He kissed Fatima then picked up Ella's satchel and his own briefcase.
'Let's go babes.'

29 Years

Into the BMW X5, Ella in the back, stereo on.
'What songs do you fancy?' and they sang in the car together. 'See you later sweetie pie; Mummy's picking you up this afternoon.'

After dropping Ella, Matt went to Charles Grech in Republic Street, his favourite place for coffee. The waiter brought him an Americano with hot milk and Matt sat outside with his first cigarette of the day. He picked up his iphone 'Hello Dad, any ideas?'
'Come over later this morning, we'll talk then.'
Matt walked through the hot streets of Valetta Old Town to his father's offices, he finger-waved hello to the girls on reception and continued past the trading floor. Nasim Navigation operated three divisions; ship owning, ship chartering and ship management.

In forty years the business had grown to a staff of seventy with an annual turnover of US$10 million, profits were modest but as Tumas Nasim and his wife were the only shareholders all those profits were theirs.

The business was concentrated in the Mediterranean; the most lucrative trades were oil shipments out of distressed nations. Some of the voyages made by the tankers were enabling devices to disguise the origin of a particular cargo. This could be helpful for a country under sanction such as Iran; the cargo would be transferred at sea and transferred again to another tanker some days or weeks later. This practice had become a lot harder to keep secret with GPS satellite tracking, however those clients that had been helped in difficult times remained grateful and good customers.

Now their principal trading business was with the emerging economies around the Caspian and Black Seas such as Azerbaijan, Iran, Kazakhstan, Georgia and Russia.

Latifa was waiting in the car outside the school; the back door opened and a small hot-looking child got in and slammed the door. She turned around, 'hi darling, how was your day?' The little girl looked tired.
'It's been boring and hot and the aircon in our classroom stopped working.'
'Well, it's nice and cool in here,' Latifa clicked the climate control down to 19C. 'Would you like to go somewhere on the way home? Shall we go and get an ice cream?' She looked enquiringly in the rear view mirror.
'No, I'm tired and I just wanna go home.' They drove in silence for a while; each topic of conversation was brushed aside by the huffy child. Latifa was running out of ways to cheer up her grumpy daughter.
'Look at the nice car behind us!' Ella turned in her seat, there was an old VW beetle convertible behind them, top down, with two women, hair blowing in the wind. They were laughing and chatting, they had big sunglasses and bright clothes. 'They look like they're having fun don't they?'
'Oh yes, why don't we have one of those? It'd be much nicer wouldn't it?' She continued looking out of the back window, the women waved at Ella and she waved back. 'They're nice aren't they?' Ella cheered up and enjoyed the waving, the passenger blew her a kiss and Ella tried to blow a kiss back, at last there was laughing and giggling from the back seat instead of a cross silence.
The car in front stopped sharply. Latifa hit the brakes hard and there was a crash from behind.
'Oh no!'
The driver of the VW hadn't been paying attention; she'd been talking to her friend and had crashed into the back of the Toyota.
'Oh for God's sake, that's all I need.' The women got out of the VW and came to look at the damage.

'Stay in the car Ella.'
Latifa got out to speak to the driver.
'I'm so sorry, we were talking, I just didn't see you stopping, I'm so sorry, I don't think there's much damage. Let me get my insurance papers let me give you the details.' The woman got back into the driver's seat and leant forward to search in the glovebox, the traffic cleared in front of the Toyota.
As Latifa bent down to look at her broken lights the woman passenger stepped smartly past her and got into the Toyota. The engine was running for the aircon, she put it in gear and drove away. Latifa was astonished.
'What's she doing?! Why's your friend driving my car away!?'
The VW driver shouted at her; 'Stand back, I'll chase her, you call the Police!' She swung past Latifa and accelerated away, following the Toyota.

~

'Matt, she's gone! They've taken her!'
'Who's gone?'
'Ella! She's gone! She's gone!'
'Tifa, tell me, tell me what's happened.'
'Ella's gone' she sobbed 'I collected her from school, on the way home a car crashed into me from behind. While I was looking at the broken lights.' She broke down and wailed.
'And then what? Talk to me Latifa.'
'And then the other woman, the passenger just got in my car and drove it away with Ella still inside. What are we going to do Matt? She's been kidnapped!'
'Oh my God, oh God. Oh Ella, oh no!'
'I've called the Police, they're on the way.'
'Where are you?'

'I'm near the Town Hall, I'm waiting for the Police.'
'OK, hold on there, I'll come straight over.' He ran back to his office, got the car and raced over to her.
He parked behind the flashing blue lights of the Police patrol car.
'Are you OK?' She turned; her face was a mess with red, make-up smeared eyes.
'Oh Matt, thank God you're here. He's calling all Police stations and the ports and airports.' Her hands were twisting a damp, stained handkerchief and she indicated with her chin a policeman speaking into his radio.
'What about our baby? She'll be terrified, how could I be so stupid? How could I let them take her?'
''Tifa, who took her? What happened?'
'Two women, the Police say they staged the accident, when I got out the car, one of them just jumped in it and drove off.' He put his arms around her shaking body. She spoke into his shoulder 'the driver said; "stand back, I'll follow her, you call the Police!" And so I did, like an idiot, I stood back and let her drive away.'
'Would you recognize them?'
'They were just two dark-haired Arab-looking women about thirty. They had big sunglasses on, they could be anyone.'
'What about the car?'
'I told the Police; it was an old white VW convertible, they're looking for it now.'
'And how did the women speak? Could you tell where they're from?'
'They spoke English, with an Arab accent; they could be from anywhere. I don't know Matt; it was all so fast. I can't think straight, I just don't know.'
Matt spoke to the Police for a while:
'He says we can go home, there's nothing we can do here; they're looking for witnesses.

He said to stay by the phone and let them know if the kidnappers call.' He took her arm 'shall we go?'
They got in the car, she sobbed all the way back to their apartment and went straight to the bedroom. Matt rang his father:
'Dad? Bad news, I'm afraid that Ella's been kidnapped.'
'Oh shit, who took her?'
'Two women, on the way back from school, they crashed into Latifa's car.'
'I bet it's bloody Arman behind this, I'm going to call him now.'
'No Dad! Dad?' The call ended.

~

'Dah.'
'Have you taken my granddaughter you bastard?'
'Mister Nasim, I have nothing to do with any granddaughters, I have nothing to do with you. You have upset my clients, you are on your own, do not call me again.'

~

Matt left Latifa in their bedroom and went into the sitting room to call his father 'What'd he say?'
'He said it was nothing to do with him, he said we're on our own.'
'Christ, does that mean it's ISIL that's got her? Will they want a ransom? How can we get fifty mill'? Shit, we're in real trouble here Dad. What am I going to tell Latifa?'
'Don't tell her anything yet; I'm sure they'll ring soon. Look they're businessmen, they just want their money, we'll tell them about Dave and they can go after him. Don't worry; it'll be alright. I'll come over, I'll handle it, I'll talk to them, I'm coming now.'

Matt and Tumas sat in the study or paced around the apartment, there were televisions on in most rooms. Latifa sat in the kitchen or in Ella's bedroom, they met in the corridor 'What if they don't ring? what if they just want to keep her? Oh why take her Matt, why Ella?'
'I don't know 'Tifa' he lied.
'D'you suppose they think we've got lots of money and can pay a big ransom? How much money have we got Matt, how much can we pay to get our baby back?'
'I don't know, cash, not much fifty thousand Euro, everything else is in the business.'
'Yeah so we can borrow the money or we can ask your dad can't we?'
'Yeah, course, I'm sure it'll be OK, Dad says he'll speak to them, get them to be realistic, he's very good at negotiating, he can sort it.'
The afternoon dragged, the news channel was on every TV; Ella's face appeared every thirty minutes. The ticker tape at the bottom of the screen carrying the headline stories mentioned her every minute. Zainab, Matt's mother arrived, it was getting dark and he was hungry.
'Who wants food? I'll ring for a take away, how about some kebabs?'
'Good idea Matt, I'm starving.'
'How about you Tifa would you like something?'
'I couldn't, I feel so sick I can't eat anything.'
'Mum, what about you?'
Zainab thought she'd like a couple of kebabs and possibly some meatballs. After they'd eaten, Matt cleared away the empty packaging and plates. The air was dense with the smells of fast food, tension and sweat.
The phone rang, Latifa grabbed it first: 'Yes?'
'Mummy! Mummy I want to come home!'
'Oh thank God, are you OK? Where are you?'
'I'm fine, I'm at McDonald's.'

'Which McDonald's? where is it, can you ask someone?'
'We're at Birkirkara, it's on the Valley Road.'
'Thank God, thank God, Oh my darling are you OK? who's there with you?'
'There's no one with me, just these nice people who gave me their mobile.'
'What about the women in the car who took you away? are they with you?'
'No they've gone, they just left me here and your car.'
'Can I speak to the people who lent you the phone?'
'Yes, this is the nice man.'
'Hallo, oh thank you so much for looking after my daughter, I'm so grateful. I'll come and get her now. Oh no, there's no need, I'll drive over, can you wait for me? My name's Latifa Nasim, what's yours? Let's swap mobile numbers; will you stay with her? Keep her with you please, I'll be there in about twenty minutes, thank you so much.'
'Come on Matt let's go, she's at McDonalds in Birkirkara, my car's there too.'
Ella was back home by nine o'clock; she'd had a Big Mac and a banana milkshake, she was composed but tired. The Police came to get her statement, two uniforms and two detectives. The sitting room was full; Tumas and Zainab sat holding hands. Lola, the Spanish au pair made coffee.
'Can you tell us what happened from when the woman got in your car and drove you away?' Ella sat on her mother's lap.
'Yes, I didn't know what was happening when this other woman got in but we'd been waving to each other and she was very nice. She said she was going to drive our car to the garage to get the damage looked at and Mummy was going to follow in the other car with her friend.'
'Where did you go?'
'I don't know, it wasn't near the sea.

It was quite a long way, it was sort of in the country I think.'

'Where did you stop?'

'We stopped at a garage and drove round the back, there was a big shed with other cars in, we parked there.'

'And then what happened?'

'We waited for ages sitting in the shed; it was too hot so we sat in the car with the aircon. We played games, Amy, she looked after me; Amy knew lots of games, her daughter's the same age as me, we had ice cream.'

'Did she ask your name?'

'No.'

Did she know your name?'

'Yeah.'

'Were you frightened? You were away for a long time.'

'No, Amy said that Mummy had broken down in the old car, it was being towed in so we had to wait for her.'

'And then?'

'And then Amy drove us to McDonald's. She said go in and ask if I could borrow a mobile to ring Mummy. Amy's had run out of battery, she said she'd wait in the car but when we came out she'd gone.' Ella yawned and snuggled against her mother.

'D'you think we could continue tomorrow?' Latifa looked down at her daughter 'this poor girl's exhausted.'

'Yeah, can you come down to Headquarters in the morning?' he took a card out of his wallet: 'we're in Floriana at San Kalcidonju Square. Is ten o'clock convenient?'

Latifa put Ella to bed and turned out her bedroom light. She went back to the sitting room.

'So what d'you think happened?' Matt and Tumas were looking very relieved.

'We don't know, maybe it was a case of mistaken identity.'

'But they didn't ask her name, they knew her identity, they knew who she was.'

'Maybe they saw it all over the news and thought it was too hot to continue.'

They talked around in circles speculating fruitlessly, Tumas stood up and stretched:

'Before we go, as a treat for Ella, would you like to come out for the day with us on Sunday? We'll go for a nice little cruise round the island on Lady Zee, we can stop off for lunch at the Baia Beach Club, it'll be fun.'

'Oh thank you Tumas, that's a great idea, very kind, Ella will love it.'

'Great, all of you, bring Lola too.' Tumas and Zainab left for home.

As they lay in bed, 'Matt are you sure you don't know something about this kidnapping? Could it be to do with your business somehow?'

'No, I don't, I really don't, I'm just happy Ella's back home.'

'Yeah, but what about the future? How can we be sure it won't happen again?'

'We'll just be extra careful. I'm sure we'll be safe.'

'D'you think it's because I'm Jewish? Could it be some religious thing, you know some Arabs hate the Jews.'

'No, I can't believe that. I'm sure it's not that.'

'Was it a warning? Matt, could it be a warning?

Chapter 19

2014 - Malta

'No, it's fine you have your night off; we'll be fine. We've had enough excitement for this week, just let me check.' He called to the kitchen:
'Tifa, it's Friday night, Lola wants to go and meet some other girls for a night out in town, that's alright isn't it?'

~

After a few hot, noisy hours downstairs at the jazz club on Republic Street Lola and her girlfriends went up to the cocktail bar where they swapped nanny stories.
'How's it going with the Nasims?'
'They've got a great apartment; I think they're quite rich you know, they're always shopping. There's so much Apple stuff you wouldn't believe it, Mrs Nasim just got a new iphone 6 it's so cool.'
'Do you have to do much?'
'Not too much, just the usual, I really like it, their daughter's so nice.'
'You're so lucky my family are like pigs, they're always eating and leaving the place a mess, I have to do all the clearing up, I'm like a maid not a nanny.'
'Oh forget them for now, have another cocktail, lets get some Mojitos; I love those.'
'Hey, we had a real scare on Wednesday, did you see the little girl that went missing on the News? Yeah, well that was the Nasims' daughter.'
'No! What happened?'
'Mrs Nasim got carjacked on the school run, they crashed into her, then drove off in her car with Ella inside!'

29 Years

'No! That's incredible, is Ella alright?'
'Yeah, that's the amazing thing, she was dumped at McDonald's and they went and picked her up.'
'So what was all that about then?'
'The Nasims think the kidnappers made a mistake and took the wrong girl.'
'Yeah we've been told to be really careful and not let the kids out of our sight when we're out.'
'I can't believe it; I thought Malta was really safe. Nothing ever happens here it's just full of rich people.'
'That's why they do it isn't it? For the money.'
'I wouldn't care if my little pigs got kidnapped, less clearing up for me to do, maybe it'd teach them some manners.'
'Did you see Carlos downstairs?'
'Yeah, he's coming up later, he said he'd bring some mates, I hope they're fit, I'm gagging for it.'
The men joined them and bought a few rounds of cocktails, they went downstairs to dance, the music was good and in the slow numbers Lola found herself with Jakob. He was much older than the others but a good dancer, cool and slim. He made her laugh and she pressed against him on the dance floor sliding her hands under his silk Armani jacket; his mobile buzzed between them.
'D'you mind if I take a look? I'm expecting a message.' He thumbed the phone and read the text.
'I need to go out side and make a call, d'you want to come get some fresh air?' She followed, holding his hand. Her girlfriends spotted her leaving and one of them made a suggestive bulge with her tongue in her cheek.
Jakob took out his mobile again 'Just need to call my dad.'
'It's arrived? Great, how's everything? What! you want me to go and check now?' He looked at his Rolex:
'it's nearly midnight you know!'

'Yeah, I'll go see the Harbourmaster. Right Dad, OK, I'll call you when I get there.' He put the phone back in his pocket.
'Crap, that's all I need.'
'What's up?'
'I've got to go and check on my dad's new boat. It's just been delivered to Portomaso Marina near St Julian's Bay. Dad wants to be sure it's been moored correctly, he wont be happy 'til I tell him everything's fine.'
She looked up at him.
'I'm sorry but I've got to leave you here, you're a very nice girl Lola I'd like to see you again.'
'Me too.'
'Hey, I don't suppose you'd like to come with me and see the boat?'
'What now?'
'Yeah, why not? It wont take long to get there, about ten or fifteen minutes, my car's just here.'
'OK, sure, let's go.'
There was hardly any traffic; pools of soft yellow light from the victorian street lamps gave way to the ugly orange of sodium lights as they sped through the dark streets and then out to the marina.
They searched for the Harbourmaster but couldn't find him, looking for the boat Jakob pointed across the marina 'there she is, let's check she's moored up properly.'
He led the way across the water, black light glinting off the slop and slap of the small waves; they navigated across gangplanks and walkways to the boat.
'It's not the mooring we were promised but it'll do for tonight.'
She was moored stern on to the pontoon; they walked up the gangway to the rear deck. Lola stopped in amazement.
'Wow, what a fantastic yacht!'
'Yeah, thirty four metres and ten million dollars, she's a

beautiful boat isn't she?'

He checked the doors were all locked and the moorings were secure.

'All seems fine, I'll just call and let Dad know.'

They walked back to the car. 'Can I drop you home? I'm going back into town anyway, where d'you live?'

'Yes please, Tower Road, it's not far from here.' By this time she would have gone anywhere with the evermore attractive Jakob.

'What're you doing over the weekend?'

'We're going for a family day out on Sunday, on Mr Nasim's dad's boat; he's got a new one too.'

'Yeah I heard he was getting one, where are you going?'

'Going for a cruise around and then lunch at the Baia Beach Club.'

'It's a good place, great food you'll have a nice time, hey, how about we come round as well? My dad's a friend of Tumas Nasim, we'll give you all a surprise!'

'Oh yeah that'll be wonderful.'

'Say, why don't you give me a call when you're at the restaurant and then we'll come into the bay and Dad can make an entrance, show off his new boat.'

'Oh yes I would but I haven't got a mobile.'

'Oh, err, here, there's a spare one in the car somewhere. Have a look on the shelf by your knees.'

'Here it is.'

'Can you switch it on? has it got battery?'

'Yeah, yeah it's full.' He pulled over and stopped.

'OK, I'll put my number in for you.' Taking it from her, he smiled and kissed her 'now remember wait 'til you're all sitting down looking out at the bay before you call, we'll be just around the headland.'

Lola could hardly sleep that night; it was so exciting. Her new boyfriend was delicious.

He thought she was lovely, he even said so. What would

the other nannies say? They'll be so jealous, and he was going to arrive on Sunday on a boat even bigger than Mr Nasim's. She hugged her pillow imagining it was Jakob.

Sunday was a beautiful morning; Matt powered the electric drapes open in the bedroom. 'Just the day for a cruise, it's going to be gorgeous.'
'I hope we're going to be safe; I'm still worried, I keep thinking there must have been someone watching Ella. Watching me aswell: they knew my car, they knew her school, they knew what time I'd pick her up, what else do they know? Why're they interested in us? I couldn't sleep Matt; I can't stop my brain.' She sat up and looked at him 'you know, I'd be able to cope more easily if I knew who it was and what they wanted, at least then I could rationalize, understand, and be able to, I don't know, respond somehow.'
They packed their beach bags with swimming things: snorkels and flippers, sunscreen and towels. Ella had an underwater camera, Matt had a harpoon gun, Latifa had the latest John Grisham, Lola had Jakob's mobile. They drove to Grand Harbour and parked at St Angelo Wharf, the Lady Zee was moored at the pontoon, glinting white in the sun. Tumas waved from the flying bridge, Ella ran to the boat, Zainab stood at the gangway; arms open to catch her.
'Hello, hello, come on board everyone, this is the skipper, José, he'll be giving me a lesson today so please, any bad driving it's my fault not his.
You can put the bags down here in the stateroom,' he led the way through the sliding glass doors into the chill, carpeted interior 'if you need it later there's a bathroom here and there's another one forward down there.'
'Wow Dad, this is an amazing boat.
I didn't realize you were getting anything as' Matt lifted

his arms, palms upward, 'as amazing as this.'
'Yeah well, you know. Honestly it's only twenty six metres, look at the size of those bastards over there, they're a hundred, hundred and twenty metres, this is a modest family boat.'
'Oh yeah right Dad, very modest, how much was it?'
'Four million but don't tell Zainab, come and have a look at the bridge,' they gazed at the bank of dials and switches. 'José, can you talk us through what all these are for? No, no, I tell you what let's get going and you can tell us as we go. Let's start when you're ready skipper.'
The twin Caterpillar diesels gargled into life, exhausts burbling richly into the clear green harbour water.
Tumas cast off astern and the skipper winched in the bow anchor, then they stood on the flying bridge. As José's fingers danced over the throttle levers the Lady Zee pirouetted and pointed her long sharp prow out to sea. Tumas was purring, 'isn't she wonderful?' He had a huge grin under his Prada sunglasses.
'Now, who'd like a drink? Darling? 'Tifa how about some champagne to celebrate our first voyage' he opened the fridge and popped a cork.
'It's a bit early Tumas, it's only eleven o'clock.'
'Yeah but we only have one first voyage all together and she's named after you so I think we shouldn't worry too much about the time of day.'
He pressed a glass of bubbly firmly into Zainab's hand and then poured for Latifa and Matt. He gave Cokes to Lola and Ella.
'Cheers Dad, many congratulations on your lovely boat and many happy voyages for you and Mum.'
They motored steadily around the island; Tumas was at the controls for a while then came down from the bridge.
'More champagne Matt, I'm getting thirsty with all this work.' Matt took him aside.

'Dad, we need to talk about the money, the kidnapping and everything, 'Tifa's still really worried.'

'Yeah, I know but first I want to enjoy my boat, we can have a nice chat after lunch, just you and me on the back deck under the shade. I got some nice Cohibas, proper chat, I promise. OK? Now, more champagne.'

Lola and Ella were down below exploring the cabins and bathrooms, playing with the toys, switching on lights, TVs and the sound system.

Lady Zee was clear of the harbour roads, out on the open sea, Tumas was ecstatic he danced with delight on the sun deck, he stamped one bare foot on the teak planking 'you know how much power we got here? Hey? Three thousand eight hundred and fifty horsepower that's what we got! Skipper, show us how fast my baby can go! Come up Ella, Lola, come up and sit on the front deck with me.' They went forward and all wedged themselves into the cushions on the curved seat overlooking the bow. Tumas leaned back to call to the skipper 'OK José, lets see what she can do! Hold on everybody!'

The sea was blue and almost flat, the engine note growled and then thundered as José opened the throttles, the bow lifted slightly as the heavy stern squatted.

'Woo, hoo' he cried angling the champagne glass against the thrust, the apparent wind was strong in their faces, the girls' hair blowing straight back. The speed increased as the deep vee hull cut through the water, spray rising up the sides of the bow and a boiling white wake behind.

'How fast?' Tumas shouted.

'Twenty eight, thirty knots' called José. They powered across the water, revelling in the speed and the noise; speech was impossible on the front deck. After a five minute blast, Tumas beamed and pumped the flat of his palm downwards.

The Lady Zee slowed and settled to a more sedate cruise.

29 Years

'Pretty good eh?'
'Fantastic Grandpa I love it, can we do it again?'
'Yeah sure, we'll do it again on the way home.'
'OK skipper let's head for the Baia Beach Club, we can anchor off and use the tender to get to the restaurant.'
An hour later they dropped their anchors in the sandy bottom of the bay and got busy putting their stuff in the tender ready for the trip ashore.
Tumas had booked a table with a panoramic view of the sea, as they walked in there were many enquiring faces looking at them. The Lady Zee looked stunning, the biggest yacht in the bay, riding elegantly at her anchorage.
At the head of the table, Tumas ordered drinks and the waiter handed out menus, they were sitting in the shade, looking out over the beach to the clear blue water.
Lola excused herself and went to the back of the restaurant; she took out Jakob's mobile and switched it on. The Nokia clasped hands screensaver lit up and showed full battery and five bars of signal. She scrolled through the contacts to highlight Jakob and pressed the call button. Lola pushed her long dark hair away from her ear and lifted the mobile. She heard the dialling tone as she looked through the shadowed dining area to see the yacht framed in the sunshine.
The dialling tone clicked, connected and started ringing.
At the third ring the portholes exploded, debris blew sideways out of the Lady Zee and the call disconnected.
As Lola looked from the phone to the yacht, a deep, whumph! rolled across the water as the noise of the explosion rocked the bay.
The diners, shouting and pointing stood to get a better view as debris rained back down onto the sea.
The white yacht was starting to list as flames appeared.
Tumas leapt up clutching his head with both hands:

'my yacht, my boat, my lovely boat, what's happening?' he grabbed his wife's hand 'Zee, what's happening? José! José what's happening to the boat?'

José shook his head in open-mouthed disbelief.

'I dunno boss, I dunno; I never seen anything like this before, it's like a bomb's gone off!'

'Is it the fuel tank? Could the diesel catch fire and explode?'

'No I don't think so, it's very hard to make diesel catch fire.' The yacht was sinking.

'Oh my God, thank God we all got off; where's Lola?'

'She went to the toilet, here she is, Lola are you OK? you look terrified.' The Spanish girl shook her head and slumped into her chair transfixed by the sight of the ruined yacht.

'She's going, she's going.' The stern sank below the surface, the sharp bow pointed at the sky then slid backwards.

'Oooooohh' there was a collective noise from the restaurant as the yacht finally disappeared.

'Boss, I gotta call the Police and the Harbourmaster, this is serious, the wreck's a danger to other vessels' said José. When he finished the calls he said 'the police want us to wait here, they'll be about ten minutes.'

It was the same detectives who'd interviewed them about Ella's kidnapping. One walked José to an empty table at the back of the restaurant and took his statement.

The other took the details of the rest of the family and Lola then said 'Mr Nasim, I think we should continue this back at the police station, you and José can come with us, can the rest get a taxi over? '

In a daze they picked up their beach bags, Lola felt Jakob's mobile was burning a hole in hers.

When they eventually got back to the apartment at six o'clock Latifa made pasta:

'Eat up Ella then please go to your room, Daddy and I have things we need to talk about.'

'Look Matt, I want to know; this was no coincidence was it? Why are we being persecuted? What have you done? I'm not going to be angry, I don't want to be angry, I just need to know.' Nervously, Matt took two large swallows from his glass of wine before speaking:

'I think it's to do with a property investment in England, the money's gone missing.'

'How much money has gone missing?'

'Fifty million pounds.' Her eyes widened in astonishment, she shook her head weakly and sat down. 'You'd better tell me what's going on.'

'Dad got the money from Kazakh investors but after we'd set up a land purchase they decided to pull out and wanted the money back. The problem is that we can't find it. We think the guy running the property company in England has hidden the money; he told us that HMRC are investigating him for money laundering, he's left UK and he's hiding in Holland. He knows where the money is so that's what we told Arman – he's the Kazakh guy.

'So why are they after us if it's the other guy who's got the money?'

'I dunno but the fifty million doesn't belong to Arman.'

'Whose is it then?'

'Islamic State.'

'Oh Christ, you can't be serious, how? how?' she had no words.

'ISIL robbed the banks in Iraq, I guess the people in Kazakhstan offered to launder the money; we didn't know anything about this when we accepted the investment.'

'Yeah but if it was an above board investment why not go to a bank for financing?

That's what you did for all your projects in Spain.'

'Yeah but the banks don't want to lend on property these days, you need to go elsewhere to raise money.'

'So why is HMRC interested? You're banned from being a director of a UK company.'

'Yeah, I'm just a foreign investor. HMRC is interested because a London fund manager got nosey and started looking into why fifty million pounds was transferred from the Turks and Caicos to a small property firm in the Cotswolds. That set off some alarms about money laundering.'

'This all sounds like a real mess, how come you're mixed up with these kind of people?'

'They're friends of Dad's, he's been dealing with Kazakhs and Iranians and all these type of people for years. I thought it might be a bit dodgy but you know, I thought it would work out alright.'

'You've been a complete idiot, how can you expect to get this much money from people you've never heard of? How can they just ask for it back? What are the terms and conditions on the investment agreement?

You know I used to work in investment finance, why didn't you ask me?' She recognised the expression on his face.

'Because you knew it wasn't kosher, you knew I'd ask too many questions. You're stupid and worse, you've put us in danger, Ella in danger. You knew all this when Ella was kidnapped didn't you?' Realization dawned:

'You lied and lied to me, "oh no it's nothing to do with my business" how could you? Your own daughter kidnapped and you kept lying. What if they'd hurt her, or killed her? How could you live with yourself? You didn't tell the police, if they'd known who to look for they'd probably have found the kidnappers. You're an idiot.'

She stood, hands on hips looking down at him:

'Right, that's it, I'm leaving. Now, tonight.' She strode to

the hall cupboard and took out three suitcases. 'I'm packing, just keep out of my way.'
'Lola!' The girl came running from her bedroom:
'Si Senora?'
'Lola pack all your stuff we're leaving, we're going to London tonight!'
'Tonight?!'
'Yes, now, as soon as possible, we're going to the airport, we'll get the BA flight.'
'Matt, get on to BA and book three seats, one way.'
'Wait, wait I can protect you, I can look after you here.' She continued opening drawers and putting clothes in the suitcases; 'no you can't, obviously you can't. I'm going to stay with my sister in London, maybe I'll go back to Tel Aviv; we'll be safe there. I'm absolutely not staying here, just book the seats and print the boarding passes.'
'What's happening Mummy? Why are you packing?'
'We're going to stay with Aunty Sara in London for a few days, put out the toys you want to take, I'll come and help in a minute.' She rang for a taxi to collect them at six o'clock. The bags were packed, stacked in the hall.
'I need some money,' she opened the safe 'is this ours?'
'Yeah, there's about fifty thousand Euro in there.'
'I'll take it.' She crammed the thick packets of cash into her handbag 'give me those boarding passes.'
'I'll come with you.'
'No, I don't want you to, I don't want to been seen with you. I never trusted your father, I always thought he was dodgy and now he's really proved it. And you're just like him.' The entry phone buzzed. 'Yes, we'll be down in a minute. Say goodbye to Daddy Ella.'
The apartment door closed and Jakob's mobile went to London.

Chapter 20

2014 – Malta

'Did you call the insurers about my yacht?'
'Yes boss, first thing, I sent a preliminary loss advice and spoke to the claims manager.'
'You told him it's a Total Loss right? What'd he say?'
'He said what's the cause of loss.'
'It fucking sank!'
'Yeah, well he wants to know why it sank.'
'It fucking blew up, that's why it sank; there was a bomb or something on board.'
'I told him that, he's going to send a Marine Surveyor to come and look at the wreck, they'll have divers. Oh yeah, and the Harbourmaster's been on the phone, he wants the wreck removed as soon as possible.'
'Oh fucking great, that's all I need; that fat greasy twat breathing all over me. Well he can piss off and wait 'til the insurers agree to pay to move it. Who's the insurers on this policy? Lloyd's?'
'Err no you decided to use a Russian insurance company called Vitall Star for the Lady Zee.'
'Did I? Why?'
'They sent a very nice looking woman to come and talk to us about insurance about three months ago and you said OK we'll give them some business. The next opportunity was the Lady Zee.
'Ohhhhhh yes, I remember the woman, Tamara. Right, so did you speak with the lovely Tamara?'
'Not yet, I thought you might want to call her first.'
'Yeah, OK, right, I'll call her tomorrow.'
Tumas Nasim drove home and parked in the courtyard.

29 Years

He lived in the Grand Palazzo, built in 1647 in the style of a Venetian townhouse, Zainab had inherited it from her Grandmother. He walked past the swimming pool and pressed the button for the ancient lift. Four floors up, he stepped out onto the roof terrace, the evening view spread out across Grand Harbour and the open sea. He sat, lit a Marlborough Light and thought about Latifa and Ella leaving. He knew it was his fault and he knew he could never make it up to them. He knew the money was dirty; it had been too easy. He looked down at the berth where the Lady Zee had been moored yesterday morning; it had already been filled with another yacht. 'Shit' he flicked the butt over into the silent street and went inside to the huge old-fashioned kitchen.

Zainab was cooking spaghetti bolognese. He looked at her resignedly across the room, over the last forty years since they got married she'd got bigger and he'd got smaller. She'd helped him to start his business, her father loaned them the money and gave him the contacts to start his trading business. He poured them each a glass of wine, her family had never liked him; they had a low opinion of the Nasims. He put her glass on the table, she turned and glared at him 'Latifa's gone to London; she's taken Ella and Lola. She say's she's too frightened to stay here. What have you done now?' Her lips tightened angrily over her teeth 'and what's this letter?' She pointed with the knife she was holding to a letter on the countertop, in bold, large typed letters was written:

TUMAS NASIM IS A LIAR A THIEF AND A RAPIST.

She grabbed it off him and shook it; he was scared. Scared of her, scared of what she might do to him and scared of what ISIS might to do next. They'd invaded his life and were destroying his family.

'Why Liar? Who have you lied to? Is this your business? Our business, the one I helped you build?

Weakly he explained about the money and how ISIS was behind it.

'So you lied to them and what? They say you're a thief for stealing their money?'

'Yes' knowing even worse was to come.'

'Rapist?' She looked at him with incomprehension: 'Why do they say you're a rapist?'

'I don't know.'

'I don't now' she echoed in menacing disbelief.

Then she screamed, 'How can you not know!' 'This isn't something you can forget! You'd better tell me, you know I'll find out. You sit down there and tell me right now!' She towered over him.

'I don't know, I think it must be a mistake, a misunderstanding.'

'A misunderstanding? You think I'm a fool?'

'Well, there was an incident.' He paused, not looking at her; 'a long time ago. In London.'

'When in London?'

'I don't know, about twenty years ago.'

'Twenty years ago, what is this, on a business trip?'

'Yes, it was just a bit of fun that got out of hand.'

'You better explain how it getting out of hand.'

'We went out drinking one evening and I had, I had…' he faltered.

'You had..' she prompted threateningly.

'I had some drugs, some drug I'd been given, it was supposed to make girls want you, you put it in their drink and, and..' he dried up.

'You put it in their drink and then what?'

'And then they can't resist you.'

'So what did you do with this drug?'

'I put it in the drink of an English girl.'

'Who was she?'

'I don't know, I don't remember her name.'

'Then what?'
'Then we took her in a taxi to the hotel, she didn't mind, she seemed OK.' He looked beseechingly at her, 'We thought she was OK, we left her for a few hours and she got up and went out, disappeared.'
'She didn't mind what?'
'The, the, the sex' he mumbled.
'You had sex? You had sex with her!'
'Yeah'
'How many times?'
'Twice, three times I don't know.'
She looked disgustedly at the small man cringing at the table and took a deep breath.
'You said "we"...'
'Yeah.'
'You both had sex with this poor drugged English girl? One after the other?' He nodded.
Who else was there? Who was with you?'
'I can't tell you.'
'We were married and you went out raping in London!'
With one smooth lift she picked up the hot, heavy pan of bolognese from the gas and swung it full force, slamming it sideways into his head. Stunned, he fell off the chair onto the stone floor, his face and hair dripping with burning hot sauce. She threw the pan at his chest. Zainab turned back to the stove, needing two hands, she picked up a big saucepan and sloshed boiling spaghetti water onto his crutch. He screamed and tried to cover himself with his hands.
'Who was with you!' She bellowed with rage.
'I can't, I can't..'
She tipped more scalding water. He screamed again
'It was Matt, I'm so sorry. It was Matt.' She gasped with horror.
'Our son? You took our son out raping?

He was a boy, nineteen. How could you, you disgusting animal, pull your trousers and pants down or I tip this in your face!' He screamed in pain trying to writhe out of the way as she dumped the red-hot liquid and pasta over his cock and balls.

'Now get out, get out now and never come back. You are dead to me. I'll tell your daughter, your grandchildren, your brother; you're dead to me and to all your family.' Zainab kicked him with each curse. 'You go, disappear; you have no friends you are outcast! You've disgraced me; you've corrupted and disgraced our son. I hate you, you bastard, get out of my house, I never want to see you again!' She slammed the huge heavy door shut.

29 Years

Chapter 21

Summer 1973 - France

Ward 12 was a quiet high-ceilinged, light room, pale cream walls and a polished wood parquet floor. The windows were tall with large panes separated by delicate glazing bars; they gave on to a parkland view of leafy trees and dark green grass.

She was breathing faintly, her face pallid with dark marks around the eyes. Her cheeks were sunken; the thick white hair was lank and greasy. Veins stood out, stringy on her thin white arms, there was a plastic identity bracelet on her wrist. Her skin was almost transparent where it stretched across her bony breastbone. There was a cannula in the crook of her left arm and a tube into her left nostril.

Estelle had suffered a heart attack and was now in a coma. In the emergency room, the doctors had flushed the poison out of her stomach and given her oxygen. What little remained of the cyanide was working its way around her system; she was very weak.

Ed wanted to gather her into his arms and kiss her.

'What can I do? What does the doctor say?'

'Do? You can do nothing but if you're here when she wakes then, then' she hid her trembling lower lip with the back of her fingers 'then I think it will help.'

'I'll be here' he said firmly 'right here. Can we speak to the doctor?' Hélène looked around the Ward

'You can ask the Ward Sister, she might know when he'll be back.' The Sister said it would be after lunch. 'It's twelve thirty now.' Ed looked searchingly at Hélène 'Why don't you go and get something to eat? I'll stay with Estelle, there's a café downstairs.'

'I'll go and get a coffee' she stood up, 'I won't be long.'

Ed turned to speak to Estelle; he leaned forward in the chair, his face close to hers. He spoke slowly into the silence with a long pause between each uttered thought:
'My darling, I'm so sorry.
I'm devastated that I upset you so much.
I just had to see you, to know that you were alright.
I was so excited that day, so astonished that I'd found you.
I buried my feelings for you for so many years.
And you're so beautiful; I loved you. I love you; I'll always love you. Please come back; please wake up.
Don't worry, you're safe, I'm here now.
I'll look after you. I'll always be here.
Just squeeze my fingers if you can hear me.'
Her small hand remained lifeless; she was alive but not connected to the outside world.

'Her body has had a very big shock; you must understand that it will take time for her to recover.'
The doctor's words interrupted him, Ed looked round.
'Who are you Monsieur?' The doctor stood at the end of the bed reading Estelle's medical notes with a nurse.
'Ah, yes, the Englishman, Hélène has told me that you are the.. err, that you're a friend of Estelle's. My name is Doctor Eric Benoit, I'm responsible for Estelle.'
'How is she? Will she recover, get better?'
'She's over the worst part of the poison; we're taking her blood for testing every four hours, the indications are positive, I hope that she'll make a good recovery.'
'Thank you, thank you so much for all you have done to save her' but the man didn't stop to listen.
He'd gone, moving swiftly down the ward, shoulders hunched, hands in the pockets of his white coat.

29 Years

When Benoit got back to his office he looked up the admission details of Estelle Levavasseur.

Née Estelle Dubose, born 15th April 1919, address; 25 Rue de l'Église, Valençay.

It must be the same family, Dubose. One of them, the Maquis.

He buried his face in his hands, in 1944 the Maquis, in reprisal against collaborationists in Tours had killed Paul Benoit, Eric's father. One of the ringleaders had been Philippe Dubose, Estelle's father.

Memories of that night flooded into his mind; Eric was eleven years old when the front door of their home was kicked in before dawn. He awoke in fear, a rush of heavy men broke into the house in the dark, they crashed around in the hall and shouted up the stairs:

'Benoit, you traitor get your lying, cheating arse down here.' Eric lay in bed trembling with fear, it wasn't the Germans; these were violent, angry Frenchmen, he heard them swearing, they were drunk.

'Benoit, I'm coming to get you, I'm going to do you, you filthy collaborator!'

From the top of the stairs his father's confident voice outside Eric's bedroom 'clear off, you're drunk, go home before I call the military patrol.'

'Oh yeah, get your Boche friends to help, have you forgotten you're a Frenchman?'

'Come down 'ere you Nazi cocksucker we want to ask you a few questions.'

His father had been in charge of food distribution in Tours. The French were always hungry; there were long queues for food all the time. But the Benoits didn't suffer, they always had meat and bread, they used to eat behind closed curtains.

Paul Benoit switched on the light over the stairs, he recognised the men 'what do you want here Tremant?

And is that LeBlanc? Does you're wife know what you're doing? Ah yes, Dubose I thought you might be behind this.' When the sound of his feet came to the bottom of the stairs there was a scuffle and the dull thuds of heavy blows.
Eric heard the grunting and muffled oaths, the scrape of furniture on the wooden floorboards and heavy boots stumbling as the men dragged his father over the broken door.

~

Estelle's hand moved in his, 'Are you awake?' He said softly.
'Edouard? C'est tu?'
'Yes, it's me, I'm here.'
Her black eyes opened and a sorrowful smile weakly stretched her lips.
'You're going to be fine, you're in hospital, just rest, I'll be here.'
She nodded in understanding and closed her eyes. Ed turned to Hélène,
'I think she'll be alright, I'll stay with her, why don't you go home and look after the children?'
'OK if you're sure.'
'Yes, I won't leave her now.'
At midnight Eric returned for last rounds, he'd been in the hospital library studying cyanide poisoning and the potential causes of relapse during recovery. In the dispensary he prepared a syringe and put with it a clear glass vial in a white enamel kidney dish. There were a few pools of shaded light as he walked silently through the darkened ward
Hélène was at home. Estelle was dozing; Ed was asleep in an easy chair beside her.

29 Years

The doctor sat on her bed putting the dish and syringe on the bedside table.

Her eyes opened as the mattress moved under the doctor's weight; he introduced himself and swiftly checked her over. Then, his hands in his lap he impassively explained their connection; he described how Estelle's father had led a gang which murdered his father. She put her hand out in condolence 'I'm so sorry, I'm so sad for you, those were terrible times.' He put her hand back on the bedclothes.

'I don't need your sympathy but there is something I have to do' he picked up the syringe and, rolling it between his fingers and thumb, continued talking;

'My mother was an invalid, she had a weak heart, she was bedridden. After I was born she couldn't have another child, she nearly died in childbirth. The men took my father from our house, I was a boy; I couldn't stop them. I went to my mother's bedroom; she was lying in her bed crying, I think she knew what was going to happen. I got into bed beside her, the noise of the scuffle and shouts disappeared down the street. We lay in silence; there was nothing to say. When it was quiet I went downstairs and pushed the broken front door back into place as best I could then got back into bed with my mother. We just held hands under the blankets, we couldn't sleep; we stayed awake 'til dawn.

In the morning, at school the boys shouted abuse at me about my father. They said I was a collaborator; that my father was a thief, that he stole food from honest Frenchmen. On my way home I went to see him, he was dead. His body was hanging from the gates at one of the warehouses where food was distributed. His clothes were torn and his face was battered, he'd been hung upside down, his feet were tied by wire. His shirt had come undone and hung down, showing his fat white stomach.

He was high up on the iron gates. The wire was so tight it had cut through to the bones, I could see the blood where it had run down his legs.'

He lifted her right forearm, opened the elbow and searched for her vein with his thumb. When it swelled up, he punctured the thin skin, slid the shiny needle in and looked into her eyes.

'What's the injection for?' she said unresistingly.

'What I came to say was to thank you; to thank your father really but I know he's passed away. I want to say thank you for killing my father; I hated him. He was a disgusting man. He ruined my life and my mother's life.'

He lifted the red vial 'Oh this, it's another sample, I just needed some blood to run another test. I've been doing some research; there's something else we can check for, no need for you to worry it's just a precaution.'

'But how did he ruin your life?'

'Almost every night from the age of nine, he sexually abused me, my mother knew and it sickened her but there was nothing that either of us could do. He was a big man and a bully.' He withdrew the needle and covered the little wound with a piece of cotton wool and a strip of sticking plaster to hold it in place. Kindly, Benoit adjusted her covers and stood up 'I hope you sleep well, I'll come and see you in the morning.'

Ed woke up at the cheerful sound of nurses bringing breakfast and getting the day started, he stood up and rubbed his stubble face, looking to see how Estelle was.

'I'm feeling so much better my darling; it makes me so happy to have you here with me, I won't ever do anything like that again. You didn't look very comfortable in the chair, did you sleep?'

'Yes, I'm fine, but I was tired after the drive and all the excitement yesterday. I'll go back to the Lion d'Or, shower and shave and have something to eat.

Hélène will be along soon and I'll come back later.'
An hour later, refreshed, Ed walked back through Valençay to the hospital; he looked in the windows of the estate agents for houses to rent. There were quite a few available, a farm cottage would be nice; he'd talk to Estelle about where they might live.

~

Estelle recovered rapidly and was transferred to the Saint Charles convalescent hospital in Valençay. They'd decided to rent a longère, a small old farmhouse near the château on La Basse Cour. He had described the property to her in detail. 'I've been to see the house with Hélène, she thinks it's really charming and I think you'll love it too. The garden looks south, down over the Le Nahon river. You can't actually see water from the house but the whole area is very peaceful, the river runs green and slow under the trees.' 'Yes I know it well; I often used to walk there before the war. Look at my walking now.' She laughed as she moved steadily along the floor behind a wheeled walking frame.
'The doctor says I can leave soon, when do you think we can move into the longère?'
He was delighted by her enthusiasm. 'I've ordered some furniture and Hélène will help me get the larder stocked up, I've signed the lease and they said that we can move in on Saturday.'

~

Estelle sat in the sitting room of their home; the garden doors were open to a sunny September afternoon. She was tired but it was going to be alright. At last, finally she was with the love of her life. The man she'd waited for.

Now twenty-nine years later, she was filled with deep contentment and a sense that her life was complete and had its purpose. She closed her eyes and dozed hearing the faint clink of china and rustle of paper as Ed carried on unpacking and putting things away.

Over the weeks, life assumed a pattern and they grew used to being with one another. Their senses of humour quickly returned and they had fun together enjoying each other's company. There was no shyness between them, the sexual chemistry was exactly the same and they lusted for each other. They were tender in bed and when the time was right they took delight in each other's bodies.

Mary filed for divorce, Ed was generous and they both tried to make the process as painless as possible. He took early retirement to live on his pension while Mary continued her career at the school and kept the house in Northleach.

When Estelle was well enough, though still walking with a stick, they went to a consultant surgeon for an examination of her leg. The X-ray revealed pieces of shrapnel from the war still in her leg. The shrapnel had moved around in the thigh muscle tissue and given her pain walking for years. After surgery and some months of physiotherapy she was able to leave the stick and walk normally other than a slight limp.

The winter passed with Estelle showing Ed her childhood home and memories. They visited the landing site at Luzillé and drove along the route that she had cycled on the night of her return. They drank and she reminisced at the Café de la Paix where the meetings of her réseau had been held. They walked along the railway track to where Patrice had pushed the suitcase full of explosives into the culvert. Then stood in silence at the railway station where Patrice had died under the train and Estelle had been captured.

Ed got to know Hélène and became part of the family. Hélène's children would often come over to play in the afternoon after school and on Sundays they would all come for lunch. If the weather was good they walked through the fields beside the slow green river.

By the spring of 1974 they each had part-time jobs. Estelle teaching English at the secondary school and Ed helped with marketing at the tourism office in Tours. He was promoting the Loire valley as a destination for English and American holidaymakers.

In May they went to Paris for three days. They stayed at a small hotel on the Left Bank and visited some of the well-known tourist sights; The Eiffel Tower, Les Invalides, Le Louvre, Arc de Triomphe, Notre Dame, Sacré-Coeur and took a river trip to see the city from the Seine on a bateau mouche.

To celebrate the moment Ed booked a table for dinner at Maxim's in the Rue Royale, they got dressed up and took a taxi across the river past Place de la Concorde to the Art Nouveau restaurant.

She looked around the room in delight 'my darling this is absolutely fabulous' the maître d'hôtel showed them to their table and Ed ordered champagne.

He couldn't wait any longer; 'Estelle my love, this is the moment I never thought would happen, will you marry me?'

'Yes! yes of course I'll marry you. I don't know what to say. Just, just that this is the best day of my life.' they stood up in the crowded room and to some cheers and clapping, hugged and kissed each other. They turned, holding hands and bowed to thank the other diners and with huge smiles sat down.

'May I have your hand?' she held it forward, fingertips just touching the tablecloth, he slid a sapphire ring onto her wedding finger then kissed her hand.

'Oh', she gazed in delight at the ring and at him 'oh Edouard, what can I say? I'm just so happy; it's lovely, the ring is beautiful, everything is just so perfect.'

They sat silent for a while enjoying the moment and occasionally smiling with excitement and pleasure.

He sat back drinking her in, his lover, his soul mate, the love of his life and now the she was going to be his wife.

Over a dinner they started making wedding plans.

'Do you think we might be able to have it at the Château?'

'That's a terrific idea, let's ask as soon as we get back, shall we invite all the people who helped to bring us together? especially Mountjoy and Crispin, you remember Mountjoy? He came to the Château on holiday as a young boy in 1934, that's how I got the photo of you when you were working there as a nanny for the Sagans. We really must ask your pilot in the Lysander.'

'Yes Graham Knowles, without him…'

'Yes, without him we probably be wouldn't be here, he leaned forward and they kissed again.

'How soon could we get married?'

'I think it'll be a few months to get the legal formalities sorted out then we have to do some planning so why don't we think of a day in September? After everyone's back from their summer holidays.'

~

'And this is where we sat' with a sweep of his arm which ended with a glass of champagne he indicated the wide stone steps set into the grass bank. 'The vile children sat that side and me just here, near my m'mah. The beautiful Estelle, our minder for the day, had managed to slip away for a few minutes, for a rest from the racket I imagine.'

29 Years

They were walking round the parkland of the Château de Valençay after the wedding ceremony; the September grass was tinder dry underfoot, Mountjoy was their guide and raconteur.

'In the war this place was untouched you know, yes because it was owned by the Duke of Sagan, a Polish aristocrat, it wasn't occupied by German forces. In fact it was declared neutral territory and many treasures from the Louvre such as the Venus de Milo were stored in the cellars here.'

They stood and admired the huge white building with its dark grey slate-roofed turrets and towers, on the upper floors the shutters were closed against the sun. On the terrace, green awnings had been pulled open to provide shade over the lunch tables. Guests were starting to sit down, English mingling happily with French all enjoying the occasion; the waiters bringing food and drinks.

After lunch the party continued through the afternoon, as the adults drank and chatted, the children played games in the park, some jumped in the fountain and got their party clothes wet playing under the arcs of water. Impromptu speeches were made by M. Le Juge, Hélène, Graham Knowles and of course in French and in English by Mountjoy.

The guests slowly and reluctantly left, groups walked slowly away down the tree-shaded avenue, laughter, snatches of voices and good wishes floating back to those lingering on the terrace.

Once all had left, Ed and Estelle went to a bench in the park to sit quietly and savour the moment for a while. 'How lucky we are, what wonderful friends we have. I think we're going to enjoy a lovely life living here, I'm so happy that you came and found me again.' She reached up and stroked his cheek; her gold wedding ring caught the evening sun and glittered warmly back at her.

In October, some weeks after the wedding there was a definite chill in the evening air, the trees had shed all but a few leaves, daylight was fading and the evening mist began to rise from the river below their house 'I'm going to light our first fire.'

Ed brought in the dry kindling and split logs, then boy-scout style made a little teepee of wood with newspaper in the middle; he struck a match and watched the flames lick. The chimney drew well, wood crackling quickly as the fire gained strength and purpose; presently he fed some larger logs onto the fire then closed the curtains to keep the warmth in the room. They sat side by side on the sofa in front of the hearth feeling the comfort of the little stone house around them. With his arm still around her shoulders she half-turned to face her lover 'this is the first time I've felt properly safe. The first time I'm with the one person who I always wanted to spend my life with. The first time I can look forward to the future with happiness and confidence that you'll always be here. We can grow old together and I'll always look after you and take care of you.' She leaned her head sideways against his shoulder and spoke to his shirtfront 'you'll never realize how important you have been to me in my life, you saved my life many times, you kept me alive.'

'When was that? How did I save your life?'

'When I was arrested in 1944 and taken to Paris I thought that it was the end for me, I expected to be interrogated, maybe tortured and then shot. We all heard many stories about the Gestapo and their methods, I was frightened but more about giving away any secrets than for what might happen to me.

When it was clear that the Germans knew more about the Resistance than I did and that they held many captured agents with me at Avenue Foch; I realized I wouldn't tell them anything they didn't already know.

29 Years

We knew the Allies were near and we hoped to be liberated but the Germans were too quick for them. We were taken by train and truck to a camp a long, long way east before they arrived.' She lifted her head and rested her forehead against his 'this is when you saved my life; you see the others, so many of them died because they gave up. They had nothing to live for; they'd lost their homes and their families. Mothers had their children taken away; they were frightened and exhausted. Every day we just piled the bodies at the back of the carriage. There were more dead than living when we arrived. You see it was the thought of you and the memories that I had of you that kept me alive. Because of your damaged eyes I knew that you wouldn't be sent back to fight. I had something to hold onto, something, someone to live for that kept me alive. I knew that you'd survive and that you loved me, I knew that somehow, that sometime in the future I'd see you again. So many times I could have given up in the work camps, just laid down and died like so many others did when they couldn't go on any longer. But I was different; I had you. I had a flame in my heart that kept me going and that flame was you.' She put her arms around him and they held each other close.

Chapter 22

Autumn 2014 – The Cotswolds

"James Fletcher, Director, Liberty Homes Ltd" Dave Chatham sat at his desk holding the business card in his left hand, reflectively flicking it with his right thumbnail. He had the company website up on screen and clicked on their current and proposed developments. Liberty seemed to have strong backing and capital available for new developments.

Was Fletcher the right man to approach? The Board would know that he'd failed to obtain the Little Rissington site the first time. Perhaps Dave should approach the CEO, Archie Gordon; the deal was certainly big enough. It was larger than any other development showing on their website. But before opening that line of enquiry he needed a competing bidder.

From his research Dave had discovered that Clarnis Construction was the third largest and most active developer in the south of England. He rang the Director responsible for new business and arranged a meeting at their headquarters in Reading.

They were interested and had promptly returned a signed, legally-binding Non Disclosure Agreement. Dave went to their offices taking the site plans, outline planning consent from the Council, a copy of the Land Registry Title showing the right of way over the track, the letter of intent to proceed with a sale to Cloud Developments from MoD and the landscaping contract.

~

29 Years

Simon Slocutt was a big blond man who wouldn't look out of place on a building site. He reached across the boardroom table, spreading out the documents with a meaty hand, shirt button cuff, tight on his ham-like wrist.

'We didn't bid on this one, not enough local knowledge. I couldn't see how we could build enough units to meet our internal return on capital requirements. I think you cracked it with this alternative access though.' The chair complained as he sat back eyeballed Dave and continued:

'Yeah, well on this basis I think we'd be interested. This is our sort of thing.' Eyebrows raised in query;

'What is it you're looking for? We don't do subcontract work y'know. Some sort of partnership deal?'

'As it stands, my capital providers will fund the programme and recoup their investment as the units are sold. Independent of that, and acting as their adviser, I'm also looking at the possibilities of an earlier exit from this deal than originally anticipated.'

'A sale?'

'Yes, if you'd like to make us an offer we'd be pleased to consider it.'

'Mmm' small nods with the large head.

'Who else are you offering it to?'

'I'm afraid I can't tell you that, but equally, I won't disclose your interest to any other parties that may be interested to make an offer.'

'How much did you pay the MoD?'

The purchase price on the MoD's letter of intent had been redacted.

Dave smiled and gently shook his head; 'I don't think so.'

'I know Liberty offered fifty.'

'Really? Well, as I said we'd be very happy to consider your offer if you'd like to make one.'

'OK, what's the timeframe?'

'We'd like offers in by the end of the month.

That gives the interested parties thirteen days.'
'I'll call you in a couple of days after I've put this proposal to the board. Can I keep all this?'
'Yeah but if you decide not to go ahead I need everything back including any copies that you make.'

~

Back in his office at Moreton-in-Marsh Dave was on the phone, 'Archie Gordon please.' When Archie came on the line Dave explained the reason for his call and the timeframe.
'Well that's very kind of you to think of us Mr Chatham, I tell you what I'll do' the plummy tones continued 'I'll speak to my colleague, James Fletcher, put him in the picture, you know, and then get him to give you a call later today or tomorrow. I expect he'll fix a meeting with you and err, and err we can all have a chat. Is that OK with you? Now I will also say that I'll be keeping a close eye on this one, erm, is that alright?'
He sounded genuine enough, wonder why he put Fletcher back on the case, last chance saloon for him maybe. It'll certainly be interesting to see how keen he is to do the deal this time.
The NDA had been signed and they met in a meeting room at Liberty Homes' offices on a business park outside Oxford. Fletcher was a tall man with a stoop and a large adam's apple. 'So it was you who got the site then?' He opened rather unnecessarily and with a feeble smile. The documents lay on the table.
'Probably easiest if I talk you through our plans and consents et cetera, go ahead and ask if anything's not clear as we go along.'
Fletcher took off his jacket and sat down, there was a faint whiff of nervous armpits.

He made notes and fiddled with his biro as Chatham made his presentation.
Archie Gordon came in, shook hands and sat down motioning Dave to continue and not to mind his presence.
When he'd finished, Fletcher said 'this is interesting, so you want us to take the project over for you then?
'No, we're looking at alternative exit strategies. If your firm would like to make us an offer for the site with the outline planning consent and the right of way we'll consider it. If the offer isn't high enough my backers will continue with the original plan and see the development through.'
'What sort of money are you looking for?'
'We've several firms interested and asked for offers by the end of the month. I expect that shouldn't be too difficult for Liberty as you're very familiar with the site.'
The adam's apple was bobbing in distress.
'Yes, yes. Yes of course.' Fletcher didn't know what to do with his hands, the room had got warmer and so had his body odour.
'I should add that we've got an agreement with a landscaping company for creating the gardens and an ongoing maintenance contract for the communal areas. As part of the deal we'd want your express confirmation to honour and continue with that agreement. The terms are competitive, here's the proposal that we've signed off on.'
'Ah well, I don't know about that, I can't say…'
'Yeah well, that's what's on the table. Is there anything else?'
'May we have sight of your financial projections for the development?'
'Sorry, no; each of the parties have the same information, if anything I'd say you've got the advantage having been the under bidder.

Can you let me know by the end of tomorrow if you wish to proceed? If not we'll be obliged to replace Liberty with another interested party.'

Dave turned to Archie enquiringly; he in turn shook his head and looked at Fletcher. 'Err well, no that all seems fine, we'll err get back to you tomorrow.'

~

They were on the M6, it was about an hour and half from Sherborne to Walsall, John was driving up to meet Janice and see the torc; Ed had volunteered to keep him company. They got closer to their destination, peering at the defaced road signs that named the sour streets. He parked the van in a grim side road and stepped over the rubbish in the gutter outside the shabby two up, two down, terraced house. Many of the brick-built houses had been painted, some more skilfully than others. Janice's was a dusty red, the pointing picked out by a shaky hand in a contrasting baby blue, the bell didn't sound so John knocked and waited for the door to be opened.

Janice came back into the gloomy little living room with a small flat cardboard box in her hand; she put it on the coffee table and lifted the lid. There was some crumpled tissue paper covering a yellow circlet, she slid the box towards Ed.

'Is this what you was thinking of?'

He lifted away the paper and the gleam of pre-christian gold bathed his face. 'My goodness it's just as I remember, isn't it beautiful?' He took it out and held the necklet delicately between his fingers. About 20 cm in diameter it was a three quarter circle of chased heavy gold, jeweled at the open ends.

'Yeah well: if you like that sort of stuff, Mum never wore it and it's not my kind of thing either.'

29 Years

Janice was a middle-aged Goth; everything she wore was black from her Doc Martin boots to her spiked black hair. Everything; apart from the sprinkling of shiny chrome studs in her ears, eyebrows and lips.

Ed passed it to John who held the torc almost reverently, he could see the hand engraving and the intricate workmanship in the settings that held the green and blue stones at each end 'I love it; I think it's great. This old-fashioned stuff is amazing.'

'You can 'ave it if you want, the bloke down the pawnshop said he'd give me two hundred quid for it, he's a robbin' bastid. You can 'ave it for five 'undred if you want.' John turned it this way and that, it felt right, it looked just like the ones in the Ashmolean; even if it wasn't genuine Anglo-Saxon it was still a beautiful thing. And with Ed nodding encouragement he said 'go on then, is there a Barclays near here? I'll go get the cash for you.'

On the drive back; 'Thanks Ed, I'm amazed I've got this fantastic torc; it's all down to you remembering the dig and having those photos from your days at Rissy. D'you think we should try and trace that ginger chap that you mentioned, the one who organized the dig?

'Why's that? What do you want from him? Actually I don't know if I mentioned it but we didn't get on very well.'

'I was just thinking that he might have some more of this type of jewellery, it would amazing if there was a complete set wouldn't it? We might even be able to work out who the person was, when they died and everything.'

'You might but you might also attract some attention from the authorities, they're very keen on knowing who's got these treasures, it's often mentioned in The Telegraph. I'd let sleeping dogs lie if I were you, save it for your best girl; be like Dick Torrance, save it for your wedding day.'

'You're right, one day when I know it's the right girl I'll give it to her.'
They grinned together at a good day's work; smoothly the white van peeled off the M40 and pointed its blunt nose towards the heart of the Cotswolds.

Back at Liberty Homes it was a tense moment:
'So James, how much should we bid for the site this time?' Fletcher had been up most of the night sweating over his spreadsheets trying to calculate the right number.
'Well, err, based on three hundred and fifty homes we can go to fifty three million, if we can build four hundred we can go to fifty five million.'
'And the right of way, how much is that?'
'Err we offered a million, I've err included that in those numbers.'
'And the landscaping?'
'It looks competitive, we might be able to shave a bit off but I think we can leave those costs unchanged. It doesn't really affect the headline numbers.'
'So what's the return on capital based on the fifty three or fifty five million?'
'If we maintain our current modest gearing of thirty per cent and our borrowings at an average interest rate of one point two five per cent we can make a return on capital of twenty per cent.'
'Which other companies have been invited to bid?'
'The only one I know is Clarnis but we should also expect that Bovis will be bidding as they've already built Victory Fields.'
'Fine, put together a presentation for the board for tomorrow at eleven o'clock and we'll have a chat about how much we think it's worth. Oh and tell that Chatham feller that we'll be bidding.'

29 Years

'Well gentlemen, you've heard James' thoughts on the development and the value of the site.
Can we just go round the table and get each of your views? I should say that at up to four hundred units this would be our largest development to date. Bear in mind that one of our corporate aims is an active growth strategy and we are targeting opportunities north of the A40 between Cheltenham and Oxford.
The board's general consensus was that Fletcher's figures were correct but that they were exactly what any other bidder would have calculated. The options available were to consider either how much of a hit to their margin they were prepared to take; or to increase the risk by increasing their gearing. In other words, to borrow more money from the bank but that would be at a higher interest rate. Banks would charge more because of the increased exposure. Then of course there was the timing risk, how long the units would take to build and sell, the debate wrangled around the room for an hour.
'Thank you gentlemen, I think we've talked enough, we're agreed we want the site; I'm going to write the proposed bid on the whiteboard and ask you to vote on it.' There were some pursed lips and nodding around the table, Archie stood and opened a felt tip; a brief squeaking of red marker pen on melamine was followed by the shirted rustle of a show of hands.

A similar group was discussing the same subject in Reading; Simon Slocutt was keen on the project and made a robust presentation to his fellow directors.
'So why is this firm Cloud Developments looking to sell?'
'I reckon their backers have got cold feet and want their money out.'
'Has anyone seen their annual report and accounts?'

'Yeah they're a small firm, never done anything like this before.'

'Perhaps it just got too much for them.'

'Yeah, well whatever the reason, at the moment we're in the fortunate position of having more capital than we have house-building opportunities.'

The debate was orderly, key points were raised and examined, Slocutt had good data and a very detailed grasp of the development that stood up well to the penetrating questions. The Chairman had often been shooting at a friend's estate near Little Rissington, he knew the area well and had a keen appreciation for the Cotswolds. 'The thing that strikes me about this proposal and in comparing it to the Victory fields site, which I have visited by the way. Is that this one has so much more the look of a proper village rather than a housing estate. I think that we shouldn't under-estimate the premium that we'll be able to charge for houses of this type. I don't think we will ever have to go down the traditional route of offering discounts and deals to sell off the last twenty or thirty per cent of the units.' Slocutt rubbed his chin; he'd made that very point the previous evening to the Chairman as they shared a bottle of Pinot Grigio in his office.

'So are we in agreement as to how much we bid?' He asked each director in turn around the table and they individually confirmed their assent.

~

30th September, the sealed bids were in their envelopes on the desk. Dave was in Burford at the offices of Crummond Firth, the firm of solicitors handling the process and who would also be responsible for the conveyancing.

Crummond himself opened the envelopes and read through the documents in silence.

'We've got two cash bids: Liberty has offered fifty-five million on an all as presented basis without any conditions.' He looked over his half-moon reading glasses at Dave who was stone-faced. 'Clarnis has offered fifty four million but with a sliding scale of additional payments up to a further three million payable once all the units have been sold.'

Dave didn't hesitate 'I'll take the Liberty offer, they know the site better and I prefer to have the cash now. How long will the conveyancing take?'

'We've got all the documents ready, the purchaser's details and those of their solicitor so if everyone can crack on I think fourteen days is reasonable, we can exchange and complete on the same day.'

'Good, will you give them a call now, get things moving and confirm the timeframe?'

~

'Hello Arman.'

'Meester Chatham, I'm pleased to hear from you, do you have news for me?'

'Yeah, I'll have the first tranche of funds in four weeks.'

'That is good news, where will the funds be located?'

'In a bank in south Cyprus, where d'you want the money transferred to?'

'Turks and Caicos, back to the same account that it came from.'

'No problem, anything else I need to know?'

'You may be interested to hear about your former business partners?'

'The Nasims? Oh yeah?'

'They've had some misfortune.

Tumas Nasim's yacht suffered an explosion and sank; thankfully no one was on board at the time.' Dave gave a short derisive laugh: 'that's a shame for him. I'm only sorry that they both didn't sink with it. They need a real kicking, look, I'll give you a call next month when I've got a date for that first transfer.'

Chapter 23

Autumn 2014 – Malta

'Matt, can I come round?'
'Sure; are you alright Dad? You sound a bit odd'
'Yeah not really, I'll be there in ten minutes.'
'What the fuck happened to you? You look like shit, what's all that stuff in your hair and on your clothes? have you had a fight with a waiter?'
'Your mum, she hit me with a saucepan of spaghetti and then poured boiling water on my crutch.' He sat and leaning carefully back in the chair, pulled his trousers down cradling a wet bag of ice cubes to his naked groin.
'You'd better have a drink and tell me what's going on.' Matt poured him a large glass of red. Tumas took a big swallow and sighed 'It's all gone wrong Matt, I guess you told her about the girls going to London?' He nodded. 'Well today she got a letter, a note, she started waving it at me as soon as I got home. It just said: "Tumas Nasim is a liar, a thief and a rapist."'
'Oh that's just brilliant.'
'Then she asked me about the rapist bit, she made me tell her.' Matt knew his father was afraid of his wife.
'Oh yeah! Here we go.'
'I had to tell her, I had tell her about that time in London. You know with the Rohipnol, that girl we... that girl in the hotel.'
'Oh Christ. So then she hit you?'
'Yeah and tipped boiling water in my crutch, shit it hurts.'
'Have you seen a doctor?'
'No I just got this ice from the downstairs freezer after she chucked me out of the house.

Have you got any painkillers?' he doubled forward, wincing in pain 'can I stay here?'
'Yeah sure, I've got plenty of spare rooms; take your pick. So now she's pissed at me as well because of this rape story then?'
'I don't know, you'll have to speak to her, leave it for a day or two, she's furious at the moment, she blames me for all of it, you might be alright. Oh God, and I'm starving; I haven't eaten all day can we get a takeaway or something? I can't go out like this.'
'Yeah, I'll order some pizzas, you go and have a shower, I'll find some clean clothes and painkillers for you.'
They sat round the kitchen table.
'Thanks for this Matt, d'you mind if I stay for a while, 'til I get myself sorted out?'
'No, course not stay as long as you like, in fact you might as well move in, no point in renting somewhere when there's room for both of us here.'
'Thanks, I'll have to work from here for a few days, I can't go to the office like this.'
'Sure, no problem, you can use the dining room as your office if you like.'

~

'Tamara, hi how are you? It's Tumas Nasim.'
'Yes hi, I'm fine thank you, I'm sorry to hear about your yacht.'
'Yeah it's a real shame, she was a beauty, though not as beautiful as you of course.'
'Well we have instruct loss adjuster to survey the wreck. He will be on the site today, we get his report and then we can decide how to proceed.'
'Yeah well I've got the Harbourmaster wanting the wreck removed immediately.'

'So you can tell him we are moving fast as possible.'
'He's threatening to prevent any of my ships docking in Malta if I don't remove the wreck.'
'So as I said you can tell him that we are moving fast as possible.'
'The policy includes cover for Liability doesn't it? So you'll pay for the wreck removal won't you?'
'We need to review Loss Adjuster report before we can make any decision.'
'I'm disappointed that you don't seem to be very interested in assisting me on this Tamara, d'you remember that you came to visit last year wanting a share of our insurances? We gave your company this piece of business to see how you would perform?'
'Yes Mister Nasim but our corporate strategy is changing and we are not so much interested in this type of insurance any longer.'
Great, that was no help at all; still he could tell the Harbourmaster to fuck off and moan at the insurers instead.

~

That evening; 'So tell me Dad, this note that Mum got, who sent it?'
'Anonymous, no idea, just the words I told you, nothing else on the paper.'
'So could it be Arman?'
'It must be him or ISIL or ISIS or whatever they're called.'
'Is there anyone else who'd want to turn you over?'
'I don't think so, that's enough isn't it?'
'Yeah well I don't know who else you might be working with.'
'No one like that, I can tell you.'

'So say it's Arman or ISIL, how do they know about the so-called rape? And anyway that was about twenty years ago; why bring it up now and why not challenge us face to face instead of sending a stupid note?'
'I don't know Matt, did you ever tell anyone about the date rape?'
'Yeah, probably but I never mentioned you.'
'So how does anyone know? how does this letter writer know and who else are they going to send it to?'
'Ah shit, d'you suppose all this is connected? The money gone, the yacht sinking, the kidnapping, the letter, all of this?'
'I don't know, I can't think straight, I can't sleep, my balls are killing me.'
'Why don't you have another drink, just help yourself, I gotta go through this pile of post.' He sat tearing envelopes and reading the letters.
'Oh bollocks' muttered Matt.
'What's up?'
'Have you seen one of these? It's from my mortgage company, they want an updated status on my income and repayment plan.'
'No, I never had a mortgage, what's it mean?'
'It says that they're reviewing their lending criteria, they're not happy with interest only mortgages and if they're not satisfied with my repayment plan they'll want the mortgage repaid.'
'Does that matter? Get another mortgage, sod 'em.'
'That's not so easy, I bought this at the top of the market, there was someone else bidding for it and I paid too much. Latifa had set her heart on it so I… you know. I paid two million, it's probably worth one point five now. If I had to sell quickly, maybe only one point two five. I borrowed one point five million so it's possible that even if I sold it I'd still owe them money.

It looks like I'll be in negative equity. Shit.'
'So what can you do?'
'I'll have to try and come up with a repayment plan, which will be difficult because the income from my properties in Spain has dried up, the Spanish authorities have opened an investigation because of rumours that the planning consents weren't legal, meanwhile the properties can't be let or sold.'

It was a sleepless night in Matt's apartment.
Ali, Tumas's managing director rang in the morning:
'Err boss, the Vitall Star insurance company have been on the phone.'
'Oh yeah, what's the news.'
'The assessor's report says that the cause of the sinking was an explosion.'
'Yeah we spotted that, what else?'
'He says the explosion wasn't an accident, that there was an explosive device put in the hull deliberately to make the boat sink. He's suggesting that it's either sabotage or scuttling by the owner.'
'What! What! I sank my own yacht? Is he crazy, who is this Loss Adjuster? do we know him?'
'No, he's a Greek, I never heard of him before.'
'So what's Vitall Star's view?'
'They're considering their position.'
'What is the value of our claim?'
'Four million for the yacht plus three fifty thousand for the Removal of Wreck. There shouldn't be any excess for us to pay because the vessel is a Total Loss.'
'Is Sabotage covered under the policy?'
'Yeah, but..'
'But what?'
'They're saying they think the owner scuttled the yacht for the insurance money.'

'They're saying it's fraud?'

'Yeah, I'm afraid so.'

'I want their response in writing today and you can get our lawyer round here this afternoon, prepare a file for him with all the relevant documents, we'll sue their fucking Russian arses for this.'

'OK boss, there's another thing.'

'What?'

'Err the Harbourmaster, he says if the wreck isn't moved within forty eight hours he'll arrest and detain any of our vessels calling at Malta.'

'OK, get some quotes today to move it.'

'I already did, as I guessed the cheapest is €350,000'

'When can they do it?'

'As soon as they get paid.'

'They want cash up front?'

'Yeah, so do the other salvage firms that quoted, what d'you want to do?'

'Leave it with me, I'll let you know later.'

Tumas sat alone in the dining room, his balls were either frozen or on fire. They were red and blistered; the skin had peeled off his cock like a burst barbecue sausage.

He couldn't afford a delay to any of his cargo ships; his customers would switch to another carrier if they knew his vessels were being detained, goods can't wait; there are always deadlines to be met. He had to get someone to move the wreck; he didn't have the cash to pay up front. The word was out, someone was trying to screw him, that fucker Arman. He jotted down a list of people likely to help him and started at the top.

An hour later his pad was covered with scratches and doodles but no offers of help. Everyone had an excuse: no salvage tugs available, no lifting gear, no divers, maybe next month. Shit, he flung the biro at the window. He didn't have any cash or any capital.

29 Years

Everything was cashflow. The money came in, the money went out. There wasn't even enough in the company's current account to borrow from. The only capital he had; about €1,000,000 was in the Lady Zee, the rest he'd borrowed. Oh Christ he owed Golam Bashir €3,000,000.

Bashir was a financier and money markets trader, he'd loaned the money interest free for six months, he knew it was for the yacht and once he heard it was sunk he'd be wanting his money back.

Telepathically his phone rang; it was Bashir.

'I hope you got good insurance on that yacht, when are they paying out?'

'Yeah, we're in discussions right now.'

'What's to discuss? It's sunk, they pay, right?'

'It's a bit more complicated than that.'

'I don't like the sound of this, why complicated?'

'They say it's sabotage.'

'So? that's covered, no?'

'They say it might be fraud, that I scuttled the yacht.'

'Not my problem, you owe me three million, you find it.'

Tumas knew that he was playing with fire borrowing from Bashir, they'd always got on well but he had a reputation as a hard man. Not a good person to upset, people had disappeared who'd failed to honour their obligations to Bashir.

Later in the week he heard shouting in the street and looked out of the window, down in the street in front of the apartment block Matt was confronting a man in a suit. They were standing beside the BMW X5; the man was showing him a document and shaking his head.

Tumas opened the window, he couldn't make out the words but the suit was insistent; eventually Matt slapped the car key into the outstretched hand. The man held out a document with a biro for signature, Matt scribbled angrily.

The man checked the signature then got into the car and drove away.
The front door crashed open:
'Bollocks, the fucking lease company have repossessed the fucking car.'
'What's going on? How can they do that?'
'They say my credit rating's been downgraded and they can't continue with the lease.'
'How can that happen?'
'The mortgage company have reassessed me and decided they're not happy with my repayment plan, they're part of the same corporation that I lease the car from.'
'Oh shit, that's bad, what can you do about the flat?'
'They've given me twenty eight days to find a new mortgage or they'll sell the flat out from under me.'
'We're in a mess here' and he told Matt about the problems with the yacht.
Finally he asked 'Have you spoken to your mother?'
'Yeah, she doesn't want to talk to me; oh she did say all your stuff is being sent here. It might be downstairs, I saw a load of bin liners in the hall. Also, you know that if I can't replace the mortgage we're going to have to find somewhere else to live. Have you got any cash? Latifa took all of ours.'
'Not much, about ten thousand in the bank, I better go get it out before it disappears, I've got the Mercedes, the company owns that though.'
'Someone's behind all this, it's just too much to be any kind of coincidence, how can we just lose everything like this?'
'It must be Arman, he's trying to destroy us.'
'Yeah, well he's doing a pretty good job so far. What the hell are we going to do? and why the hell's he doing it?'

~

29 Years

Vitall Star had decided that they weren't going to pay, the report from the surveyor was clear; an explosive device had been deliberately used to sink the yacht. It wasn't terrorism and it wasn't an accident. It wasn't covered. Tumas's solicitor advised that suing would be a long and expensive process particularly as the Law and Jurisdiction of the policy was Russian.

'If you wish us to proceed we'll need an upfront payment of twenty five thousand Euro.

'OK, I'll think about it, thanks for your advice.'

~

'Boss, it's Ali, about the renewal of the Iranian oil cargo contract.'

'Yeah, what's happening?'

'They've decided to use someone else, the contract expires at the end of the month.'

'Why? they've been with us for years, they're our biggest client.'

'Yeah, I know, they wouldn't say why they're moving, I checked the accounts, they're all up to date; they don't owe us anything.'

'Have we got any other oil contracts that we can use the tankers for?'

'I'm working on it but there's only odd one-off voyages available at the moment, no long term contracts are out for tender.'

'We need long term to pay the hire on the ships.'

'I know boss, I'm on it.'

The next morning after another sleepless night:

'It keeps going round in my mind Dad, if this is all about the rape how could Arman know?'

'Someone told him – a witness, one of the other girls from the bar in South Kensington?'

'Or someone from the hotel, maybe a guest or one of the staff; maybe he was at the hotel and saw us.'
'Maybe, but why should he care and why wait so long, why lend us the money? Speaking of the money, where's Dave?'
'No idea, he won't answer my calls or texts or emails, he's disappeared, vanished.'
'Has he got the money?'
'I don't know but if he has, good luck with ISIL they'll probably kill him. No wonder he's disappeared, I guess Arman's after him too.'
'So what can we do?'
'I can ask Arman and find out who's behind all this bollocks and why.'
'OK, I s'pose it can't get any worse.'
Tumas picked up his phone and called Arman.
'It just rings once then goes straight to voicemail.'
'Sounds like he's blocked your number, try him on my phone.' Matt slid it across the kitchen table, Tumas tapped in the number.
'Yeah, Arman? it's Tumas Nasim.'
'We have nothing to discuss.'
'Oh yes we have, why are you trying to ruin my life.'
'Why did you try to ruin my life Meester Naseem? Why did you hide my money? Any problems that you have are of your own making. I've told you; you are on your own, I don't know you, don't call this number again.'

~

'Yeah, you're right Matt, I think it's him. He said:
"any problems that you have are of your own making" he knows, but how does he know and what's it matter to him?'
'I'm not so sure that it is him.

Look, we thought the kidnapping was ISIL and then they let Ella go. We thought the explosion was ISIL, who else could carry out an act of terrorism like that? Who'd have the expertise? Then there's the letter to Mum, now that starts to make sense.'

'Not to me it doesn't.'

'Well look what happened straight afterwards; the Iranian oil cargo contract was cancelled. You know how you got that account, I remember because I was involved with it when I was with working for you. The guy, Faruq, running the Iranian company was an old friend of Grandad's, they'd met and been friends in Paris and done some business together. When Faruq took over the company he gave the oil cargo contract to Grandad who passed it on to you.'

'Yeah, so?'

'So whoever's got that contract was the person who sent the letter to Mum, knowing it was up for renewal and that she would chuck you out and try and ruin your business in revenge.'

'Well, it's a thought; I'll ask Ali. What about Latifa and Ella, will they come back once you convince them that ISIL is no longer a problem?'

'I hope so, if I've got somewhere for us to live. She told me yesterday that she's going to move to Israel, to stay with her family in in Tel Aviv.'

They went to bed with sleeping pills.

In the morning: 'Ali, which firm took over the Iranian oil cargo contract?'

'Global Oil.'

'Global? but they're a huge corporation, this must be a small account for them.'

'Yeah but I heard that one of their lady directors is shagging Faruq's son so he moved it to guarantee his sex-life.'

'That's nice, thanks, anything else?' He thought sadly of his own disintegrating cock; that wouldn't be seeing action anytime soon, if ever again.
'When are you coming back into the office?'
'Next week, Monday.'
'There's some other stuff I need to talk to you about.'
'Oh yeah what sort of stuff.'
'The staff are nervous, there's been a lot of gossip about the yacht and the kidnap and you not being in the office and stuff.'
'OK I'll get them together for a team talk on Monday.'
'Quite a few are talking about leaving now we've lost the oil account.'
'Have you found anything for the tankers?'
'Nothing serious, just bits and pieces so far, and we've got them on charter for another eighteen months at a million dollars a month.'
'Well you better find some work for them try the Libyans and Nigerians.'
'Oh yeah and the bank's been on the phone, they want to see you, can you ring to arrange an appointment?'
Arrange an appointment? he'd been friends with Mustapha for thirty-five years; they had lunch together once a month.
'Hello Mustapha, it's Tumas.'
'Oh hello, thanks for calling back, yes could you come in for a chat?'
'About what? we normally have a chat over lunch, can't it wait until our next meeting?'
'No, sadly not, we've got some new shareholders and things are being done differently round here now, is Monday convenient?'
'I can do Monday at three pm.'
'Yes that's fine Tumas, see you then.'
Tumas was wearing nappies his burns were bad.

29 Years

The doctor was seeing him every day and he had to change his dressings every six hours.

The weekend was miserable, the flat was for sale; punters were viewing with the agent all day. No wonder, the mortgage company had put it on the market at €1.25 million to stimulate interest. There was no peace, Tumas just wanted some quiet but there was none. Matt had gone out flat hunting, looking at rental properties to tide them over. He went out on the small balcony and looked out to sea, leaning on the railings. He'd gone from 'have yacht to have not' in two weeks. He was dizzy with fatigue, pain, lack of sleep, stress and too many cigarettes. He put his right hand inside his shirt on his chest; he was surprised he hadn't had a heart attack.

Tumas was a chancer; he'd always been led astray by the lure of easy money, he liked to think he was street-smart, a savvy businessman. The superficial signs of success were very important to him; eating at the best restaurants, hand made suits, expensive watches, cars and boats.

He didn't have anywhere to turn to; he was under no illusion, he had no real friends who would help him; his wife's family despised him. His own parents were dead and his one brother was in Africa somewhere working as a teacher. It was getting dark, time to change the dressings again and apply more ointment. It even smelled a bit bad now. He sat on the bidet with his trousers around his ankles and his head in his hands. He wanted to weep but the tears wouldn't flow. He sorted himself out and stood up, blew his nose and looked at the old man in the mirror:

'Where do we go from here Tumas?' he said to himself 'where do we go from here?'

Matt was back at the apartment; 'I've found a flat for us; it's not in your favourite part of town, it's down near Sliema Creek.

The fact is that without references or a guarantor and with my credit rating down the pan the agent told me that I can't get a lease to pay monthly. I've got to pay a year's rent in advance plus a deposit. We've only got ten grand so I worked on a budget of five hundred a month and you don't get much for that.'
'I'm seeing the bank on Monday, they asked me to come in, I'll see what I can do.'
'Why do they want to see you?'
'They've been bought out, new rules now, Mustapha's going to explain when I see him.'
'Yeah I saw they'd been bought by a German bank, that should be OK then, they're a big secure firm.'
'I hope so; I don't need any more surprises at the moment.'

Monday morning:
'You alright boss?'
Tumas was wearing a sweatshirt and baggy jogging pants.
'You don't normally dress like this, I mean it's a bit casual isn't it?'
'Never mind Ali, it's not important.'
After the team talk, Tumas was grey-faced with pain. He went into his room, sat at his desk staring blindly at his blank computer screen.

Ali came in and shut the door, Tumas didn't look up.
'Boss? I need to talk to you.' No response. He came over to the desk.
'Boss, I'm sorry but, but it's not working is it? Something's wrong, we've just lost two more contracts. No one wants to deal with us, I've been on the phone over the whole weekend. There's no business for us out there, why now all of sudden?

Is this all connected, you know with the yacht and the kidnapping?' Without looking at him Tumas said
'I don't know, I just don't know.'
'The thing is my wife's been hearing stories and she's worried, she doesn't want me working here any more. She knows Latifa; she's been talking to her about, about, about your family situation.' He took a deep breath. 'I'm sorry but I'm going to have to resign.' He put a white envelope on the desk. Hesitated, couldn't think of anything else to say, so walked out closing the door softly behind him. Tumas's head sank slowly onto the blotter.

Tuesday afternoon:
Tumas took a taxi to the bank and was shown into a meeting room. Mustapha came in and raised his eyebrows at Tumas's choice of clothes. He introduced a German executive, Herr Blumenthal, the Director responsible for Compliance, they sat across the table from him, Tumas was on his own.
'We have been through the bank accounts which are dealing with those countries where we have money laundering concerns Mister Nasim. We note that your firm is mainly dealing in those areas. We have a responsibility to report all suspicious transactions to the Regulator and we are tightening up our procedures. Bluntly Mister Nasim, your business has a history of dealing with clients that this bank would not accept under our new rules. There are historic transactions in here that we are most uncomfortable with. I am therefore required to inform the Regulator that we are proposing an internal inquiry into our relationship with your company.
In the meantime and with immediate effect your accounts are frozen.'
Tumas's heart was thumping; his pulse was loud in his ears. His face was red with anger.

'Once our inquiry is complete we will send our report to the Regulator for his review and approval. I'm aware of the Regulator's view of matters such as these and expect that we would be directed to cease providing banking services to you or your company. In view of the seriousness of the offence of money laundering the Board has decided to pre-empt the Regulator's likely recommendation and to cease our relationship with you with immediate effect.'

'That's bollocks, that's right out of order, what about my staff? How are they going to get paid? What am I supposed to do? How can I live? I've got no cash. Mustapha, we've been working together for thirty-five years, doesn't that count for anything?' Mustapha was silent and wouldn't meet his eye. 'What about my personal account, I assume that's not affected.' Blumenthal continued;

'All of your accounts, business and personal are frozen and closed. If, after the inquiry, there are funds to be released, then you will notify us of your new bank and the funds will be transferred.

We hope to avoid notifying the Police in this matter but it can't be ruled out at this stage.' The German stood up and left the room without another word.

Tumas took a bus back to Matt's apartment 'I'm stuffed. I've got one hundred and forty seven Euro in my pocket, and that's it. I'm going to have to declare myself bankrupt to avoid my creditors, fuck knows what I'm going to tell Bashir.'

'What about your father-in-law, will he help?'

'Not after Zainab's finished with him, he'll do whatever she wants.'

'Does that mean we can't get the ten grand from your personal account?'

'Yeah that's frozen as well.'

'Shit, that's all you need, look, I might be able to get some money from Spain, various people owe me but I've got to go there and bring it back in cash, I can buy a flight on my credit card.'
'OK, you better go then, I need to speak to my lawyer and ask him how to proceed with the bankruptcy and winding up the company, I guess he'll have to appoint an administrator or receiver or something.'

Wednesday afternoon:

'Dad, I've got twelve and half thousand Euro' he came into the dining room and put a pile of notes on the table, that's it for now, there's other money owing but no one's got any cash.'
Hi father just sat there in a dirty tee shirt and a nappy, a bowl full of cigarette ends and pile of papers sat on the table.
'Come on, I'll get the flat lease signed and we can move. I've accepted an offer on this apartment. The agent managed to get three people interested so they bid it up to just over €1.5 million. They worked it so that their fees are covered and the mortgage is paid off so at least I don't owe them any money.'
'Good' said Tumas 'at least that's some good news. My company's being wound up. The accountant's been appointed as the Receiver, I've said goodbye and apologized to the staff, they were in tears; they couldn't believe it. I felt so bad, it was bloody awful, what a mess.'
'I'll make a you a cup of tea Dad.' Tumas doodled on a foolscap pad. 'Bashir's been on the phone, I told him I'm going bankrupt, he's not happy, I'm going to assign the yacht and the insurance to him; he can sue the insurers and take care of the wreck.

I told him it's his best chance of getting any money back.'
'Yeah well, they'll have a rough time dealing with him, he's a nasty bastard.'
'Speaking of nasty bastards, I saw the doctor yesterday about my burns. He's not very sympathetic; I think Zainab's been at him. He said there might be an infection so he's given me some antibiotics. He said if that won't cure it he's going to have to cut my cock off.

Chapter 24

Autumn 2014 – The Cotswolds

Pip, Liz's elder sister, had come to stay for the weekend; her husband had taken their boys on a cycling weekend to Wales and dropped her off on the way. Pip was fun, good to have around, she got on well with Dave and Liz and loved their boys. Aunty Pip was much in demand when she visited.

The children had finished supper and Liz opened the red wine; Pip was on the kitchen sofa flipping through a small pile of brochures that gave details of country houses for sale. 'Wow these are nice, you thinking of moving?'

'Well you know it's always nice to look, can I top you up? Now, would you like some snacks to be going on with? I love these taramasalata and hummus dips.' Liz started unwrapping some Waitrose packages.

'Yeah but this is serious looking, these are all two million plus. Business must be going well, and I notice a few nice new little additions since my last visit. Did I see a new Range Rover on the drive? and that' she pointed 'is a very nice bracelet.'

'Oh yes I love it, my birthday present from Dave.' She elegantly arched her arm and wrist to model the heavy woven gold cuff bracelet.

'So, is there something you need to tell your big sister?' Liz went and sat beside her, cupping a large glass of wine. 'There is but it's a bit of a long story.'

'Now you've really got me interested.'

'Do you remember a long time ago, twenty years ago, I was date-raped.'

'Oh God yes, how could I ever forget? I was so worried

about you. You were so brave; I don't how you coped. I remember that nice counselor that saw you a few times, d'you still speak to him?'
'I do, yeah, sometimes I visit him if I'm in London otherwise we do it on Skype or Facetime.'
Pip looked a bit uncertain 'so how do we get from date-rape to country houses?'
'Yeah, you may well ask there's a lot to tell, probably best if we tell it together when Dave's back.'
After supper they sat in the living-room and talked:
'You know Dave always kept work and family quite separate? well he didn't tell me who his business partners were, just that they were some foreign businessmen who wanted to get into the UK property market. They'd done well in Spain but that country's in such a mess they wanted somewhere more stable. Dave was asked by one of these people to run the UK company, they couldn't do it themselves because they'd been barred from being a director of a UK company for previous tax irregularities.'
'Sounds a bit iffy, so Dave, you were the front man and the manager then?'
'Yeah, it all went fine, we did a few residential projects and made some money, I was really enjoying it. Then an old school friend came to me with a big deal. He did landscaping for the MoD and they told him about a proposal to sell off the other side of Little Rissington airfield for a housing development. It was much bigger than anything we'd done before but this guy, my backer, Matt, he'd done large-scale developments in Spain and was fine about it. I didn't see how he'd find the money, the site was going to cost fifty million and another fifty million for the construction and infrastructure, anyway they told me that they'd secured the funding and to go ahead.'
'Yeah that's when Dave showed me the plans for the

project, I was stunned at the sums of money involved and asked him who the backers were.'
'And who were they?'
'The Nasims, the father and son who had raped me.'
'No, you're kidding, my God, I don't believe it' Pip stared at them goggle-eyed 'so what did you do?'
'I told him to go ahead, complete the project take the salary, earn the bonus and then walk away, resign, not deal with them anymore.'
'How could you? I mean how could you do business with these men after what they'd done to Liz?'
'It was Liz's call; she said it was too much money for us to walk away from, about two hundred thousand.'
'That won't buy one these' she nodded at the stack of brochures 'so what happened?'
Liz took up the story:
'You know that guy Damien who lives in the village, bald and very tall; he's renting The Old Forge on Back Lane? He used to be in the Fraud Squad, now he's a private fraud investigator. We were just chatting about his work and how he has to travel so much. I asked him where he went most and he said the Turks and Caicos because it's a territory favoured by money launderers, as well as Malta and Northern Cyprus. I did a bit of digging on the internet and it started me thinking that there could be a way of getting my revenge on the Nasims.'
'That's quite a leap of imagination.'
'Yeah well, you know me' she looked down and peered up under her eyelashes eyes in mock-modesty.
'It wasn't just me, if Dave hadn't had his knowledge and contacts from his clerking days we couldn't have put it together.'
'That's where it all began, with me helping out the Nasims, when I was a clerk.
I always knew they were dodgy but I thought it was just

their financial dealings that were, umm a bit creative, I never thought they were such a pair of little shits.'

'So what was the deal? you'll have to tell me the whole story.' Dave got up, unscrewed the top off another bottle of Malbec and filled their glasses.

'The project continued as normal like Liz and I had agreed. Once the first transfer of funds arrived at the solicitor, the fifty million, I hacked into Matt's email account and sent the solicitor an instruction to transfer the money to an account that I'd set up with the same MoD name but with a different sort code and account number. De Salis, that's the solicitor, made the transfer thinking nothing wrong.

I deleted that email from Matt's sent mail box, went into his contacts and amended de Salis's email address to a new one that looked similar but was actually set up by me. Then, when I asked Matt to send him an instruction to transfer the money, the email would go to this dummy address and he wouldn't get a bounce-back. I had to do that otherwise it would have alerted de Salis that the first email may not have come from Matt.'

She nodded appreciatively 'neat.'

'Liz came up with a scheme about the HMRC, you know the tax office, saying they'd had a report of a suspicious transaction; the Nasims are terrified of HMRC.

A few days after they'd made the transfer I told them I was under investigation for money laundering; I expect they shat themselves. We didn't know where they'd got the fifty million from to buy the site but we were pretty sure it wasn't legit money. I told them my passport had been confiscated and I was going on the run so I didn't get arrested.'

'Oh God' she squeaked 'where'd you run to? Where did you hide?' Dave laughed.

'No, no, you must remember we'd invented this story

about HMRC so I didn't actually have to go on the run but I did it in order to convince the Nasims that it was serious. I went to Amsterdam, on my bike.' She shook her head not understanding 'why on your bike?'

'I often go across the Channel on my bike so I know that UK Border Patrol don't check bikers' passports on the way out. When I got to Amsterdam I rang Matt Nasim and told him I needed cash and ID. Of course I'd got my own passport but I had to make him believe that it was all for real. He then told me that their backer, a Kazakhstani named Arman, had decided not to go ahead with the project and wanted his money back. I told Matt that the money from Turks and Caicos had been received by Carson de Salis and was now in an escrow account in favour of the MoD as required by the bid process.'

He paused 'are you with us so far?' Pip nodded and held out her empty glass.

'So Matt calls de Salis and asks for the money back.' He looked admiringly at Liz 'then this was another one of your ideas. I'd been to see de Salis and asked him to take a few days off and if Nasim rang to say he'd been suspended due to HMRC investigations. I know Carson very well, and said there'd be a nice Christmas present in it for him. So when Matt rings Carson, he tells him that he can't get the money back, that HMRC are all over him and he's given them a copy of the email instruction from Matt Nasim! You remember that Matt's banned from being a company director for fifteen years and during that period he's not allowed to be involved in the running of a UK company. Well this instruction proves that he is and so he's facing up to two years in prison.'

'Brilliant, so this Nasim's right in the shit then?'

'Yeah, and it gets better. In fact the money isn't Arman's, at all; he's laundering it for ISIL.

And they've nicked it from the bank of Iraq.' Pip put her

hand over her mouth and looked worried:
'This sounds like it's all getting a bit bloody dangerous.'
'The Nasims didn't know who to be more frightened of HMRC or Arman or ISIL. I nearly crapped myself when Arman told me the money had come from ISIL, god knows what the Nasims thought.
So, Arman's furious with the Nasims and reckons they're trying to steal the money, they deny it and tell him I'm going to pick up some cash and ID from the left luggage in Amsterdam train station. I guessed that the Nasims might tell Arman so I had a little plan to distract anyone waiting for me.' Dave described the scenes with the homeless man, the Dutch police and the bags of caster sugar. 'Course Arman thought the Nasims had tipped me off and that we were working together to steal the money.'
'Classic, so how did you do it without cash or ID?'
'I still had my own remember, so I went back to England, telling the Nasims and Arman that I'd sort it out with the solicitor and get the money back somehow. When I saw Carson I got a print out of the incriminating email instruction from Matt, photographed it and sent it to Arman. I also sent him a copy of a bank statement showing the fifty million was in an account at Encip Bank in Northern Cyprus. So now I'm on his side working to get the money back for him. I tell him it'll take time and how I'm going to do it by running the money from Northern Cyprus to banks in south Cyprus. By the time he gets it back it will be thoroughly laundered and can be used for any purpose anywhere in the world. He's pretty grateful and asks if there's anything he can do in return for me.'
'Yeeees,' Pip is wincing in anticipation of something she can't guess at.
'So I told him the story of how the Nasims raped Liz.'

'Oh my God' her head swivelled from one to the other 'that's so neat, fantastic, so what did he do? He's really pissed off with them already, right?'
'Yeah he went to town on them, he blew up the dad's four million dollar yacht and told the insurers that Nasim had done it himself for the insurance money so they're refusing to pay out.' Pip snorted with laughter.
'Then he had Matt's daughter abducted for a day but returned her unharmed, Matt's wife was so worried and upset that she's left him and taken the daughter to go and live in Israel. Arman also fucked up Matt's credit rating so the mortgage company foreclosed on his loan and sold his flat from under him.'
Liz interrupted 'and don't forget the letter to Zainab.'
'Oh yeah, this one's brilliant. Arman sent her a note, it just said:
"Tumas Nasim is a liar, a thief and a rapist."
'Oh my God, what did she do?'
'She's a big girl and she beat him up, poured boiling water on his privates and threw him out of her house. He's in a bad place and now he's lost his biggest contracts. His shipping firm's gone bust and the bank's investigating his accounts for money-laundering deals that he did in the past for dodgy sanction-busting oil shipments from various middle east countries.'
'So both Nasims have gone bust, been thrown out of their houses and lost their families then? That's some revenge Liz.' She looked appraisingly at her little sister 'remind me never to upset you.' They cleared the table and tidied up, Pip refilled her glass and sat down again. 'He turned out to be quite a good guy then didn't he that Arman?'
'Yeah I'm sure if you're on the right side of him he's lovely but I bet he's right bastard when he wants to be.'
'Where are you now in the masterplan? Yeah and where's

all that money and what happened with the housing development?'
'Now it's getting interesting.'
'Interesting! What was all other stuff then? other than bloody terrifying.'
'Oh that was setting the scene and putting everything in place, this is the real point of the scheme. You see once the solicitor transferred the money to the account I'd set up, I got the bank statement then I transferred it to the escrow account as required by the MoD, so it was in the right place for the bid to be accepted. Once I'd got Arman happy he was going to get his money back I started a tender process to sell the development site with the planning permission.'
'You're piece of work Dave.'
'Yeah well y'know, just teamwork really.'
'Some team! how's the sale going?'
'Going well; gone well in fact. A firm called Liberty Homes bought it, the deal completed last week and I transferred fifty million pounds to a bank in Northern Cyprus. I'll move it to south Cyprus piecemeal over the next few months and then to Arman's account in the Turks and Caicos where it originally came from.'
'Wow, that's perfect, and you're best friends with Arman!'
'We hope so.'
'Have you heard anymore about the Nasims? They must be trying to work out what the hell's happened to them.'
'We're not expecting a Christmas card.'

Chapter 25

Autumn 2014 – The Cotswolds

'Hello John, I thought I heard your car.' Ed was sitting in his garden on the white wooden bench. 'Come and sit down, I'm just looking at the river, d'you see the grey heron fishing? He stands right out there in the middle, in the weeds for hours. It's gravel, sort of shingle on the bottom. The small fish and crayfish like to feed in amongst the weed, there's always been a heron here, solitary old birds; a bit like me.' He laughed shortly, 'If you look down to the right, below the weir, you can see a family of swans on the river, there's always a family there, they come back each year and have more young.'
They sat companionably, sheltered from the wind by the wall and buildings. After a while Ed began talking:
'I started telling you about my French SOE agent, Jeanne, didn't I?'
'Yeah, I remember you talking about her ages ago, did you say that you were going to try to find her?'
'I did say that, yes. And yes I did go to look for her in the summer of 1973, in fact I went with my wife.'
'Wasn't that a bit complicated? I mean how'd she feel about you looking up an old girlfriend?'
'Honestly I don't know how she felt, I think it was a woman's thing, she'd rather be there to see what happened than be left behind. Mary's a strong woman and I suppose she decided to fight her ground. Maybe she thought if we found Jeanne she'd see that I had a wife who was sufficiently confident in her marriage that it would survive meeting an old flame.'
'Mmm that's pretty brave stuff.'

'Yes it was and I'm glad she did come, I didn't want to go off searching France on my own, inventing excuses for my trips. I felt bad enough about my behavior as it was without having to add further lies.'

'Why did you feel the need to go and find her after all that time?'

'She'd never really left my mind; she'd never left my heart. There'd always been a special place for her but I'd decided to close that memory, to put it in a box if you like and never let it out. I thought I'd lost her, would never see her again. It was most likely that she'd have been killed in the war; so many of those agents died you know. I think I mentioned the exact moment that the box of memories broke open; it was watching the television, a programme called "The World at War" in 1973. We went on our search and with great help from a French Judge who was an old wartime friend of mine we found Estelle in a village called Valençay, near Tours.'

'Wow, that must have been an amazing meeting, I mean really emotional for you, for both of you.'

'It was, bear in mind I didn't know what sort of reaction to expect, turning up out of the blue and with my wife. We went to her daughter's house; Hélène opened the door and with some astonishment I can tell you but she invited us in and went to fetch her mother. Estelle, as I then knew her real name to be, was marvelous. Charming and beautiful; now with white hair and walking with a stick but otherwise still the same girl that I'd fallen in love with in England all those years ago.'

He faltered as the memory flooded through him again. 'Shall we go in? I'll make us a cup of tea if you like.' Once they were inside he continued:

'I left my wife in 1973, Estelle needed me more and I was in love with her. Our children had left home and Mary's career at the school was very important to her.

29 Years

I think we just grew apart; when I went to be with Estelle, we lived in France for many years until Estelle passed away. Until I lived in Valençay I didn't realize quite what a centre for the Resistance it had been.

There was a memorial erected in the summer of 1991, look in that packet, there's some photos of it. You can't make them out but the names of the agents are engraved on it. I made a note on the back of one of the pictures.'

John arranged the photos on the coffee table and turned them over 'yes here's some writing, it says ninety one men and thirteen women, wow, were they all from the same town?'

'Oh no, I think they were from all over the world.'

'Who's this in this photo? she looks familiar' John held it up for Ed's inspection.

'That's Queen Elizabeth the Queen Mother, she unveiled the monument, there was quite a crowd as you can see. Yes she was there, in fact I'll tell you who else was there the woman who was responsible for F Section, Vera Atkins. I remember that she came to the annual memorial service each year, there was quite a group of them, they used to put up at the Lion d'Or, the hotel where I stayed when I first came to search for Estelle. It was a big occasion in the village, people came from all over the world to remember their comrades, still do I expect but there can't be many left alive now.'

'This is Princess Ann isn't it?' John held up another photo.

'Yes, I'd forgotten that, she came out for the memorial many years later.' John turned it over 'it says 2011 on the back' and he passed it over to Ed.

'That's right, not very long ago. Look at those great big sunglasses she's wearing you couldn't see her eyes at all. I shook hands with her; she was very friendly. I'm told there's a film of the event on the internet.

It was on national television you know, everyone was talking about it for weeks afterwards. You could see us all, we were all in the film and Princess Ann had a yellow dress, yes and a big hat.' He gave the photo back to John 'actually that's the last one I attended; you see I stayed on in France to be with Hélène and the family but I got these eye problems. I came back to Moorfields but my eyesight kept deteriorating and I found it too difficult to travel back and forth. Eventually in about October 2011 I decided to stay in England. It's a bit of a circular story you know, me living in the annex at Brook Cottage. It used to be called Bennett's Farm when the Smiths lived here. Then Tom my nephew and Denise, they took me in. It's wonderful being here.' Ed looked around the room.

'Of course you realize this is where Estelle stayed whilst she was recuperating during the war, I sleep in the same bed that Estelle slept in, I look at the same view, the truth is, I feel she lives here with me, that any minute she'll come through that door and we'll go for a walk together; down there, across the field and along by the river.'

'Do you mind that you've got so many memories here?'

'No, funnily enough, I find it very comforting; it was such a special period for both of us. I belong here now more than anywhere else.'

John picked up a silver framed photo of young woman, 'is this one of Estelle?'

'No it's Hélène's daughter, she's called Amandine.'

'She does look like Estelle doesn't she?'

'Yes she does and she's a real career girl. She's over here now working at the French Embassy in London and often comes to see me at weekends.

May I say John, how much I appreciate your visits and you taking an interest in me and my life. It's been fun for me and we've done some interesting things too.

I'd very much like you to meet Amandine and she'd like to meet you too.'
'How come? she doesn't know me.'
'Well I must confess that I've told her rather a lot about you, erm she's coming on Saturday, we're all having supper here.'
'Here?'
'Well actually we'll be next door at Brook Cottage, Denise is doing the cooking, we'll be having boeuf bourguignon; it's Amandine's favourite.'
'That sounds great I'd love to come, can I bring something?'
'That's a nice idea; yes, some wine would be nice, could you run to a couple of bottles of Gevrey Chambertin? I think that would be absolutely perfect.'
The little dinner party was a great success, Tom and Denise enjoyed entertaining and Amandine hit it off with John; he offered to take her out the next time she was down.

.

Chapter 26

Autumn 2014 – The Cotswolds

The following morning after her third cup of coffee and as her head cleared, Pip's eye caught the house brochures again. She did some strained thinking and with a quizzical expression said:
'Err what you were saying last night about Liberty buying the site, how much did they have to pay in the end?
'Fifty-five million.'
'And you paid the fifty million back to that Arman guy, so there seems to be a spare five million, is that right? Is that where the country house comes in?'
'Yes it is' said Liz delightedly 'that's the profit on the deal so we get to keep it.'

~

On Tuesday evening when Dave came home, Liz said 'I saw in the local paper that Liberty have got their show homes on the market.'
'Yes, they look good don't they?'
'And they've used your design on the hoarding of what the village will look like. It's called Rissington Hill. It's rather nice, all the roads are in and they've rebuilt the track so it's like a proper country lane, they must've spent a fortune.'
'Yes, I was thinking it's time I went and showed them some old black and white photographs.'
'What old photographs?'
'Well there's an ancient burial ground on the site and some Anglo-Saxon treasures were found there in the war.